ÐECRYPTEÐ
PHISHING FOR LOVE
BOOK 2

DECRYPTED

PHISHING FOR LOVE
BOOK 2

Meribeth Richards

Contents

Dedication

To all those whose love language is sarcasm.
Be a good little brat.

Lincoln and Sierra's Playlist

▶ **Slow Hands**
Niall Horan

▶ **Starving**
Hailee Steinfeld

▶ **Bad Blood (Taylor's Version)**
Taylor Swift

▶ **Addicted**
Saving Abel

▶ **Dirty Little Secret**
All-American Rejects

▶ **Bad Things**
mgk, Camila Cabello

▶ **I Need You**
Saving Abel

▶ **Far Away**
Nickelback

▶ **Pony**
Ginuwine

▶ **If You Love Her**
Forest Blakk

▶ **Sweet Child O' Mine**
Guns N' Roses

▶ **Warmness On The Soul**
Avenged Sevenfold

▶ **In My Daughter's Eyes**
Martina McBride

Content Warnings

This book is intended for an adult audience. There are scenes, including those with sexual content, that are not suitable for children.

Please review this list for any possible triggers:
Body Shaming
Mentions of Depression
Financial Abuse
Death of a Parent (off page)
Mentions of Cancer
Child Abandonment
Kidnapping
Possession of Firearm
Torture/Dismemberment
Anal Play

Your mental health matters. If you feel additional content warnings need to be considered, please reach out at author@meribethrichards.com

Chapter One
Lincoln

"**A**re you sure you're okay?"

My mother lets out an exasperated sigh at the question I've asked at least a dozen times within the past couple of hours.

"Lincoln, I'm alright and I am capable of taking care of Charlie. I swear, you act like we haven't had this arrangement before. Now you go out and have some fun. My granddaughter and I will be fine here at the house, spending another Friday night together like we typically do. We'll eat spaghetti and watch those little pony things she loves so much. I can't wait to hear for the millionth time the differences between a Pegasus, a unicorn and that other doohickey one."

My daughter climbs up onto the stool at the kitchen island as I finish cleaning up from the meal I've prepared for them. "It's an Alicorn, Grammy. And they're the most specialist and prettiest ones of all. It's a unicorn with wings. So freaking awesome."

"Watch your mouth," I warn my daughter, who immediately puckers her lips and narrows her eyes in an attempt to do just that. Her actions make me pinch the bridge of my nose and release an irritated breath. "I don't mean literally, Charlie."

She stops her endeavor and leaps down from the stool. Standing across from me, she crosses her long arms and juts her tiny hip out with all the sass in the world. "Well how was I supposed to know? You shouldn't say things you don't mean. And you told me that I could say the word 'freaking' so long as I stopped saying the word fucking. Which isn't fair because you say that word all the time. Like all the time, Daddy."

"I don't recall having that conversation with you." I rub my forehead. This kid of mine is going to be an attorney like her Uncle Camden one day, I have no doubt.

"Well you did. Didn't he, Grammy? He said it last week right after I said 'I don't fucking like grilled cheese sandwiches.' Do you remember? Remember when I said the word fuck? That vein in his forehead popped out and his face got all red. Daddy's like the Hulk, only not green. Right, Grammy?"

The vague memory clears up. "Well then, good job for listening to me, I guess. But you really shouldn't be saying that word, either."

"I don't think it's fair to tell me what I can and can't say. You say things like, 'Be strong, Charlie. Stand up for what you believe in, Charlie. Make your voice heard, Charlie,' and then you get mad about the words I say. What's up with that?"

Raise strong, independent women, they say. It will be fun, they say. Well who is they? Because I would very much like to tell them to fuck right off.

My mom beams at my daughter, a special smile reserved only for the most incredible person on the planet. I wrap my big hands around my tiny girl and toss her in the air before catching her.

Pulling her against my chest, I kiss her head. "You're right, Charlie, but you were wrong about something."

She leans back and scrunches up her little nose. "About what?"

"Alicorns aren't the specialist of them all. I am, Little Bit, because I get to be your dad." I begin peppering kisses on her face, the scruff on my chin and neck causing her to squirm.

"Daddy, put me down. Your face is too hairy," the laughter coming from her makes her protests weak. "Besides, you aren't that special. You can't even fly. And you don't count because you aren't a pony."

Nothing like a six-year-old spitting facts to humble yourself real quick. I place my spitfire down on the ground and look back at my mother. "You're really sure that you—"

"Lincoln. Charles. Fisher. If you ask me if I'm okay one more time, I will scream. I will admit that some days I'm not at my best, but today is not one of those days. I'm fine. And Charlie and I will be alright long enough for you to go on a date." I know not to argue with Mama when she breaks out the full name and places her hands on her hips like she's doing right now, so I keep my mouth closed and give her a little nod. You wouldn't think a woman who barely surpasses five feet and struggles getting out of bed most days would be formidable, but she has taken my two brothers and me down a peg more than a time or two.

It isn't that I don't want to believe my mother when she says she and Charlie are going to be okay on their own tonight, but as her main caretaker the last several years, I've seen good go to bad too quickly for me not to be concerned. Sharon Fisher was the best mom ever to the three of us boys. In our elementary days, lunches would be packed with little notes inside of them wishing us the best or offering up words of encouragement. She was at every single one of our ball games, an impressive feat when football and basketball schedules overlapped. Summers were spent with trips to the waterpark, the zoo, the aquarium and our backyard. She also had this magic about her where she managed to make tiny traditions that would stick around. All three of us can whip up a mean batch of pancakes thanks to our Saturday morning ritual. Birthday cakes continue to be made from scratch. We will still often get together, building forts and shoving our way too big bodies into them for a movie night in the living room.

But one dreadful day wiped away the opportunity for new traditions and happy memories to be created. When I was in high school and my father passed away in a car accident, it was as though we lost the mom we grew up with right along with him. Grief never truly sets you free, but Mama wears hers like a badge of honor. She has let that grief completely consume her to the point she won't even leave the house anymore.

"A date?" My daughter gasps from behind me. Shit. I don't generally let her know that I'm dating so I don't risk getting her hopes up. "Are you gonna kiss her, Daddy? Is she pretty? Have I met her? Am I going to meet her? Where are you taking her? Did you buy flowers? You should buy her flowers. Pretty ones. Don't get those ones from the grocery store either because they're always dead or have brown edges. Oh, I know! You should get her French fries. Girls love French fries."

I roll my eyes at my mother as she mouths the word sorry at me, but then she gives me the out I need. "You know what, Charlie, girls do love French fries. What do you think about the two of us eating this spaghetti with a side of fries? I can whip some up in the air fryer so fast they'll be finished by the time I plate our food." Leaving my family with the sounds of my daughter's victory cry behind me, I hop into my Bronco and peel out of the driveway.

Dating in a small town like Cheatham can be dangerous, especially when you're a single dad, so I have been meeting my dates in the next town over recently. There's been the accountant. Too quiet. The real estate agent. Too loud. The woman who quite literally signed her divorce papers hours before we met. Too weepy. But I keep going out in hopes to find Charlie the mother that she desperately deserves.

Let's hope that tonight I find the one.

Chapter Two
Sierra

I bring my wine glass to my lips and savor the taste of ripe blackberries, warm vanilla, and a whisper of smoky oak that lingers like a secret on my tongue. It's my second glass of the delicious Cabernet Sauvignon my waiter suggested in this adorable restaurant that is a lot more upscale than I expected. Two glasses of wine is probably too much to start out on, but I didn't want to risk being late. Besides, I had nothing else to do in the small town I recently moved to before heading to the next town over to meet up with the man I matched with on the dating site I've been a part of for the past few years.

Being single has been my lifestyle all through college. I still had fun (I mean, a nunnery would turn me away) but a long-lasting relationship? Nothing like that has been in my sights for some time. Now as a recent college graduate, I'm ready to start that journey in my life. I'm eager to start my career as a therapist and meet someone so I can fall in love for the first time. Maybe Cheatham is the place for all of that to happen. Maybe this man will be the one.

He's only five minutes late, so I straighten in my seat, tugging my dress down that's slightly too tight in my midsection. I look around at all the beautiful couples surrounding me in the dining room. There are a few on their phones not looking at one another and I can't help but frown and hope that the love I do find doesn't look like that. I know having a device in your hands is the norm these days, but I'd rather look like the couple sitting in the corner, with their arms stretched across the table, embracing one another. They're staring longingly into each other's eyes as their fingers are entwined and he rubs his thumb across her knuckles. There is no doubt in the world how the two of them feel about one another, and I crave that. No doubts.

I continue scanning the restaurant and take in another couple sitting to the left of me. As I watch them for a bit, it appears like they're on a first date, too, with the way he's asking her questions. From my perspective, things seem a little one-sided with him trying to get to know her; she's pulled out a compact from her purse and looks to care more about her lipstick. And her eyebrows. And her hair. And well, everything but him.

Having freshly graduated with my psychology degree, it is my professional opinion that this woman is batshit crazy. Her date is jaw-droppingly gorgeous. He has a sharp jawline covered in stubble that I just know would scratch my face and between my thighs deliciously. His hair is trimmed super short, but with his serious features, it works for him. I swipe the metaphorical drool from my mouth as I silently stare at the man who had to have been molded by the gods themselves. I watch the way his muscles move under his crisp white shirt that's tucked neatly into a pair of navy slacks. His matching suit jacket hangs on the back of his chair.

Expensive footwear completes his attire. Okay, admittedly I don't know how much his shoes cost, but if it was anything more than the thirty dollars currently in my purse, they get my respect.

My hands begin to twitch with the desire of running them over his toned body and finding out if his hair has enough length I could still run my hands through it. Abruptly, I snap myself out of my lustful stupor. I mean, she could. She could still run her hands through it. His date. The beautiful woman he is on a date with that continues to look at herself more than him.

Maybe I can run my hands through my own date's hair tonight. If I'm lucky, we could go back to his place, or to the cute bed and breakfast I'm currently staying in, and he can distract me long enough to ease the nerves I have about starting my new job tomorrow. But before I can find out if things will lead to that, he's going to have to show up.

I look back down at the dainty, diamond-encrusted watch that hugs my larger-than-average wrist a little too tight. It may not be the most comfortable thing I own, but it's the last thing of my mom's I have and I will wear it every day. My date is now ten minutes behind and a sick feeling forms in my stomach. I may not be every man's ideal type, but I can't say I've ever been stood up before.

"What the hell?" I'm startled by the deep voice and movement to my side. The man I'd been checking out way too intently has gotten to his feet and a wet spot soaks his perfectly sculpted abdomen.

"Oh, calm down. It's white wine." The woman he's with bites the words out.

"I'm drenched," he says, motioning to those abs that the fabric of his pristine white shirt is now clinging to. I lick my bottom lip with the knowledge that those muscles would taste sweet and fruity.

The woman abruptly stands at her side of the table, knocking me from the incredibly inappropriate thoughts I was having about this total stranger. "Listen, if you're gonna get all worked up over me spilling just a little bit of wine, then I don't see this working out between us. I'm gonna go ahead and get out of here. I wish you and your little girl the best. You've got the check, right?"

He mumbles something gruffly as he throws several dollar bills onto the table and then storms to the back of the restaurant as she makes her way to the front.

My eyes can't help but follow her in the sparkly gold dress she's wearing, and as they do, I see a man in a black t-shirt and ripped jeans walk in. I can't help but think how out of place he looks compared to her, but he also looks slightly familiar.

The young man who can't be much older than my twenty-three years says something to the pretty little hostess and she leads him my way. As he gets closer, I can see the resemblance from the one photo he had of himself on the app. In that picture he had on a hat and sunglasses and was making a kissy face at a large fish I assume he had caught that day. The blonde hair that's long enough to curl behind his ears is the same, though, and relief washes over me to know my date has finally arrived.

I smile and wave as the hostess stops where I'm seated. "Hi, I'm Sierra. Are you Elton?"

"You've got to be kidding me," he mutters, but it's still loud enough for me to hear.

The hostess gives me an apologetic look and walks back to her stand as Elton sits down in the chair across from me. I look him over and realize he's not exactly what I expected, but that's okay. His profile said he was an entrepreneur and I wrongly assumed he would have been a bit older to have established his own company. I suppose it's rude of me to make those assumptions knowing there are creative geniuses of all ages and some of today's wealthiest entrepreneurs got their start in their teens or while in college.

"It's so nice to meet you. Have you had a good day?"

"It was good," he says, "now I'm here." He leans back in his chair, looking like he can't wait to go home even though he arrived mere seconds ago.

"Oh? Did something happen on the way here? Is that why you're late?"

Elton scoffs. "I just got here and you're already nagging me?"

Taken aback by his accusation, I try to recover, but I have a feeling it's going to fall on deaf ears. "No, I'm not nagging. I simply wanted to make sure everything was okay."

He scratches the back of his head before he stands up. I can't help but take in the fact that he's not the six foot fella he claimed to be. Not that it matters, height isn't important to me. It's just that I've noticed most guys prefer to be taller than their partner and at five feet and eleven inches, finding those taller men hasn't been incredibly easy.

"No, everything isn't okay." Elton says loud enough to garner attention from the nearby tables. "I was excited to hook up with this girl, but she insisted we go somewhere nice. After having to ask my dad if I can borrow his car so I could come into town at this fancy ass place, I notice that I've been catfished."

There are so many things to process about his confession. First of all, he doesn't have his own car? Secondly, catfished? The fuck?

"I'm sorry. What?"

"You should be sorry. The pictures you posted didn't show a fat loser that nobody in their right mind would want to date. I mean, I'll admit, you've got a pretty face, but I can't be seen with someone like you. People might think I'm into that shit."

I shouldn't do it. I know I shouldn't do it.

"What shit?" I ask.

I did it.

"Some fat fetish or something. I had to agree to use my own money to fill my dad's car with gas and pay to take it through the car wash and I don't even get to have my dick get wet." He looks at me, flicking his tongue over his bottom lip. "Well, I mean, if you wanted to get down on your knees under this table and suck me off for playing me like you did, it would be the least you could do."

Is this guy fucking serious? I stand up too, so I can look him in the eyes. "The least I could do? Who the hell are you to judge me? I get it, maybe my body isn't to your liking, but you think you're such a catch?" I take a deep breath. I refuse to sink down to his level even though this boy in front of me right now is less than to be desired.

More of the restaurant patrons are watching the scene I'm now a part of and I just want this humiliating moment to be over. I take a deep breath before I speak again. "I think it's best if you go ahead and leave."

I look across the table and he's standing there with a confused look on his face. "So, no blowy then?"

This dumbass. "Leave. Now," I grit out, clenching my eyes tight, trying to will him away. It does the trick, because when I open them again, I see Elton's back as he retreats from the restaurant.

Good riddance.

I sit back down at the table with my head down, not wanting to see the pity on all the faces around me. I only wanted a nice night out. I wanted a good start on my new life. But, like always, Sierra Thomas doesn't usually get what she wants.

Picking up my wine glass, I sigh as I realize it's empty. Again. I sit it down and finally bring my eyes up to scan over the restaurant and see if I can't find my server so I can get the hell out of here. I manage to find him and flag him down, but also note the hushed whispers and a few stares of the people who were only trying to enjoy their meal, but instead had to bear witness to my humiliation.

"Can I get you another glass of wine, Miss?" The man, only a couple years younger than myself, asks in a soft voice.

Three glasses of wine would probably put me in a much better place than I'm currently in, but knowing I have a lonely trip back to the small town of Cheatham ahead of me, I decline the offer and instead ask for my check. Looks like I'll end this depressing evening with one of my battery-operated boyfriends.

Chapter Three
Lincoln

L ooks like I won't be finding the one tonight.

This date is the fucking worst. When my assistant insisted that her cousin's friend was beautiful and exactly my type, I thought I'd take a chance on meeting up with someone I haven't known for my entire life. When you live in a small town like Cheatham, Kentucky, your prospects end up being pretty slim. But I'd rather know that a girl peed her pants in the third grade or slept with the entire baseball team in high school than deal with the woman sitting across from me.

I should have said no to Amanda from the very beginning. "Just your type," she had said. I don't even have a type. I was with my ex all through high school and college, but the second we found out a baby was on the way, she started getting distant. I insisted on us getting married, but she said she wasn't wearing a wedding dress while she was swollen and pregnant, so I agreed to wait. But as the due date grew closer, Nicole started getting farther. She moved to a different bedroom in our small apartment above the diner we had managed to talk the owner into renting to a couple of poor kids just starting out. Anytime I would bring something home for the baby, she would huff about wasting money and that she needed things, too. I didn't see how a warm blanket or a couple of cute pink bottles after finding out the gender was a waste of money, but getting a full set of nails every two weeks and new throw pillows were more essential.

Turns out I was purely a waste of her time. Well, we both were, I suppose. After Nicole had our baby girl, Charlie, she stayed in the hospital another couple of days. When I went to bring the car around to load them up and take them both home with me, Nicole said no thanks. Her friend picked her up, she took off and has never looked back. Good riddance, if you ask me.

When Camden got his law degree, one of his first jobs was filing a petition to terminate Nicole's rights. She hasn't cared enough to see or contact Charlie since she left the hospital that day, so it was an easy enough process. I haven't seen her since that ruling was finalized and I thank my lucky stars that Charlie never had to love her and lose her the way that I did.

But now I'm on a mission. As much as I'd like to find love like my brother Keaton has with his wife, Anna, I'm actually on the hunt for a mother. Charlie deserves more than only me. Sure, my mom lives with us and has been essential in helping me raise my daughter, but she has her own battles to face and I can't always rely on her to step up when I need it.

So here I am. On what feels like my thousandth date of the year, hoping like hell this one will work out, but it was clear early on that wasn't the case. As soon as we entered the restaurant, she started in with the money bullshit. "Oh, this is such a nice place. I bet you go to really expensive places all the time, don't you?"

I don't. At least, I try not to. When my brothers and I started our cybersecurity company, we didn't have a penny to our names. I'm not entirely sure how my oldest brother, Keaton, managed to con someone into giving us a business loan and then scraped up enough to put a down payment on the building we've been in since day one, but I'm sure as fuck glad he did. Phisherman's Cybersecurity has evolved over time into one of the most reputable tech companies in the country. We have people from all over, fucking billionaires, calling us up and wanting to install our equipment for their multimillion dollar companies. In turn, we've managed to put several million into our own pockets.

The money is nice, but I honestly hate the fancy ass places we have to go sometimes. I also hate that women I date seem to expect it. "Truly, I prefer the small town lifestyle. Give me a diner or a local dive over a place like this." When I gave her my answer, her nose wrinkled and not in that adorable way.

It continued once we were seated, making demands of our server, and insisting we splurge on the most expensive bottle of wine on the menu. Whatever, just drink it and put me out of my misery. When the server poured her a glass, she swirled it around and gave it a sniff. I highly doubt she's a wine connoisseur and is only mimicking what she's seen in the movies, but when she took a sip, I knew instantly she couldn't stand the stuff.

"You've brought us a bad bottle," she insisted, "this one is clearly spoiled. Bring us a new one."

The server looked at me confused, so I tossed him a bone. "Could you bring us a bottle of this instead, please." I pointed to the only Moscato on the menu, knowing she would prefer the sweetness to the drier Chardonnay she had chosen.

When our server returned and poured her a glass, she thanked him for bringing the correct bottle this time, then proceeded to order the filet mignon, well done. I ordered the same, but in a medium rare. What kind of monster desecrates meat like that? I try to make things easy on the poor boy who was clearly not used to the customers of this restaurant making outlandish demands and butchering the pronunciation of a common cut of beef.

"So, Amanda tells me that you're in sales." I try to make conversation.

She leans forward, crossing her arms on the table and then positioning herself so her barely-there cleavage can attempt to make an appearance. A thin strap of her gold dress slides off her bony right shoulder. "Part time, I suppose. I work at the county clerk's office, but on the side, I sell sex toys."

I choke on the bourbon I ordered, thinking there's no way I heard this woman correctly. "Excuse me, what was that?"

"You know. Dildos, vibrators, cock rings, butt plugs. Don't tell me you're one of those men who don't believe in little helpers in the bedroom."

"No, it's not that. I just," I'm fucking stammering over my words, "I've never met someone who does that for a living."

"Well, I do it more for the discount. A girl's gotta have her toys. If you play your cards right tonight, I could potentially introduce you to them. Tell me big boy, have you ever used a strap-on?"

I choke back a laugh, "Umm, I've never needed one. I have something of my own."

"No silly," she lets out a laugh. I'm fairly sure she thinks it's sexy, but it's totally missing the mark, with me. "I would use it on you."

Well that's a big fucking nope.

I try to get us back into typical date banter, "Anyway, umm, so you like kids?"

She lifts herself from the table and shrugs her shoulders then begins digging through her purse. "They're fine, I guess."

"You do know I have a daughter, right? Her name is Charlie." I smile as I think about my six-year-old little spitfire. She's the best thing that's ever happened to me, and I know she deserves two parents who can give her everything she'd ever want. That's why I try and force myself to make things work with, well, shit I forgot her name.

She fixes her hair in the little handheld mirror she pulled out, and then checks her fire-engine red lipstick. "Yeah, Amanda mentioned it. I guess that's fine."

"You guess?" I can't help but laugh. "She's kind of a big deal in my life."

She doesn't look at me as she answers, keeping her gaze on herself as she tilts her head left to right, seemingly considering things. "Yeah, but she's old enough to be in school, right? So I would only have to deal with her for a few hours after that and then she would go to bed. I can handle three to four hours a day, I suppose."

Is this woman fucking serious? Obviously this date isn't going anywhere, so I'm going to gently let her know that this isn't going to work out and she can take her damn overcooked "feel-it mig-none" home with her. But just as I'm about to open my mouth, she leans for her wine glass, her eyes still fixed on that damn tiny mirror, and it tips over.

As it falls, the lip lands on my edge of the table, causing the cool liquid to seep into my shirt.

"What the hell?" I jump up, trying to pull my soaked shirt away from my body it's currently clinging to.

"Oh, calm down. It's white wine." My date spits the words at me.

"I'm drenched," I say, motioning to the huge wet spot on the front of me.

She huffs. "Listen, if you're gonna get all worked up over me spilling just a little bit of wine, I don't see this working out between us. I'm gonna go ahead and get out of here. I wish you and your little girl the best. You've got the check, right?"

"You sure as hell don't have it," I mumble as I retrieve a handful of twenty dollar bills from my billfold and toss them onto the table. At least the server will get a good tip out of tonight.

She retreats out the front of the restaurant as I turn on my heels and head to the bathroom to see if I can dry off.

I can't fucking do this anymore. I'm sorry Charlie, but it looks like it may just be you and dear old dad.

Chapter Four
Sierra

It's completely humiliating to walk through a restaurant where everyone inside just watched you get belittled by a blind date. I keep my head down so as not to make eye contact with anyone. When I reach the bathroom, I push the door open, then quickly slam it behind me and turn the lock. Leaning my head against the door, I can feel my shoulders begin to shake, wanting to give into the sobs I've been holding back, but I refuse to let myself feel inferior from the words of some fish kissing idiot.

"Can I help you?" A deep voice has me startling and lifting my gaze from my feet that have swollen from being shoved into the strappy sandals that adorn them. I turn my body around and instead of puffy pedes, my eyes land on the insanely attractive man that had been sitting beside me earlier.

In the most ladylike way I can manage, I squeal. "What are you doing in here?"

He smirks and calm as a clam, provides his response, "Cleaning my shirt. What are you doing in here?"

It must have been the startling awareness that there was a man in the women's restroom that kept me from noticing that the man's torso is completely bare, but now that my senses are once again firing on all cylinders, my eyes can't seem to look away.

Ink is stretched across his top half like it's a second skin. It traces over his back and both arms. A vine of what appears to be Morning Glory dances from his wrist to his impressive biceps that are adorned with even more ink. Seriously, I am not a small girl and I bet this man would have no issue bench pressing me.

A throat clears and I realize I have been openly ogling the man. He's clearly waiting for my answer. "I have every right to be here. This is the women's restroom." I cross my arms under my chest, pushing my breasts up. Am I doing it to show assertiveness or to show off the solid C-cups that look quite impressive in the flattering milkmaid style dress I'm wearing? One may never know.

"I'm pretty certain those would say otherwise." He points across the way and my eyes track his finger to the urinals against the wall. Great, I'm the one in the wrong. It seems to be a recurring theme in my life.

He continues, "Either way, take a piss if you need to. I'm just gonna run my shirt under the dryer so I shouldn't hear you."

My jaw drops in shock, "I don't need to take a piss, as you so eloquently stated."

He shrugs, "Fine, take a shit. Doesn't bother me."

My eyes widen. I cannot believe he would think I would even consider doing either of those things with him standing in here. "That's not why I came in here."

"So you didn't come to the bathroom to actually use the bathroom?" He asks, frown lines forming between his eyebrows and somehow the grump look only makes him sexier.

I let out a deep sigh. "No," I admit, "I only came in here to take a moment after a date went horribly wrong."

He holds his shirt up, "Did yours spill wine on you, too?"

I like that he's attempting to commiserate with me and I smirk a little, but it quickly fades away as I remember why I am currently standing in the men's bathroom. "I wish that's all he did. Instead he ever-so-kindly explained to me that I didn't look as fat online as I do in real life and since he wasn't attracted to me, the best he could do is let me suck his dick."

I didn't mean to unload the humiliating confession to this tatted stranger, but here I am awkwardly standing in the wrong restroom saying the wrong thing. Classic Sierra.

"The fuck?" I stare down at the floor and attempt to count the tiles, avoiding looking back at the handsome man with the chiseled jaw and the defined abdominal muscles. A pair of feet keep me from reaching double digits in my counting mission, and my eyes slowly ascend. With him standing this close to me, I can make out the complex images that adorn his skin. Both of his arms are trailed by the vining flower, and his entire chest has an intricately detailed tattoo of a map of the world. The word 'daddy' is inked above his right collarbone.

I would totally love to call this man daddy.

It would take me days to explore all of the beautiful artwork that adds to his attractiveness, and I would willingly take on that challenge. But when he reaches out and touches my chin so that he can tilt it to where I'm looking into his eyes, it's an even better view.

Where my eyes are more of a deep navy, his are such a light blue they're almost white. They're like the sky on the most perfect day and I could easily get lost in them, but his deep voice breaks me from their trance. Even though we've only just met, I can feel the anger radiating from him, but somehow his voice is gentle. "Is he still out there?'

Shaking my head to let him know the idiot took off, he breathes out what sounds like relief. "Good, I would have hated to have to murder someone tonight."

A giggle begins to bubble out of me, and then another, and another. I have gone into full blown hysterics in front of this gorgeous man and I can't seem to get a grip. I try to apologize through gasps, and he softly smiles at my attempt, making my heart flutter. This man had to have wandered in here from a runway. Seriously, how are his teeth so perfectly straight and white?

When he speaks again, his voice sends electric signals over me, charging me with desire. "Please tell me you told that fuckface to fuck right off."

"Not exactly." I shake my head and attempt to lower my eyes to avoid his piercing gaze, but he regains his grip on my chin and doesn't allow me to budge. His thumb brushes over my cheek and my eyes flutter shut at the gentle caress.

"Look at me," he demands.

Opening my eyes, my body freezes as I realize how close his face is to mine. "Any man who looks at you and doesn't immediately want to worship this incredible body and run his hands over your goddamn gorgeous curves, has no clue what he's missing out on."

"You're just being nice," I whisper breathily, still terribly close to the dark stubble that runs along his jawline and chin. I breathe in his scent and immediately rub my thighs to create friction and keep the moisture that has built up between them from venturing south.

He chuckles, deep and warm. "I'm really not." Without warning, his lips crash against mine and he moves his hand from my chin to the back of my head, the other gripping my waist in a move that's only meant to claim a partner. I wrap my arms around his neck and decide to explore his mouth with my tongue, forgetting my surroundings and the fact we're locked in a men's restroom.

Suddenly, he takes a step away from me and runs a hand down his face. "I'm so sorry."

I can hardly focus after the most handsome man alive literally sucked the breath right out of me, but when I realize what he said, it feels like a punch in the gut. "Oh, it's okay."

"It's not okay. You deserve better than being manhandled in a bathroom. I don't even know your name."

"It's," I begin, but my name doesn't get to leave my lips when his mouth is pressed against them once again.

This time when he breaks the kiss, he doesn't go far. He leans his forehead against mine and speaks softly. "Don't tell me. I have a request. It's a pretty crazy one, but can I ask?"

I nod my head so that it brushes against his.

"Could you simply be the beautiful stranger I need tonight? Please?" I can hear the desperate desire in his voice. He's a man who has been let down and I want to be the comfort he craves even if it's only for this one night.

Nodding again, I whisper. "Tonight, I'm yours."

An animalistic growl bellows out of him as he lifts my thigh, granting him easy access to slip his hand within the slit of my dress. He yanks down the matching red satin thong I had paired with it down to my knees. "Need these off. Now."

I lift my legs one at a time so he can slide them the rest of the way down. Then I watch as he shoves them into his pocket. When I lift an eyebrow at him, he simply smirks. "Gonna need a souvenir after I visit such a sweet fucking pussy."

"What makes you think it's sweet?" I sass, biting my lip.

"Ooo, is there a bit of a brat inside of you?" He grips my right thigh and hikes it up to curl it around his leg. "I can't wait to tame it."

Suddenly the hand that was behind my back is now pressed against my mound, rocking back and forth as he teases the bud that's begging for all of his attention. "See how your body responds to my touch, Brat? See how your pussy is weeping for me to take care of it?" He runs a finger through my slit, collecting the arousal he has so quickly helped build. When he puts the finger in his mouth, closing his eyes and moaning as he takes in the flavor, I grind myself against his other hand that has relentlessly been bringing me to the edge. I'm so damn close, which is a completely foreign concept to me. I've never been able to get off without penetration before.

Who the hell is this man?

"Mmm, I was right." He says after pulling his finger from his mouth with a pop, "so fucking sweet."

I don't mean to do it, but a scoff bursts out of me before I can rein it in. He cocks an eyebrow and runs his finger back down my body to collect more of my flavor. Then, he places his wet finger against my bottom lip and rubs it, coaxing me to open up and taste myself. I oblige and can't help but suck as he probes the inside of my mouth, crooking his finger around my tongue so that I don't miss a drop. As he retracts his hand, I let out a tiny whimper, and he leans forward to whisper in my ear, "Told ya."

My entire body trembles as his warm, minty breath hits my face while his other hand applies more pressure. The finger that was just in my mouth seconds ago is now gently squeezing my neck with the rest of his digits. "My dirty girl has a sweet tooth, hmm?" I moan so loud at his words that I'm pretty sure the entire restaurant heard me. I don't care. The orgasm taking over my body has me oblivious to the fact we're in a public place.

As I come down from the unexpected high, I look into those beautiful sky blue eyes of my sexy stranger and say the first thing that comes to mind.

"Thank you."

Chapter Five
Lincoln

I 've been on my best behavior over the years, so maybe I'm a bit off my game, but I can't recall any other time a gorgeous woman said those words to me after providing her with an earth-shattering orgasm. "Did you just thank me?"

Those round cheeks of hers turn pink in a blush, "I like new experiences and this was my first time doing anything like this in a public place, so yeah, thank you. And thank you for the kind words. And for taking my mind off things tonight. I should probably clean up and let you get back to your night, though."

Is she serious? She thinks she can walk her fine ass into this bathroom and give me a taste of her sweetness, mixed with the bite of her sass, and think I'm finished with her? "What the fuck are you talking about?"

She blinks at me. I love that she's on the taller side and I don't have to strain my neck to look into the deep ocean blues of hers. "Oh, I mean, I figured you had other things to do tonight. It's still pretty early." Now that our moment is over, the confident woman grinding against my hand and sassing me has been replaced with the same defeated beauty that waltzed into the restroom earlier.

I knew she was trying to be strong when she walked in, but I couldn't help but notice the sound of her sucking back sobs.

We can't have that again. This curvy goddess is going to know exactly how desirable she is if it's the last thing I do. "Yeah it is. But I recall you saying you were mine tonight. And the night is far from over."

"You don't even know my name."

"I don't need to know your name to know I want you."

She raises an eyebrow at me, a sign that the savage sweetheart is still under that pretty exterior. I haven't had a brat in my bed for some time and I can't help but think of how much fun I'm going to have with her all night long. "Besides," I continue, making a show of licking my lips, "dessert was delicious, but I didn't get a chance to eat dinner yet, did you?" She shakes her head, biting her lip in the process.

I pull it from the hold her teeth have on it. "Let me get you something to eat and then we can go from there."

I was surprised to hear that we actually both lived in the small town of Cheatham. With a population hovering right around fifteen hundred folks, I thought I knew everyone there. Since we both had driven to the restaurant here in the slightly larger town of Laurel, we each took our own vehicles back to meet at Pizza Papa.

"You're sure this is okay?" I ask as we both step out of our vehicles.

She nods her head excitedly, "Pizza is my favorite, and I haven't tried this place yet."

"I take it you're new in town?" The question slips from me as I hold the door open for her. I can't risk getting to know this beautiful woman in front of me aside from what she's like in the bedroom. I'm over being disappointed when things don't work out in my daughter's favor. But I can't help my healthy dose of curiosity when it comes to this beauty who is far too young for me, far too sweet for me, and far too delicious for me to pass up on tonight.

We're greeted and seated quickly, so her answer comes once we're settled in our booth. "Yeah, I actually just arrived yesterday. I haven't even moved into my new place yet so I'm staying at the bed and breakfast. It's a really cute place, have you seen it?"

I can't help the smile that forms. "I've lived here my entire life, so yeah, I'm familiar." She bites her lip and I have the urge to pull it from her grip, but I ask the question that's been on my mind the whole ride back to town. "So why Cheatham of all places?" While I prefer the small town life, we've noticed more and more people have been moving to the city, especially the younger crowd. Lord knows Nicole couldn't wait to get out of town. Knowing that this woman chose here to start her life has me curious.

"Oh, I got a job here. I'm really excited, but also incredibly nervous. It's," I hold my hand up again to cut her off and shake my head.

"If you tell me where you work, that's basically the same thing as telling me your name in these parts."

She crosses her arms on the table and leans over them like she's about to tell me a secret, "Why don't you want to know my name? Some weird fetish of yours?"

I bite my lip to hold back the smile and lean into her, my hands brushing up against hers. "Keep up with the smart mouth, Brat, and I'll punish it later."

She smiles big showing rows of perfectly white, straight teeth, and fuck. It does something to me. Her next words are a whisper so that only the two of us can hear. "Maybe I don't mind being punished," she hesitates for a split second, "daddy."

Well fuck, my dick liked that. He's straining against my slacks, demanding I knock this table over, bend her over, flipping up that red dress of hers with the fucking slit that shows off her gorgeous long legs. The way the whole thing covers her curves has taunted me all night. He wants me to take her right here in the middle of my favorite pizza joint, letting the whole town know that this new arrival belongs to me. I would only have to move that slit over a tiny bit to see that bare pussy I know she's sporting, thanks to the panties of hers that are tucked in my back pocket. My dick strains against my pants so hard I'm sure an imprint of my zipper is going to form, but I can't risk not letting this girl get supper a second time tonight, so I adjust myself and try to settle down.

"Before you so rudely cut me off," she gives me an adorable look of disapproval, causing me to snort, "I was going to tell you that it's my first official job. I recently graduated from Georgetown College this spring."

Damn, I knew she was young, but that puts her way below anyone I would have ever considered dating. Good thing this is solely a one night fling and not a forever type of situation. I could do a deep dive into why I'm connecting with someone so much younger than my thirty-eight years, but thankfully, a local girl, Jillian, bounces up to where we're seated and brings me back to reality before I can allow my brain to derail my mission here tonight. "Hey, Mr. Fisher, twice in one day is a bit unusual, but it's always good to see you."

The teenager's cheeks blush at her confession, and while I will admit that it's nice to know the younger female population still finds my thirty-eight year self attractive, the woman sitting across from me has me toeing the line, but the young waitress is a big fuck no. Hell, Jillian is young enough to be my daughter. Still, she's a sweet kid, so I don't draw attention to it and embarrass her more, simply carrying on the conversation. "Well I had to be hospitable and show our newcomer in town the best pizza place. Can you give us a few minutes?"

"So what kind of pizza do you like?" I ask my new date for the evening as Jillian walks away. Instead of seeing the relaxed woman I had just been speaking with, my stranger now appears to be fighting an internal battle. Her shoulders are stone, tensed up in a way that is a stark contrast to the turning and twisting her hands are doing. She's nibbling her bottom lip like she's trying to solve the world's problems, and her eyes are doing everything they can to avoid me.

"Is everything okay?"

Chapter Six
Sierra

"Hey, Mr. Fisher," the young girl's words had me stopping the trajectory of my drink coming to my lips. It has to be a coincidence, right? I am not sitting with the man who could very likely be my new boss. I'm sure there are plenty of "Mr. Fishers" in this small town. This small town of barely more than a thousand people. Shit. If he isn't the Mr. Fisher I'm supposed to be working for, then he's probably at the very least related to the one I am.

When I was hired, a lovely lady named Janine did the entire process, but she made it clear that it was on the behalf of her employer. I will be the first nanny and caretaker for a Mr. Lincoln Fisher, the father of a six-year-old sassafras named Charlie, and the son of a reclusive mother who lives with them. Those were Janine's words, not mine. She explained they wanted someone with a degree in psychology who could possibly help his mom, a troubled woman who refused to seek counseling services. The fact that I had my degree, along with experience working in a daycare all through college, is ultimately why she felt like I was the right fit.

The pay was more than I ever expected to start out with, and it came with a place to live. Everything about it seemed to be too good to be true, so I imagined the family had to be absolutely horrid beings. Something akin to the beast that locked the beautiful woman in his tower in exchange for her father's freedom. But if this man is the one who hired me, then the only thing I'd need to fear from this beast is trying to somehow maintain my distance and keep my legs from opening up every time he's near.

I watch the older man as he interacts with our server who clearly has a crush on him. I'm not bothered by it in the least. He gives no indication that he is at all interested in the very illegal, very off-limits teen, and I can't blame her for the googly eyes she's giving the man. He is gorgeous. But if this dangerously attractive man is my new boss, then this is a very bad plan and I definitely shouldn't pursue what he was very much insinuating.

Even though I want to.

So damn bad.

"Is everything okay?" Mr. Fisher asks me.

I nod slowly, but I genuinely don't know. If the man across from me is the same man I'm supposed to be working for, then this is a major conflict of interest and could make things incredibly awkward and tense in my new job. A job that I desperately need and am actually excited about starting. But if he isn't, then I risk giving up on something I truly desire, because let's face it, one look at this man has me ready to give in to every single one of his demands.

"Are you sure? You look like you just took a bite of pineapple pizza."

"You really don't want to know my name or what I was hired to do here?" Maybe if I give him the chance to learn more about me, it will clear things up and I won't be torn on the decision I should make.

"No, please," he shakes his head, and leans back on his side of the booth looking defeated. "I'm going to be really honest with you. I've been on the dating scene for far too long and I can't take it anymore. I want one night with no strings attached. One night with a beautiful woman who makes me so fucking hard I see stars. One night with you."

I gulp and have to rub my legs together since I can feel the moisture begin to pool between them, knowing there's no fabric since he took his little souvenir. It's time to make a decision. Do I give into the carnal desires that have taken over my body since he first kissed me in the men's bathroom? Or do I trust my instincts and training and take a step back and end my night with this handsome man who may or may not be my new boss? I know what I should do. I know what the right thing to do would be.

"For the record, I love pineapple on my pizza." He scrunches up his nose and somehow the movement makes him even more attractive. "But the more important question is, what kind of pizza do you like...daddy?"

Apparently I am a horrible decision maker, but the way this man's hands are on me doesn't have me caring in the least. We devoured dinner at a ravenous pace so that he could follow me back to the bed and breakfast where we are now in my room and he has yet to stop touching my body.

Thank god.

I should probably be self-conscious about the overflowing curves of my frame. Society tells me I shouldn't be proud of the extra skin that hangs at my belly. Or the arm flab that keeps jiggling long after the rest of me has stopped moving. It even tells me I shouldn't be proud of these strong, thick calves that could protect me if I needed them to, simply because they aren't dainty.

But I've come to terms with my body and have said a big "fuck you" to society. Apparently the man roaming every inch of me feels the same. He untied the bow at my chest the second we shut the door to my room here at Sheets n' Sweets, and it fell away from my skin, allowing my breasts to become bare and exposed, since I decided to skip an uncomfortable bra tonight. He eased the smooth fabric over my skin, pebbling it with goosebumps.

Since he had taken off my panties earlier, when the dress hit the floor, every inch of me was opened up to him. The way his eyes raked over me told me he liked what he saw, and the fact he is still fully clothed has my words coming out breathy, but whiny. "It's your turn. Get naked. I want to see you. All of you."

A slow smile spreads against the handsome stranger's face. "It's cute how you think you get to make the demands here. I'll let you see all of me tonight, but first I need dessert."

My eyes roll before I can think better of it, "I thought you said you ate dessert first?"

He moves to stand behind me, his hands cupping my breasts before trailing down my sides. "Hmm, maybe I have a sweet tooth, too." A loud crack sounds around the room and a sting has my right ass cheek tingling. "And that's for rolling your eyes at me. Now, get on the bed."

This man did not just spank my ass. And I did not seriously like it as much as I did, right? Is this something I need to tell my therapist about? It feels like there's a lot to unpack here.

"On the bed. Now. Don't make me say it again." His firm tone has my body shuddering, but in pure desire.

"Or what?" I ask.

A slap against my left cheek this time has a yelp coming out of me and I scurry over to the bed in anticipation. But how does he want me? Why is this so difficult? I've had sex before. I'm good at it. Well, I'm decent at it. I mean, I guess I'm fine at it. How does one even know?

The man doesn't allow me the time for my internal battle because he pushes me to the side and climbs on the bed himself. "Fine, if you won't sit on the bed, then you can sit on my face."

Umm, what? "I can't do that."

"You absolutely will do that." He settles himself so that his head is resting on a pillow and his long body extends past the end of the mattress. "Climb up here and sit on my face."

I shake my head. "Are you trying to make me a murderer? I will suffocate you."

He laughs and the deep sound has my core throbbing. "The only thing getting murdered here tonight is your pussy. Now do as you're told, and sit."

I climb onto the bed, straddling him, and manage to waddle on my knees until my pussy hovers over his chiseled face. His hands reach up and squeeze my thighs so tightly that my knees weaken and my body begins to lower. "I don't want to hurt you," I whisper.

"Then stop denying me. The longer you keep this sweet pussy from me, the more pain I'm in. Now squeeze your tits and let me fucking feast."

It's embarrassing how quickly my hands give into his demands and I reach up and palm my breasts. They're each a solid handful and the pressure I put on them feels good, but nowhere near as incredible as when the man beneath me runs his tongue along my seam, parting me so that he can devour my core.

His hands still grip my thighs and he continues tugging me towards him to the point I know he has to be struggling to breathe, but you wouldn't know it with the relentless way he attacks my core. While his tongue laps up the absolute mess leaking between my thighs, I throw my head back and pinch my nipples until I'm crying out and shaking on top of him. Everything with him feels so good, but I need more.

"I need you. I want to taste you, too."

"Not finished," he manages to mutter while brushing his tongue against my sensitive clit.

My hips begin to rock as I ride his face until he has me coming completely undone over top of him. I'm crying out, my body thrashing against him, but his tongue continues to thrust in and out of me until my body goes lax.

"There. Now I'm finished." He places a gentle kiss against my mound before helping me off of him.

My body is exhausted, but the pleasure brimming inside it has me needing to see him. Touch him. Taste him.

"Good," I say, "because now it's my turn. Strip."

Chapter Seven
Lincoln

"**F**uck, Brat, your mouth feels so good." I look down at this beautiful woman on her knees in front of me and grip the chocolate strands of her hair at the base of her neck, feeding a little more of my cock into her mouth. At nine inches, I know I'm big, so I give her the time she needs to adjust to my size before I completely thrust myself in. The sound she makes as she gags on my length almost has me ready to shoot straight down her throat, but I'm able to hang on to my sensibilities long enough to get things back under control. I may have her tasting my cum tonight, but it won't be until after I've dipped my dick into that glorious pussy of hers.

The thought of her sucking her own taste off me until ribbons of white are filling her mouth has me so fucking hard I can barely last much longer. I enunciate each word as I thrust into her mouth. "Need. To. Fuck. You. Now."

She releases her grip on me with a pop of her mouth. Taking the grip I have on her hair, I haul her up to me and slam my lips against hers. Kissing this woman is something I could make a living off doing, and if I only have her for one night, I'm going to take every opportunity I get.

The whimper she releases has my dick twitching in need, and I push her back against the bed so that her stunning long legs are hanging off the edge. This woman was built for a man like me. She's strong and beautiful and I know she's going to take my dick so well.

I bend down and pick up the pants I had discarded moments ago, pulling out my wallet and retrieving the condom I hid in there earlier tonight. Rolling the latex down my length, I watch the beautiful woman who has her eyes fixated on my hardened cock. "Don't worry, it will fit."

She smirks at me and it is quite possibly the most beautiful thing I've ever seen. "I was just thinking about how I could handle more, but I suppose this will do."

"Fucking brat," I shake my head and line up at her core, filling her up in one painfully slow movement so she can feel every single inch of me, but not allowing her time to adjust. "Then you'll take it all at once," I say as I bury myself to the hilt.

Her cry is the most beautiful melody. "Yes, oh it feels so good, you're amazing." I could get used to her praise and fucking this tight cunt of hers, but I remind myself that I've limited myself to one night with her and one night only. No matter how well she takes my dick.

It's time for me to stop trying to find something that's never going to happen. Taking the time to go out on dates every weekend is keeping me away from the person I'm trying to be better for in the first place. Charlie is my everything and I have to put her first. I've been invested in finding her a mother for so long, that

I've probably slacked at being the best dad I can be. For the night, I'll indulge in this fascinating, curvaceous lady. Then tomorrow I'll put all my focus on my family.

But as this beautiful woman takes me better than anyone has in, well, quite possibly ever, my daughter is the last thing on my mind. I continue to pound as she cries out, making the sweetest sounds. "Look at you being such a good girl and taking all this cock," I manage to grunt out. "You like how I fill you up?"

"Is that all you've got?" I smile at her sassy retort. That bratty mouth of hers is absolutely delicious and going to get her into some trouble. I move my left hand down and cup her ass, squeezing it until she releases a cry that's mixed with equal parts pleasure and pain.

"Not even close," I continue to let my fingers trail around her plump posterior until they find that forbidden erogenous zone. I gently push against it, causing her to gasp. "Tell me, Brat, has anyone ever had you here?"

She shakes her head back and forth, but catches that bottom lip of hers between her teeth. Desire lights up those deep blue eyes of hers and she pushes her ass against my fingers, causing me to chuckle lightly. "I've filled that smart mouth of yours, and now this fucking fantastic cunt. Do you want me to fill this hole of yours, too?"

She whimpers in confusion, wanting to feel the pleasure, but I can sense the nerves in her, too. "I won't shove my cock in there, but how about I tease you the way you've been teasing me all night?" I pull myself from her pussy and stroke my length to collect the wetness she's left on me before I shove two fingers deep inside her, pumping that tight heat until her legs are shaking. When my fingers are wet enough, I return my finger to press against her back hole, causing her to moan.

"You're gonna be a good girl for me and take my cock while I take your ass. Aren't you?" She nods her consent and I slide my finger past the barrier. The beauty beneath me bucks against my hand, making her pussy impossibly tighter and I need her to come so badly. Slowly I pull my finger out and push it back in, performing the same motion with my cock. It's euphoric and there's no way I will be able to last much longer. "Come for me. Come on my cock like the good fucking girl I know you can be." My words and the overwhelming sensation of her being filled to the brink has the two of us exploding together.

We lay there for a few moments, nothing but the sound of our heavy breaths filling the small space. My beautiful girl rolls over and slowly trails her fingers up and down the patterns of ink that vine up my arms. "I know this is only for tonight, but could tonight last until I fall asleep?"

Her sweet question tugs at the heart inside me that hasn't beaten for anyone but my daughter in so long. The feeling is foreign, but makes me want to grant her every wish. "Close your eyes. I'll be right here."

I wake to my phone buzzing in my left hand while my right arm is curled around the softest skin. I didn't mean to doze off, but something about laying next to this woman feels so good that sleep easily pulled me under.

As I check my phone I note that it's half past three in the morning and there's a string of text messages from my brothers. Shit, they're not gonna let me live this night down anytime soon.

Camden

> Linc, where you at? Mama says you were supposed to be back hours ago.

Keaton

> Thought he had a date tonight. They never last this long.

Camden

> That's exactly why Mama called me to see if I'd seen him. Where you at big bro?

Keaton

> Maybe this one actually panned out and he's getting his dick wet for once.

Camden

Geez, Keat. You kiss your wife with that mouth?

Keaton

Yes. Yes I do.

Fucking idiots.

It's too late to message back, but that also means I left Mama alone with Charlie all night. I really hope she hasn't slipped into one of her episodes. The Dad Guilt has been piling on and the thought of my daughter possibly being neglected while I'm out getting my soul sucked out of me by the young succubus beside me is the last thing I need at this moment.

Careful not to wake my sleeping stranger, I extract my arm from beneath her and climb out of bed. As I gather my things I'm at war with myself. It's been a hot minute since I've had a hookup like this. Do I leave a note? My number? Do I simply walk out the door and never look back?

We both knew it was only one night. But man, what a great fucking night it was.

I decide to forgo leaving any trace that I've been here, knowing it will only have me wanting more. After placing one last delicate kiss on her puffy lips, I sneak out the door, closing it softly so I don't wake her.

Descending the stairs, I hear a painfully familiar voice. "Sneaking out of here in the middle of the night, Lincoln Fisher?" Turning in the direction of the check-in counter, I see a small woman in her sixties, her thin lips smiling at me like she's the cat who ate the canary.

"Hazel," I tip my head at the innkeeper's girlfriend who also happens to be my younger brother's, well, what do you call the woman who runs the entire operative of his law office? Seriously, of all the people in town to catch me in my walk of shame, it had to be the one I know for a fact can't keep a secret from my brother. Or her hairdresser. Or the ladies she goes to the diner with every Saturday morning. Fuck my life.

I refuse to slow down, but I should have known I'd never make it out the door. For an older woman she still has quite the spring to her step and intercepts my escape route. "You know, you and that new girl sure made quite the racket, but I think Herb and I have you beat on who could scream the place down." She smirks at me as I process the horror of her words, visualizing an unpleasantness that has no business residing in my mind. I try to eradicate the image of her and the owner of the town's only bed and breakfast in bed together, but unfortunately it has burned itself into my brain. What should be dreams of my fun, curvy, one night stand is now replaced by the nightmare of whatever Hazel and Herb do behind closed doors.

"Way to ruin a man's night, Haze," I grumble and pivot around her so I can reach my desired destination. When the old, pink door closes behind me, I can hear the woman cackling behind me.

The drive home has me contemplating what life will look like now. For so long it's been work throughout the week, taking care of Charlie and Mama, and dates to find the woman who can somehow fix my broken family on the weekends. My little girl is strong and spirited, and you wouldn't know that the lack of a mother has a strong impact on her, but I hear her sweet prayers at night. I see the lists she writes to the jolly man who lives up north. She may be fine with what she has for now, but she wants her family to be complete.

As I walk into the silent house, I spot my mom's frail body on the sofa, a rush of memories from the time we almost lost her springing to my mind. "Mama!" In my head I'm screaming, but the sound barely comes out as a whisper. My heart doesn't begin to slow down until I watch her chest rise and fall with her deep breaths, knowing that tonight won't end with a trip to the hospital. Gently, I shake her. "Mama, let's get you to bed."

Her eyes are a bit disoriented when she wakes, but then I know she's good when she slaps me against my chest. "You could have let me know you planned on being out all night."

I can't help but smile when Mama lets her fire come out. It's been a long time since I've seen those flames fan and the little embers that spark from time to time always have me grinning. "I'm sorry. I should have said something. Didn't exactly plan on staying out."

"I take it the date went well then?" Her face is eager, but I shake my head, knowing I let her down when her face begins to droop. I can see now that her eyes are puffy.

"Mama, have you been crying?"

She mumbles that she's fine, but I refuse to let her hide. "What's going on? Is everything okay with Charlie?"

"Charlie is perfectly fine, I swear." Her shoulders begin to shake and I brace myself for the floodgates that are about to open. "I put her to bed and then, well then, it's not fair, Linc." Tears begin to fall down her still so beautiful face. "I can't do this life without him. I wasn't supposed to. We were in it together." It's the same words I've heard for over a decade now, and they haven't gotten easier with time.

"I know, Mama." I rub her back and try to console her as her body crumbles. She shudders as she tries to suck in breaths through her tears. I hold her and repeat the words I always say when she's going through one of these moments.

"I know."

"I love you."

"I'm sorry."

Several minutes pass, but when her body begins to still, I cradle her into my body and carry my mother to her room. Placing her in her bed, I pull the covers around her exactly how she did for me so many years ago.

Mama deserves to be healed. Charlie deserves a mother. And I deserve some help.

I hope like hell the woman that's supposed to arrive tomorrow can do all that.

Chapter Eight
Sierra

I wake in a panic and all alone. The man from last night must have crept out of the room shortly after I passed out from the coma-inducing orgasms he gave me. While I wouldn't mind another round or two, I'm not surprised the handsome grump is gone, and I'm really glad he wasn't here to bear witness to the night terror I just had.

Glancing at my phone, I see that it's 3:47 in the morning. Again. It's the same time my mother took her last breath, and the same time I have frequently woken up since. The night terrors began shortly after her funeral and the one telehealth visit I had with a therapist didn't do enough to shake them.

Having a psychology degree myself, I know that one session isn't enough for me to overcome the internal struggles I've been dealing with, but the financial strain of therapy is a cold hard reality, and sadly the people who need it the most are often the people who can't afford it. So I try to regulate my breathing and center myself like I always do after a fitful night of sleep.

Searching the room I look for five things I can see. My dress that was a little too tight is now a loose ball on the floor. The sandals I kicked off as soon as I crossed the barrier are peeking out underneath it. I take in the barely there indentation on the pillow beside me. The edge of the fitted sheet that popped off after orgasm number two. Or was it three? And finally, a button on the bed from when that damn shirt of his wasn't coming off as quickly as I needed.

I pick up the button, running my hands over its smoothness and counting it as one of the four things I can feel. Putting it down, I run my hands across the slightly scratchy sheets on the bed. I allow them to caress my skin, remembering my stranger's touch. I mimic his touch and run my fingers over my own skin, shivering in their wake. Finally, I graze them over my lips and release a sigh that I will never feel his pressed against them again.

My ears perk up as I try to find three things I can hear. My mind immediately tries to tell me there's nothing but silence. Silence that overruns the loneliness I have felt since my mother's passing. I know it's purely a cruel trick, so I close my eyes to sharpen my senses. The air conditioner is running to battle against the heat that still lingers this late into the fall. There is a creaking of the hardwood stairs or floors. Quiet giggling accompanies it. Sounds like someone else had their own romantic rendezvous tonight.

Two smells come next. I take a deep breath in and immediately I smell him. His masculine scent of sandalwood mixed with something strangely sweet, like birthday cake. I pick up the pillow he collapsed on after the events that took place and press it to my nose. Another smell hits me. Sex. The messy kind where you're unashamed of all the dirty desires you act out, but then blush about it the morning after. I can feel the heat pooling in my cheeks as I think about all the filthy, but wonderful, things we did.

Finally, one thing I taste. My tongue darts out across my bottom lip, and maybe I'm imagining things, but I can taste him. My sexy stranger. The man I got for one night and one night only.

With my breathing regulated and my heart no longer trying to escape my chest, I lie back down in the bed that's now filled with so many memories. Never have I ever had the mind-blowing orgasms that man delivered. And the way he touched me was like he owned my body. He practically did. I would have let that man use me in any way he saw fit. I have been a firm believer in the "things go out, but don't go in" mantra of that forbidden hole, but when he asked to explore, there was no saying no to him. And Lord knows I enjoyed it far more than I ever imagined possible. The sensation of being so full was intense and I was almost coming undone simply from the pressure he put there when he pressed against me. When he finally slid his fingers into my ass at the same time his holy huge erection pushed into my pussy, well I'm pretty sure I went blind.

But it was so much more than just the sex, too. Our conversation through the night was easy. And the way he handled my smart mouth? It felt empowering to talk back at him the way I did. I've always been scolded for my quips and comebacks. It isn't ladylike. I should be seen and not heard. I'm a lot prettier when I keep my mouth shut. But this man didn't say any of those things. The way he reacted sent electric pulses through my entire body. I'm pretty sure that man could have me crying out his name with only his dirty words.

Well, that is, if I knew his name. A sense of dread comes over me as I remember the words of that young waitress last night who delivered us some of the best pizza I've ever tasted.

Mr. Fisher.

It can't be him. The man worshipping my pussy like it was his own personal deity can absolutely not be the father of a six-year-old daughter and the son of a woman in serious need of healing. The daughter and woman I am supposed to be taking care of and helping. The family that I'm supposed to live with for the duration of my position.

I run my hand down my face and groan. How have I managed to already complicate things after only spending one night in this sleepy little town?

Rising from my bed, I plod my way over to the bathroom to get ready for the day. Reluctantly I brush my teeth, replacing his taste with the mint of my toothpaste. I pull my chocolate brown hair back into a braid and cover my face with some minimal makeup. After I pull on some black leggings that somehow shape my ass beautifully, and a University of Kentucky sweatshirt, I head downstairs for a cup of coffee. The first of many I'm sure I'll need today.

As I go downstairs, the first thing I notice is the sweet older couple making out like teenagers behind the front desk. It's still dark out being as how it's only around four in the morning, so I'm sure they thought they were all alone, but I'm in desperate need of caffeine, so I clear my throat.

"Umm, excuse me," I interrupt, "I hate to break this up, but could you please tell me where the coffee would be?"

The couple release one another once my voice reaches them, the man looking as though he's ready to run away and hide, but the woman with a smile a mile wide. I think I like her.

"Oh, hi there, Sugar! I can fix you a cup right up. Why don't you come on into the kitchen with me?"

Leaving the blushing man to tend the counter, I follow the older woman into the small, but pristine kitchen space. Everything inside it is red and pink with dainty little cherries speckling the wallpaper. A tea towel with the phrase, "Life is as sweet as cherry pie," sits on the counter in front of me.

"So you're up mighty early this morning," the woman begins. "Had a tough time sleeping? Was something wrong with the bed?"

I shake my head and give her a smile, "Oh, no. Everything here has been wonderful. I'm just not a great sleeper."

She smiles knowingly and hands me the cup of coffee she freshly made. As I take a sip "Did it have something to do with a handsome man slipping out of here in the middle of the night?"

The coffee comes flying out of me like a bat out of hell. "I am so sorry," I sputter, "but, um, what?"

She motions to the tea towel sitting in front of me and I use it to clean my mess as she continues, "Oh, I saw him not too long ago trying to sneak out of here. Thought you might know something about that."

"Um, it was only a one time thing," I explain, ignoring the way my stomach drops with that confession.

"Is that so?" She cocks her head, studying me, but then changes the subject. "So what brings you into this small town of ours?"

I take a new sip of coffee, managing to keep it in this time. "I'm actually supposed to start a new job today."

"Ooo, tell me about it," she pries. Something about this woman's curiosity tells me she loves to be in on the gossip, but also loves to share it.

"Well, I was hired to be a nanny for a local businessman."

A smirk crosses the woman's face, "Oh, were you now?"

"Do you know anything about that?" I ask.

Her smirk transforms into a full-on grin, "Oh, sugar, I know everything that happens here in Cheatham."

Jason

i need more money

I roll my eyes at the message from my good-for-nothing stepfather. Jason. He came into my mom's life while I was away at college, only a few months before she was diagnosed with stage four breast cancer. The day she was diagnosed they should have explored options on how we could prolong her life and make her comfortable. Instead, he took her down to the courthouse and they got married. She seemed happy, but I had my suspicions it was all so he could swindle her out of every dime she had. Since her passing, I feel I was right to not trust the man.

Sierra

I just graduated college, Jason. I don't have any money.

Jason

then get off that fat ass of urs and get a damn job

That was rich coming from him. He had worked for a trucking company before marrying my mom, but when they got married, he insisted he needed to take early retirement and be with her so he could take her to all her treatments. While he took her to some, it was me who was at the hospital with her the majority of the time, and now that she's passed, he has yet to try and find himself a new place in the workforce.

Sierra

What do you need money for anyway?

Jason

none of ur damn business

Jason

get me my money

Jason

u wouldnt want me to start selling off all this precious shit of ur moms would u

I gulp, knowing that he would definitely get rid of all the memories I have inside their home. I rub the watch on my wrist, knowing this little piece of her isn't enough.

Sierra

> I'm starting a new job today. I'll message you when I get my first check.

Throwing my phone against the bed, I pick up the pillow and scream into it. That son of a bitch sucked the life out of my mother, drained her bank account, and now he's trying to steal from me. I hate him.

Unfortunately I don't have time for a tantrum because across town is a little girl waiting for me. I toss the rest of the things I brought in yesterday into my suitcase, then zip it up and head out to my vehicle where I place it with the rest of my life's belongings. It's time to start my new job, live in my new house, and hope like hell it's a new man that I meet this morning.

Pulling up to the farmhouse, I take in how absolutely stunning the place is. The board and batten siding is the cleanest white that has me immediately scouring the place for the pressure washer they must have recently used. Beautiful flower beds are in front and you can tell someone is really dedicated to making sure they remain in tip-top shape. The covered porch looks like the perfect place to sit and rock in one of the black chairs while talking about your day.

I walk across the sidewalk that I can't wait to fill with chalk drawings alongside the little girl I just know will become my new best friend. If this November continues to be warm, we will have plenty of days we can spend out here.

As I climb the steps and raise my finger to the doorbell attached to the house, I chant to myself, "Please don't be him, please don't be him."

When the door inches open, I peek through squinted eyes to find a man only slightly shorter than the one I was with last night, and maybe an inch or so above my 5'11". His smile is bright and his hair more silver and spiked, rather than the short cut my fingers sadly couldn't seem to get a grip on. The relief washes over me and I find myself releasing a tense breath I had been holding.

"Hi there, I'm Keaton Fisher." He extends his left hand out to me and I notice a simple gold band sits there. Interesting, I wasn't aware there was a wife in the equation. I had thought three people lived in this household. Not that it's a problem. I don't mind him having a wife at all. In fact, it's better that way, really. That whole single dad and nanny trope? Total cliché. "You must be Sierra."

I let out a breath or relief and feel my face pull into a smile, nodding. "That's me, it's so nice to meet you Mr. Fisher. You have a beautiful home."

He chuckles and it's a smooth sound. "Thanks, I appreciate it. Though, it isn't my home anymore. This house belongs to my mom and my younger brother, Lincoln. He's who you will be working for, but he's a little busy trying to get bubble gum out of his daughter's hair." He leans in a little closer to whisper, "I hope you aren't opposed to some cussing. My youngest brother, Cam, is going to get quite an earful once he shows up."

"Oh, no," I say with a laugh, "that sounds like quite the story."

Just then I hear heavy footsteps headed in my direction. "Is that Cam, I'm gonna wring that motherfucker's throat for buying her a pack of gum. What was he thinking?"

A large hand pulls at Keaton's shoulder and pushes him to the side, so that the grumpy man with a bubble gum aversion is standing in front of me. When his pale blue eyes stare down at me, I lose my breath.

"What the fuck are you doing here?"

Chapter Nine
Lincoln

"Where did this even come from?" I ask my daughter who is squirming under the grasp I have on her hair. Her beautiful, long brown hair that matches my shade and is now caked in bright pink bubble gum.

"Uncle Cam got me some when we went to the store. It's really cool because you can pull it out like a piece of tape and chew as much of it as you want! But I guess I probably should have spit it out before I fell asleep, right Daddy? You probably can't sleep and chew at the same time. Can you? Google it."

I roll my eyes, "I don't have to Google it. You should always spit out gum before you fall asleep. And exactly how the hell much were you chewing? Half your head is covered in this mess. We're gonna have to run down to Becca's shop and see if she has time to get you in and cut this out."

My little girl who has something to say twenty-four hours of every day completely tenses under my touch and goes deadly silent. This is not good. The wail that releases from her mouth pierces my ears and I reach up to cover them, forgetting the sticky substance that covers my hands. Gum sticks to my ear lobes, but it's the least of my worries as my baby girl begins crying huge tears at my thoughtless words.

"Do we really have to cut my hair? I don't want it to look like yours." She chokes her words out between sobs and it absolutely breaks my heart.

"Your hair is beautiful and we're going to fix this. Your hair will not look like mine, I promise." I wrap her in my arms and pull her to me in an embrace, not caring if the gum transfers over to me. I'm absolutely going to murder my brother for this.

The doorbell rings and Keaton hollers that he's got it. My oldest brother was here early this morning trying to help me coax our mother out of her bedroom. I may have failed to mention to her that not only have I hired a nanny to help out with my daughter, but that I plan on moving her into her home. When I broke the news this morning, well, she was not so kind in her response.

"You may legally own this place now, but make no mistake that this is my house. It is not okay for you to bring people here and house them without my consent. I raised you better than that. And what the hell does Charlie need a nanny for anyway? Am I not enough?"

Sadly the answer is no, and I don't have the heart to tell her that. She went to a dark place after my father's funeral and we almost lost her at one point. The night I came home to see her lying in her bed comatose was one of the worst nights of my life. I called up Keaton and we managed to get her to the hospital in time for a full recovery, but it was only a physical one. She hasn't left the house since that day.

When Nicole rode out of town and left me and our three day old daughter behind, I thought maybe the new addition would help turn things around. And it did, for a while. Mama loves being a grandmother to Charlie and she helps me every chance she gets, but when Charlie started school last year, Mama's dark days returned.

The final straw was when I walked in from a date a couple of months ago and found Charlie all by herself while Mama was basically in a comatose state. I couldn't get her attention at all and finally had to put Charlie to bed, then pluck Mama up and put her in her room. The next morning I walked into a complete mess. She had soiled herself and continued to do so over the next several weeks. She refused to move from her bed. She refused to speak. It was as though she had completely given up on life.

When Mama found out that Keaton had drunkenly gotten married to his new assistant when they unexpectedly met in Vegas, that finally snapped her out of her stupor. She popped out of bed and cleaned herself right up, eager to meet her new daughter-in-law. I suspect with the way those two are so sickeningly in love, Mama will have more grandbabies to love on soon enough.

But until then, she has moments like she did last night. Crying fits where she can't seem to get past the grief and the loneliness. She's a good woman. She deserves happiness. She deserves a life worth living. And I'm doing my best to help her see that.

My brothers do the best they can to help out with her, but since I live here with her, I feel it's my responsibility to make sure she's taken care of and gets the treatment she needs. The last time we tried convincing her to go to therapy, well, it made me realize real quick where mine and my brother's colorful vocabulary came from. The nanny I asked our human resources director, Janine, to help me find has a degree in psychology. I'm hoping she can put that expertise to good use while she's here and maybe I can get a 2-for-1 special and get the help I need for both Charlie and Mama.

Needing to find out whether I need to greet the new nanny or beat the shit out of my younger brother, I extract Charlie from my hold. "I'll be right back, Little Bit, and we will get this mess taken care of."

"Without a haircut?" She whimpers, crushing my soul.

"Without a haircut," I reply, praying that I don't have to break my promise.

I walk across the house to the front door where Keaton blocks my view from whomever is on the front porch. "Is that Cam, I'm gonna wring that motherfucker's throat for buying her a pack of gum. What was he thinking?"

Taking my hand, I push my oldest sibling out of the way to rip into my youngest one, only it isn't Camden standing on my porch. Instead it's the navy-eyed beauty with all the right curves that I had to walk away from in the middle of the night. I'm taken aback and don't think twice about the words that come flying out of my mouth, "What the fuck are you doing here?"

Chapter Ten
Sierra

S hit. Like, bad shit. Like really, really, really bad shit.

I open my mouth, but no sound comes out as I stare back at the handsome man who had his way with me last night. Every which way with me last night.

Lincoln Fisher. My new boss. Well, maybe. Oh, shit. Did I screw myself over on this job when I screwed him? I mean, it wasn't like I knew who he was when we saw each other in the bathroom at the fancy restaurant. I may have kinda sorta assumed it could be him when we were at the pizza place. But it was his dumb no names rule that kept us from identifying one another and is now the cause of this incredibly awkward situation.

His glare is furious and has me wanting to go back to my car. "Are you stalking me?"

I physically draw back from the accusation, crossing my arms under my chest and noting that the movement pulls his eyes to my cleavage. Enjoy the view because you'll never touch them again, motherfucker.

"Excuse me?"

He fixes his eyes back on my own. "I told you last night was a one time thing. Why are you at my house? Did you fucking follow me here? I'm calling the cops."

Why are the ones that give such good dick always the biggest dicks themselves?

"I am here to start a new job as a nanny. My name is Sierra Thomas." I hold my hand over my mouth, "Oops, was my name still supposed to stay a secret?"

His shoulders draw back and I watch his fists clench. "You're my new nanny?"

"Yup," I reply smugly, allowing the last letter to sound off with a pop.

"The new nanny who will be living in this house with us?" I watch as he takes a deep breath in through his nose and releases it with a shudder of his body.

I hitch my thumb over my shoulder, "Bags are in my car, boss."

The heated and electrically charged conversation between myself and my new boss had me completely forgetting that his brother was standing in the doorway taking in the entire scene, so when he speaks up, I jump. "Oh, this is gonna be so good." Keaton rubs his hands together. "It's nice to meet you, Sierra. If your car is unlocked, I can go grab your bags."

I give him a warm smile, "I appreciate that. I see who the well-mannered brother is around here."

Keaton smiles back at me, "That's actually gonna be our brother, Cam. You should meet him soon. But don't worry, I'll let him in on all the dirty details so you don't have to repeat them again."

As Keaton walks towards my car I can hear Lincoln mutter, "Asshole."

"I know you are, but do you plan on letting me enter the house or am I going to be forced to sleep on the porch tonight?" I uncross my arms and place them on my hips.

Lincoln steps to the side to allow me entrance into the beautiful space, but as I cross the threshold, he reaches out, grabbing my elbow in the process, and pulls me to him, whispering in my ear, "Keep it up Brat. I'd love to punish that smart mouth of yours."

My core clenches and it takes everything in me to not go weak in the knees and instead grit out my next words. "In your dreams, boss. You'll never get near my smart mouth again."

When I enter the room, I hear a sweet, but small voice. "Who are you? Are you here to cut my hair?" Sobs begin to fill the space around us and big crocodile tears are falling down this lovely little girl's face. My heart begins to break for the sweet soul I've just met and I find myself dropping to my knees in front of her.

"Oh, sweetie. I'm not here to cut your beautiful hair. What's going on?"

Her blue eyes match her father's and she cuts them over to him so he can speak on her behalf. "She somehow managed to get gum in her hair and I've been struggling to get it out this morning."

"Do you have any peanut butter?"

Lincoln grunts, "You want a fucking snack?"

"A snack would be lovely, thank you, but if you can also get me a jar of peanut butter, I can get this gum out of your daughter's hair."

This man is completely unnerving. One minute my body wants to open up to him and let him have his way with me. The next I want to punch him in that stupidly handsome face of his.

He stomps off in the direction of what I assume is the kitchen and I'm left alone with the little darling full of big emotions in front of me. "Hi, I'm Sierra. What's your name?"

"I'm Charlie," she manages to choke out. "I got gum in my hair and Daddy said we may have to cut it out." Internally I roll my eyes. Of course the abrasive man jumps straight to the extreme.

"Oh Charlie, we won't have to cut it. All it takes is a little oil and a lot of elbow grease, but we will get your hair back to beautiful in no time."

Loud footsteps have me turning and watching Lincoln walk back into the room, a jar of creamy peanut butter in his hands. "You wanna do this here?"

"A bathroom would be preferred," I admit, and the three of us head in that direction. It's a strange way to go about getting a tour of the house, but it's also a strange predicament I've gotten myself in.

As we walk into the bathroom, I instantly notice the black walls and white accents. It's the exact contrast to the outside of the house and I'm absolutely obsessed with it. The beautiful granite counter tops are clean with the exception of a glittery hairbrush featuring cartoon ponies of all colors. I set the jar of peanut butter beside it and screw off the top. "Do you have a spoon or would you prefer I just scoop this out with my hands?"

Lincoln pulls a spoon out from his back pocket and hands it over to me. As I go to reach for it, he draws it back to his body.

"Get the gum out and the job is yours, otherwise I'll find someone else." With that, he turns and walks out of the decently sized space, leaving me alone once again with his bawling beauty and her gummed up hair.

Un-fucking-believable.

"Okay, Little Bit, I'm going to spread some of this peanut butter over the pieces of hair that are covered in gum. I'll use my fingers to get in there and make sure all of it is covered and I'm going to be as gentle as possible, but if it hurts at all, you be sure and let me know. Can you do that for me?"

She sniffs, but then straightens her shoulders and makes her stand taller. "I can do it. I'm tough."

I smile at this strong, sweet girl. "Oh I have no doubt at all about that. Okay, my tough girl, here we go."

Dipping some peanut butter out of the jar with the spoon, I then transfer the slick, but sticky, substance to my hands. I begin massaging it into Charlie's hair and try to come up with something to talk to her about to help take her mind off things. "So Charlie, how old are you?"

"I'm six and I'm in first grade. My teacher is Miss Hynes, she is the sweetest lady. One day, she kept bragging on me and I got to give her five hugs!"

A small laugh escapes my lips, "Oh, wow! Five hugs is an awful lot. I bet your hugs are the very best."

Charlie begins nodding her head vigorously, "Slow it down there, girl, I don't want to pull your hair or make it more tangled."

She instantly straightens, standing as still as a statue. After a few seconds pass, she speaks again, "How old are you? What grade are you in?"

"I'm twenty-three, and I actually just finished school."

She scrunches her tiny nose, "I guess that's why your boobies aren't as big as my Aunt Anna's. She has really big boobies because she's really old. She's thirty."

I somehow manage to contain the laugh that wants to bubble up out of me. "Is your Aunt Anna your dad's sister?" I ask, wanting to know a little more about the family I will hopefully be moving in with.

"No, my dad doesn't have any sisters. Only brothers. Aunt Anna is married to Uncle Keaton. They're cool, but Uncle Cam is my favorite. Only Daddy says it isn't nice to have favorites, so don't tell anyone I told you that. But sometimes I say that Uncle Cam is my favorite. Does that mean I'm not nice?"

I shake my head, "No, Little Bit, that doesn't mean you aren't nice. I know we just met, but I think you are very nice."

"I think you're nice too, Sierra."

My heart melts as I massage the oils of the peanut butter into her matted mess of goo that is currently her hair. "Okay, Charlie. I think I've got it all covered. We're gonna let it sit in there for a minute, and then I'll wash your hair in the sink. Can you do me a really big favor?"

"Do I gotta carry something? I don't have big muscles like my daddy and so sometimes carrying things is hard." She leans in closer to whisper the next part, "Sometimes I pretend my muscles are too weak when my daddy asks me to carry something so that I can get out of it. Does that make me not nice?"

I put my finger to my chin, "Hmm, I don't think that makes you not nice, but it does mean you could be a little on the sneaky side."

"Sneaky? Me? What?" The little girl looks everywhere but in my eyes and I know for a fact she's going to be a little troublemaker, but so much fun.

I roll my eyes dramatically at her. "Uh huh, so, can you go get me a towel and your shampoo?" Charlie shoots off like a rocket, literally jumping into the bathtub to grab her shampoo, then heading out into the hallway for what I can only presume is to get a towel.

"Charlene Elizabeth, stop running in the house!" Her crotchety father yells from another room. I can't believe of all the men in all the world, the man I slept with last night is now my new boss. And then on top of that, he accused me of being a stalker. If I wasn't in desperate need of this job, I would have held my head high and turned right back around on that adorable front porch.

Maybe.

Probably.

Oh, who am I kidding, being close to this handsome man is not a hardship, even with his sour personality. And I know I've just met her, but I could see myself easily falling head over heels for Charlie. I hear her little footsteps approaching and she slides into the bathroom with her sock feet. "Got it all. Let's do this!"

Her announcement has me giggling, "I know you're eager, but slow down there, Little Bit. I need to try and pull the gum out of your hair before we wash out the peanut butter."

With a very serious nod, Charlie turns in the opposite direction of me and I begin weaving my hands through her medium brown locks. The gum easily begins to pull away and I say a silent thank you to the heavens above that I will get to keep my brand new job. When the last of the gum has been retrieved, I make quick work of washing my hands, then hoist Charlie onto the counter top.

"Alright, girl, it's time to get you all cleaned up. Can you hand me the shampoo?" She passes it my way and when I click the little lever to snap it open, I instantly get a whiff of the birthday cake fragrance. The smell lights up my brain to the events that happened last night, and I close my eyes and smile at them.

"Umm, Sierra. Are you okay?" The tiny voice snaps me out of my daze and I shake my head to clear the memories that want to linger.

A nervous giggle releases from my lips, "Ha, I'm fine, thanks. Charlie, just curious, do you and your dad use the same shampoo?"

Charlie cringes, pushing her shoulders up and tilting her chin down, wriggling her adorable nose and looking like the cutest thing I've ever laid eyes on. "Well, I really wanted to take a bubble bath the other night. I kept asking Grammy if I could take one and she just kept staring at the dumb black and white show she was watching. I even tried showing her the time on her phone and she just kept staring at it like I was a ghost and she couldn't even see me."

I bite my lip as I realize why Lincoln may be in need of a nanny instead of depending on his mother who is clearly struggling with something. "So you used your dad's shampoo to make a bubble bath?"

"Yup," she says proudly, popping the last letter, "lots and lots of bubbles. We will just say that Daddy wasn't too happy about it." She leans into me and whispers, "He said the word 'fuck' like twenty bajillion and eight times."

A laugh roars out of me because I can totally picture Lincoln walking into a bathroom of bubbles and realizing he now has to share his daughter's sweet-smelling shampoo as a result. "Girl, you are a mess. Now let's get this mess cleaned up and go see your dad."

Chapter Eleven
Lincoln

I walk away from the stranger I met last night who is now supposed to work for me.

And live here.

In my home.

Every day.

Fuck my life.

Keaton is sitting on the sofa, a leg crossed so his ankle rests against his knee, and a shit eating grin on his face. "So you and the new nanny know each other?"

"We've met," I manage to spit out between gritted teeth.

"Yes, but I meant in the Biblical sense." I look at my brother's smug face as he raises his eyebrows up and down. I want to punch him so fucking hard.

"Fucking grow up. Yeah, okay. We ran into each other last night."

"And exactly how many times were you in her last night?"

I release a heavy sigh before offering my confession, "Listen, we had both just ended horrible dates and happened to meet up in the bathroom. I didn't know who she was when we met. Fuck, I didn't even know her name and she didn't know mine. We were supposed to be two strangers who never saw each other again."

"And so when she showed up on your doorstep this morning, that's why your automatic thought went to she must be a stalker?"

I run a hand down my face, "Fuck. I'll admit, that wasn't my finest moment. But I never would have expected of all the people in the world for her to be the nanny Janine hired."

"Janine does have a tendency of hiring the women we sleep with, doesn't she?" I glare at my older brother as my younger one saunters in.

"Well aren't you the biggest motherfucker that ever mother fucked?" I rage at Camden, who at least has the decency to look sheepish.

Camden holds his hands up like he's under arrest, "Easy killer. Want to tell me what's going on?"

"Oh simply the fact that my daughter has been in tears while I spent the morning trying to get a gob of gum out of her hair. Gum that she says you gave her."

His wince causes his black frames to slide down his nose a tad, "Did you manage to get it out of her hair? I hear peanut butter helps with that."

"The new nanny showed up this morning and is trying to get the gum out as we speak. Way to break her in on the first day."

Camden's brow furrows, "I may have bought Charlie the gum, but I didn't tell her to sleep with it in her mouth. Did you not make her spit it out last night before she brushed her teeth and went to bed?"

Keaton stands up from the couch, stretching his arms above his head. "He wasn't here to put Charlie to bed last night, remember?

He went on that date last night. Why don't you ask him how that went?"

I glare at Keaton, but turn back to Camden's confused stare. "I went on a date last night. It didn't end well."

"If it didn't end well, then why were you out so late?" Cam asks.

Keaton smiles brightly at my baby brother, "Because he was out fucking the nanny."

I can't help it. Before I realize what's happening, my hand is balled into a fist and colliding with his stomach. As Keaton stands there, hunched over and sucking in air, Camden's words run through my mind again. "Shit. Mama was watching Charlie last night. She swore to me she was okay and in a good mood, but if that's the case, how did she not catch that she had gum in her mouth? Did she not make her brush her teeth?"

Camden looks at me with the sad face he always reserves when we talk about Mama, "Where is she now?"

I jerk my head to her bedroom door. "Hasn't come out of there. Refuses to believe that we need an extra set of hands around here to help take care of Charlie."

"Doesn't help that she was kind of blindsided by it," Keaton wheezes, still hunched over. Good.

"I didn't mean to blindside her, okay? But you know how she reacts to these types of things. I didn't want to make things worse." I sit on the edge of the couch and put my head in my hands. The whole point of hiring a nanny for Charlie and a caregiver for Mama was so I could avoid this feeling that is currently plaguing me and has for the past several years. Inadequacy. I'm not enough for Charlie and I'm not enough for Mama. But hopefully if I can get some help, I can begin to balance things better in my life.

Camden sits down beside me. "We know you're doing the best you can, and you're doing a great job. Now that this new girl is here, hopefully that will alleviate some of your workload and stress."

"Not when I have to fucking fire her before she even begins," I admit.

"You're firing me?" I look up to see Sierra and a gum-free haired Charlie walk into the room.

"Hey, you got the gum out," I say, avoiding the question.

Sierra raises her chin and crosses her arms. "I told you I would, now let's get back to the part where you said you were firing me. Is that true?"

I gesture my hand between the two of us, "Don't you think this is a little awkward?"

"I mean, maybe a little," she admits, "but I also think that I'm a professional and I was hired to do a job. A job that I would very much like to keep."

I look at the woman with the dark brown hair and the curves my body craves to explore again. Last night she was sexy as fuck in that dress that hugged her body in all the right ways, but today she's gone for a more casual look. Her jeans are paired with a dark yellow tee that has orange ears of corn on it and the saying 'Fall is A-maize-ing." She's the most beautiful woman I've ever been lucky to lay my eyes on. And that's a fucking problem. I shake my head and she huffs a breath.

"I do believe you said the job was mine if I could get the gum out of Charlie's hair. Take a look, I did a pretty damn good job, if I do say so myself." The brat in her is coming out and my dick stirs at the thought of taming it. Nope. Can't have that.

"Tell me, Miss Thomas, as a professional, do you think that language is appropriate to use in front of my child?"

Her mouth drops open. Got her.

"Don't listen to him, Sierra. You can say whatever you want. My dad says fuck all the time."

"Charlene Elizabeth, I have told you to stop saying that word," I fuss at my kid, but she doesn't miss a beat.

"I don't say fuck, Daddy. You do. You say it all the time. We just talked about this last night. Do you remember? Maybe you don't remember because you're so old. Do we need to get you some remembering medicine? Maybe you need to go to the doctor. Maybe they can give you medicine so you don't say that fuck word all the time, too. But not me, I don't say that word. You do."

Sierra bites that plump bottom lip of hers to keep from laughing and I somehow manage to suppress the groan that wants to emerge from inside me. Why is she such a tease? "That's enough, Charlie. Why don't you and Uncle Camden go outside and play. Take Uncle Keaton with you."

"That's okay," Charlie says, "just Uncle Camden and I can go."

Keaton puts a palm to his chest like he's been shot. I hope those words hurt, motherfucker. "That was rude, Pipsqueak. I'm coming anyway." He chases my daughter out the back door and

Camden follows, shaking his head, leaving me alone with the temptress giving me a death glare.

"I know that last night was a one time thing, you made that abundantly clear," Sierra starts, "but I also know that I was offered this job. A job that I was specifically chosen for because of my credentials. I can do this, Lincoln. I want to do this."

I shake my head, "I really don't see how this is going to work out. It's never a good idea to mix business with pleasure, and well, last night was a helluva lot of pleasure."

She bites that goddamn lip of hers again, and a flirty glint is in her eye. "It was for me, too. But I can put all that to the side and focus on being the best nanny for Charlie. Oh, and I can work on helping your mom," Sierra looks around the room, "Is she home?"

"She's never not at home," I grumble. A wicked idea pops into my brain. "How about we run this like a trial? Your first task was to get the gum out of Charlie's hair, and I'll admit, you did a great job with that."

"Thank you," Sierra says, her eyes lighting up with my praise. Oh how I would love to see what a good girl she could be for me.

I shake off my lustful thoughts and continue, "You will have one week to prove to me that you are capable of this position, while maintaining a respectful and professional relationship with me. But there's another condition you must meet before I will consider you the right person for this job.."

She rolls her eyes, and my hand twitches with the need to slap that plump ass of hers. "I was under the impression I was the right person for the job when Janine, your hiring manager, said the words," she taps her lips and pretends to remember, then sticks a finger in the air before continuing, "oh, when she said the words 'Congratulations, Sierra. You're hired.' Or do those words mean something different in your much older version of the dictionary?"

"Would you like to look in my version of the dictionary to see what the word fired means?"

The glare she gives me causes me to smirk, "What is the condition?"

"The job is yours, if," my smirk grows into a full-on smile, "you can get my mom out of the house."

Chapter Twelve
Sierra

I squeal like a fucking pig as I practically throw myself at Lincoln, wrapping my arms around him in an embrace. "Thank you, thank you! I won't let you down, I promise. I'm really excited for this opportunity."

The truth is I needed this job. My mom passed away from breast cancer just three weeks shy of seeing me graduate college. I was the first in my family to make it to higher education and even though I insisted it was unnecessary, she was determined to throw a big party for my graduation. Unfortunately, her illness progressed quickly and we weren't able to make that dream come true.

When she passed away, I was holding her hand in her bedroom. I sat there for hours as I watched the Hospice workers come in and check her vitals one last time before declaring the time of death. 3:47am. The time I've woken up every night since. I remember the time well, because I looked down at the watch she gifted me and made sure it said the same.

My stepdad, Jason, played the doting husband through her funeral preparations and the service, but the moment we stepped back into their home, he made it clear that I was to get my things and get out. Since he had made sure they were married, he was able to claim her assets. He gets the house and all the memories I have of her that linger inside. The only thing of hers he didn't seem to have was money. The cost of cancer treatments, hospital stays, Hospice care, and medications added up, even with her health insurance. I suppose that's why he's demanding I help him financially, though I owe him absolutely nothing.

Within the week of the funeral I was completely moved out, and the following week, another woman moved in. I hope they're happy together. Who am I kidding? I sure as hell don't hope that. I hope the hag gives him syphilis and his dick rots off. I hope he writhes in pain knowing how much my mom loved and supported him and knowing he deserves the agony he's in for the way he disrespected her and treated me.

But since that apparently hasn't happened yet, I'm here in Cheatham, in dire need of a job and remembering that I'm still clinging to the man who seems to give me exactly what I need. I breathe in the same spicy cologne he wore last night and can't help but release a soft moan.

Lincoln clears his throat and gently pushes me away, reminding me that I've now created yet another awkward moment between us. "Like I said, the job is yours, but I think it's important that we establish some boundaries."

Right. Boundaries. I nod my head at him, "I agree. Boundaries are important. What did you have in mind?"

"Well, for starters, I think we should refrain from physical touch. No hugging or anything." I begin to wilt as I realize he didn't want to touch me, but I notice the subtle movement he makes to adjust himself. I can't help but smirk knowing that my touch impacted him as much as it did me. And yup, that's exactly why no physical touching is an important boundary.

"Okay," I say, "anything else?"

"No keeping secrets from me. If Charlie does something, I want to know about it. Don't protect her from me by withholding information or lying about it. Understand?"

His tone is all business and his face is super serious. This man needs some fun in his life, and I would love to be the girl to bring it to him. "Yes," I sigh heavily, but then I tack on the word I know he likes to hear from my lips, "daddy."

If I wasn't watching, I would have missed the flare of his nostrils indicating that I managed to get under his skin. I'd like to get under so much more than that, but I know these boundaries are important and I need this job more than I need another sexcapade.

"And no more calling me 'daddy,'" he grits out between his perfectly straight, white teeth.

I pout my lips at him and watch the fire build up as he blows out a breath and crosses his arms, causing his muscles to bulge like he's that green dude that you can't really figure out is a good guy or simply destroys a bunch of stuff.

"One week, Sierra. You have one week to show me that you can do this job. You have one week to get my mother out of this house. Otherwise, you're out and I'll bring someone else in."

If there's one thing I've proven in this life, it's that I'm up for the challenge when the odds are stacked against me. I'll make sure this is the best damn week of Lincoln Fisher's life. By this time next

Saturday, he'll realize he never wants Sierra Thomas out of his life. I extend my hand so we can shake on our terms of agreement, but Lincoln looks down at it and tsks.

"Already forgetting the boundaries, Miss Thomas?" He leans in and whispers in my ear, "I love seeing you struggle with the desire to touch me."

My breath catches with the feeling of his against my face, but I manage to cover it up with a scoff. "You see, I know back in your day that they signed agreements with a quill and ink on parchment paper," I watch the corners of his mouth turn up, "but these days, we would call this a handshake agreement. Put it there, pal."

I wiggle my fingers at him, taunting him to make the first move and touch me. Sadly he doesn't take the bait. "Follow me. I'll show you to your room."

I step back and smile as I look at the biggest bedroom I have ever had in my life. Since I didn't have many personal belongings, it didn't take long to fill the dressers and the closets with my clothes, and place my makeup on the vanity. I add my threadbare blanket that started out it's life in a beautiful shade of pink, but has managed to fade into some strange gray you wouldn't find in a crayon box, and the completely worn stuffed piglet I've had for as long as I can remember, to the massive bed.

Fast and tiny footsteps alert me to the whirlwind of energy that bursts through my doorway. "Hey, Sierra! Aunt Anna and Skyla just got here with sandwiches. Let's go!"

I laugh at Charlie's enthusiasm, "Wow, these must be some incredible sandwiches to have you all excited like this."

She nods her tiny head ferociously, "You have got to try the pickles."

Laughing again, I take her hand and Charlie and I make our way to the crowded kitchen. The company Lincoln owns must be some sort of modeling agency because the people standing around are some of the most breathtakingly beautiful folks I've ever seen. The handsome, bespectacled man I saw earlier walks my way and manages to tower over my fairly tall frame. His beautiful blue eyes instantly have me recognizing him as one of the Fisher brothers, and standing at every bit of 6'5", the tallest one at that. He extends his hand out to me and I take it because Lincoln's stupid boundaries don't apply here, "I'm Camden."

"Ah, the well-mannered brother, I hear." His smile dazzles and he glances over to his older brothers, one with a smile equally as bright as he looks at who I assume is his wife, the other glaring our way.

Camden shrugs, "I'll accept that title, but it's not much of a flex when the competition is those two."

I let out a small chuckle and survey the room. I point to Keaton and the gorgeous, voluptuous blonde with the great rack he's standing beside. "I'm going to assume that is Aunt Anna?" Camden nods and I move my finger over to the adorable curly redhead with a smattering of freckles and sporting the cutest pink dress. "And she would be Skyla?" I look over at the man standing next to me and watch a blush creep into his cheeks at the sight of the precious woman standing in his brother's kitchen. Never taking his eyes off of her, he swallows and nods.

"She's pretty," I say.

Camden's voice is barely a whisper, but I manage to hear him say, "She's beautiful."

I decide to leave Camden to stare at the woman he's obviously crushing on and head over to introduce myself. I go to extend my hand, but the bubbly firecracker of a woman pulls me in for a hug. "Oh my goodness, it's so nice to meet you!" She's a tiny thing and I tower almost an entire foot over her, so her face is pressed right up against my breasts, but she makes no indication that she's bothered. As she steps back, she looks me up and down before she speaks. "I'm Skyla, and I already know that you're Sierra. But I didn't know you were such a big, brave beauty."

A small laugh escapes me and I have to ask, "Brave?"

Skyla jerks a thumb over her shoulder in the direction of Lincoln, who has now transferred his glare from his brother to her. "Anyone who is willing to live with this man is brave in my book," she leans in closer to me, "he's kind of a grumpy pants if you haven't figured that out yet."

I laugh as I see him grow redder in the face, and a vein in his forehead begins to pop out. "Oh I have most definitely figured that out," I wiggle my fingers in Lincoln's direction and he storms off in the direction of Cam.

"Hi, Sierra. I'm Anna, Keaton's wife."

Anna is also considerably shorter than I am, but somehow manages to loom over Skyla. I extend my hand, and while Skyla's hug wasn't the worst thing ever, I'm thankful for Anna returning my gesture. "It's so nice to meet you. Charlie has already mentioned you to me."

She shakes her head, "I love that girl, but I have a gut feeling she told you I'm old."

Laughing I nod in agreement and Anna continues. "That girl is something else, but I have no doubt you'll be good for her. And for Sharon. Have the two of you met yet?"

I release a defeated sigh, "No, and I'm really hoping to meet her soon. She's kinda gonna seal the deal on whether or not I get to keep this job."

"What do you mean?" Skyla asks.

"Lincoln says the job is mine on a trial basis. In order to keep it, I have until this time next week to get her out of the house." I watch as both women cringe in unison and panic begins to bloom inside of me.

They must notice the sudden fear in my eyes and immediately try to console me. "It's going to be alright," Anna soothes, "I'm sure Lincoln wouldn't have tasked you with that if he didn't think you could do it. He really needs a nanny and I'm sure he wants you here."

Looking across the island, I see the man who wanted me last night, but is now doing his best to get rid of me. I look back at Anna and Skyla, smiling with all the confidence in the world, "I'm sure Sharon and I are going to be the best of friends. And Lincoln is going to have a hard time keeping her inside this house by the time I'm through with her."

Skyla laughs, "Oh, I like you. Let's get together one night and go to Kalli's."

Anna offers me a sandwich. "This one is my favorite. It has extra pickles," I smile remembering Charlie's words from earlier. Anna scoots in a little closer to me, "I really am glad that you're here, Sierra. Lincoln really needs the help, and I know he's so thankful to have you here. I think you'll come to love him and the town of Cheatham."

I smile at my new friend around a bite of a truly delicious sandwich. I may already be falling for this small town, but there's no way I will be falling for the single dad.

Chapter Thirteen
Lincoln

"You have been struggling for so long. I thought you genuinely wanted help, Lincoln." My sister-in-law followed me out to the backyard and has been scolding me as I go around picking up the toys Charlie has left scattered all over the place. I needed out of the house for at least a minute. Away from my brothers who taunted me every chance they got, and away from Sierra looking absolutely perfect and like she belonged in my kitchen.

I stop when my hands are so full I can't carry anything else, "I do want help. Obviously," I wave my full hands at her.

"Then why in the world would you set that poor girl up for failure? Tasking her with getting your reclusive mother out of the house is cruel, Linc, even for you. You're asking her to do something you haven't been able to do in a decade."

I groan, knowing Anna is right. "If she isn't capable of using that fancy degree of hers and figuring out how to help Mama, then I need to move on to someone else who has that skill set. It's not personal," I lie.

"Don't listen to his bullshit," Keaton comes up to us, immediately reaching for Anna and planting a passionate kiss on her lips. I think I'm gonna be sick. "It's definitely personal."

Anna scrunches her nose as she looks up at her husband, then she turns to look at me. "Do you know her, Lincoln?"

"No," I say at the same time my older brother says yes. He's really being a pain in my ass today.

"One of you better explain," Anna looks between the two of us, "now."

Since Keaton would figure out how to walk on water if Anna demanded it of him, of course he's the one to speak up, "Lincoln and Sierra actually met last night. They ate dinner together and then they had a little special dessert after."

Anna's gasp is loud enough for the neighbors to hear and they're a solid mile to the right of us. "You slept with your nanny?"

"I didn't know she was my nanny," I defend, "and technically we had dessert, then ate dinner, then had a nightcap. Or three."

"Damn, baby bro. Didn't know you had that in you," Keaton says and I think about how nice it would be to punch him for the second time today.

Anna looks at me confused, "How did you not put two and two together that she was your nanny? Did her name not tip you off?"

"They didn't exchange names," Keaton says and I really hate that he's so fucking happy.

Blinking slowly at me, Anna asks, "You slept with someone and didn't even know her name?"

"Don't you two judge me. You got married to one another and didn't know anything *but* each other's names," I accuse.

Keaton pulls Anna into his arms and looks down at her with so much love it's nauseating, "That's not true. I knew she was the most beautiful woman I'd ever met. And that she was way too good for me."

Anna smiles up at him, "You're perfect for me, Keaton Fisher."

I can taste my ham sandwich from Crumb and Get It rising up in my throat, "If the two of you will excuse me, I'm going back into the house to be sick. I'd rather not vomit on my freshly mowed lawn."

"Seriously, Lincoln? It was white wine." I pinch the bridge of my nose as my assistant, Amanda, berates me for the bad date I had this weekend. According to her cousin, I was the reason things didn't work out.

"Seriously, Amanda," I mimic, "she doesn't even like kids."

Amanda waves her hands in a dismissive gesture, "Oh, please. There is no way that anybody couldn't absolutely fall in love with Charlie. But if things didn't work out with Katrina, then let me see who else I can think of. Oh! My friend Charlotte recently got divorced. Totally not her fault, by the way. I can see if she's available."

I let out a sigh. "No more dates. I'm done for a while." I'm done forever. I think back to the pact I made with myself. I can't keep going through this awful process. It's only leaving me bitter and keeping me away from Charlie. I would much rather spend my time at home with my kid, my mom, and, unfortunately, the new nanny.

The new nanny who stepped out of her bathroom this morning in nothing but a towel that gaped at her thigh and gave me a vivid reminder of what lies beneath. The new nanny that had me gripping my dick so tight I saw stars last night when I was in the shower. The new nanny who is a total fucking temptation and completely off-limits.

"Probably for the best, I'm not sure when Charlotte is ready to put herself back out there. But as soon as she is, I'll set the two of you up."

"Looking forward to it." My sarcastic reply falls on deaf ears as Anna strolls up to Amanda's desk. That's right, my brother's wife is also his assistant. Seems like too much togetherness for me, but whatever works for them, I suppose.

Amanda picks up her purse and tosses it over her shoulder. "I'm going to get coffee, you want anything?"

I point to the high-end machine in my office that spits out the most delicious Colombian roast. The machine that Amanda has full access to and uses at her convenience. The gesture doesn't deter her.

"I'll take that as a no. Be back soon. Ish," she adds.

"Bye Linc," Anna hollers and I wave, but the pair has already headed down the hallway towards the elevators. Nothing good can come from the conversation those two are about to have.

The day is dragging and I glance down at my watch to see it's only ten o'clock. I debate whether or not I should check in with Sierra. I left her to get Charlie to school this morning and then she said she was eager to help my mom on her path to recovery by getting her outside and into the garden. I smiled at her realization that gardening was a passion of my mother's, but knowing how Mama feels about our new roommate, there was no way Sierra was going to be successful in her mission today. Hell, I'd be surprised if Mama even spoke to her.

"Meeting in ten," I look up to see Keaton standing at my door, "with our favorite new clients." I groan. Caruso Enterprises has been a pain in our ass since the day they signed their contract. A day my brother almost missed because his drunk ass got married. I wonder how many fewer headaches would occur in my life if I hadn't called and woken him up in time for that meeting.

I give him a head nod, "Be right there. Finishing something up real quick." As he walks away I pull out my phone.

Lincoln

Just checking in. Charlie make it to school okay? Everything alright with Mama?

I watch the three little dots fade in and out for so long I worry that I entered Sierra's information in wrong. Right when I'm about to call and make sure it's really her, a message pops up.

Sierra

> Well don't you know it was my lucky day when the sweetest motorcycle gang drove by just as I was about to get in my car and take Charlie to school. They offered to save me the trip and take her for me. She made quick friends with a man named Snake and looked so cute wearing that big biker helmet as she climbed onto the back of his bike and wrapped her little arms around him. I think I may get her a little leather vest for Christmas.

What the fuck? I hit the little phone button at the top right of my screen next to her name.

"Oh, hello Lincoln. What a lovely surprise to hear from you." Sierra sing-songs and I can't help but picture my hand slapping her bare ass for the way she's taunting me right now.

"Do you care to explain what the fuck you're talking about? Where is my daughter?"

She laughs and it has me flexing my hand in a fist. "I'm teasing you. Gosh you're so easy to do that to, by the way. Lighten up a little."

"Where's Charlie?"

"She's at school, Lincoln. Safe and sound. I drove her there myself. We didn't so much as pass a motorcycle."

A ding on my phone has me looking down at a message from Keaton.

Keaton

> Where the fuck are you? I need my CFO.

Shit. "I've gotta go, but it's nice to know you're in the business of lying," I fuss at my nanny.

"I'm simply in the business of messing with you. Now go back to work. Things are hunky-dory over here."

"Fine, but I'm issuing a new boundary. No more teasing me."

"Really? Or what?"

"Or I'll have to smack that ass of yours until it's as red as a cherry."

"Don't make promises you don't intend to keep, Mr. Fisher."

My dick threatens to spring to life. "Goodbye, Sierra."

"Goodbye," she pauses, "daddy."

I hear the click signaling the disconnect and curse under my breath. So much for fucking boundaries. Pocketing my phone I rush off to the conference room. Caruso Enterprises is a pain in my ass, but I fear this new nanny of mine may be an even bigger one.

Chapter Fourteen
Sierra

I really didn't mean to be in the business of lying, but I may have told a tiny fib to my new boss when he asked if everything was okay. Charlie really is fine and we had the best conversation about what they do with the donuts after they take out the donut holes on our way to school. We never even saw the first motorcycle speed by. However, when I returned from the school and found Sharon locked in her bedroom, well things definitely aren't hunky-dory over here.

I've tried to coax her out of there, but to no avail. I even offered up some of the donuts that were calling my name after mine and Charlie's little talk, but the Fisher matriarch refused to unlock this door. She's a grown woman and I wouldn't be too concerned other than the fact that she hasn't spoken one single word to me since I arrived and I haven't heard the slightest sound come from her room all morning.

"Mrs. Fisher? Sharon? It would be really lovely if I could meet you." Silence continues to greet me behind her door, and I try to breathe through the panic that begins clawing at me. I search my mind for the strategies that were taught to me in my psychology courses, and exhale a shaky breath before trying again.

"I can understand that having a stranger come into your home can be invasive. I promise I am only here to help. Charlie is such a fun little girl, isn't she?" I wait to see if bringing up her granddaughter will draw a response, but when no words are spoken, I carry on, "I was an only child, so I didn't have any experience with them when I was younger, but I did work at a daycare all through college. I was mostly in the three-year-old room and, shew, those little boogers are mischievous things. From what I know about Charlie, I am sure she was quite a handful as a toddler. Am I right?"

I press my ear to the door, hoping to hear some semblance of noise beyond the wooden barrier. "You and Lincoln have done such a wonderful job raising her. She's truly such a smart and delightful little girl. I would love to fix her a little treat for when she comes home from school. Do you have any suggestions?" Nada. "Well, if you can think of anything, I'll be in the kitchen. I'd love your input."

Walking away, I head to the kitchen to search for the ingredients to make the chocolate oatmeal no-bake cookies I loved from my childhood. I may not have gotten Sharon outside of the house yet, or even gotten her outside of her room, but I refuse to give up.

I can do this.

"This morning I came out to watch a little bit of television. There was a black and white show on where these two women were working in a factory and shoving chocolates in their mouths and oh my goodness how I cackled when they started shoving them in their hats and down their dresses. I was laughing until literal tears were streaming down my face. Have you seen that episode?" Per usual, silence comes from behind Sharon's bedroom door.

"That show reminds me of my mom. When she was in her hospital room at night, it would come on. She and I would somehow manage to squeeze into that tiny, uncomfortable bed, and the two of us would cackle at Lucy and Ethel's antics. She had the greatest laugh. Sometimes when I see something funny, I listen to see if I can hear it. Is that crazy, Sharon? To listen for the laugh of a ghost?" I sit on the hardwood floor, lost in the memories of my mother. I barely hear the voice behind the door.

"It's not crazy," she whispers.

I gasp at the response. We're making progress. Nervous laughter bubbles out of me, "Oh good, I'd hate to go crazy this early in my life."

Silence greets me again and my heart falls. If I can't speak to my mother again, I sure would love to speak to this one. To my surprise, the soft click of the door sounds. I turn and see a beautifully broken woman standing in the doorway. Her voice is quiet when she chokes out a sob. "How did you lose her?"

I stand up and look at Lincoln's mother for the first time. There's not a stitch of makeup on her face, and she wears her nightgown even though it's the afternoon. Still, there's no denying that she's the mother of the three incredibly striking men who are the Fisher brothers. Her blue eyes match that of her boys and they're currently filled with tears. "How did you lose your mother," she repeats.

My breath catches in my throat, "Cancer."

Sharon nods, "Such a horrible disease. When did she pass?"

"This spring," I choke out, "only a few weeks before I graduated."

She nods again, "I'm so sorry. I know from experience those words don't help numb the pain, but I truly am so sorry that you lost someone you loved so deeply."

Silent tears begin streaming down my face as Sharon steps past me into the living room.

One door down.

"So, Mama, what did you do today?" Lincoln asks, but instead of his sights set on the woman he's questioning, he's staring and smirking at me. It's been a long and disappointing week failing in my mission to get Sharon out of the house.

The day I shared with her about the loss of my mother was painfully beautiful. It's also the most we've spoken all week. Each day I would stand outside her door and try to coax her out. I only succeeded twice. Occasionally we would meet in the kitchen and I would ask if there was something I could help her with. Apparently that was the wrong question to ask.

It's been a defeating struggle all week, and to make matters worse, Lincoln is so damn smug about my failures. While I've tried to dodge him and avoid his stupidly handsome face all week, we've eaten dinner together every night. And every night he enjoys tormenting me.

Sharon sighs, "You know what I did. Same as I do most days. I watched my shows. Did a load of laundry."

"You didn't go with Sierra to take Charlie to school? Or pick her up?"

Snorting, Sharon says, "Have I ever gone with you to take Charlie to school or pick her up?"

"No, Mama, you haven't. I simply wanted to see if anything had made you change your mind this week." He raises his dark eyebrows at me and I wish I could rip them right off his face.

I've failed. I know I have. And that means I'll be without a job and struggling to survive on my own. This world is not kind to those trying to skimp by on minimum wage. But more than that, Sharon will remain in her reclusive ways. I hate that so much for her. Sharon is still young and very beautiful. I've loved getting to know her this week. She has so much life left to live ahead of her if she can move past the grief that she's allowed to overtake her. I hate that I won't be here to see when that happens.

"Well, this supper is delicious, Mama. You know meatloaf is my favorite and this may be your best batch yet," Lincoln leans back in his seat, patting his flat stomach as though he's bloated. The man has probably never had an inch of body fat on him his entire life and it makes me roll my eyes.

Sharon smirks, "I do know meatloaf is your favorite, and Sierra did a fantastic job of fixing it tonight." Sharon winks at me, keeping the little secret between us when I asked her what meal her son might enjoy. I reply with a small smile, though I'm beaming inside with the brief interaction she just graced me with. But when I look down at my portion of the meal that still remains on my plate, my stomach bottoms out again. Turns out you don't have much appetite when you know you're mere hours away from unemployment.

I don't need to hear his gratitude. I only want to hear that even though my mission was unsuccessful, Lincoln is going to keep me in this role. Still, I glance over at the man who only a week ago called me his good girl and I wait to hear some acknowledgement or compliment similar to the one he gave his mother. Instead of his deep voice that admittedly sends flutters through my entire body, a grunt comes from Charlie and we all turn to look at her.

"Thanks, Sierra. This is some mighty good meatloaf," Charlie growls out, imitating the deep voice of her father.

She switches to a high-pitched tone, "Oh, thanks, Lincoln. I made it special, just for you."

I can't help but to giggle, though I can tell her dad is less than amused.

"That's enough out of you, Little Bit," Lincoln scolds his daughter. "You need to head in to the bathroom and brush your teeth. It's almost bedtime."

"Umm, it's Friday, Daddy," she reminds him, "I don't have school tomorrow, so I get to stay up a little later. I thought maybe we could all watch a movie together."

Lincoln clears his throat before muttering, "Yeah, I guess we could do that."

I smile at the way that little girl is wrapped around his finger. The man is a grumpy asshole, but one thing I've learned this week is that he's an incredible father. He's firm, but fair, and he adores his daughter.

"But no flying ponies," he adds on.

"Aww, man!" Charlie complains, jumping down from her seat and taking her plate over to the island. "I'm gonna brush my teeth and get my jammers on, then I'll choose something for us to watch."

Sharon yawns, "I think I'll skip out on movie night. I'm tired and I'm gonna head on to bed."

Lincoln scowls, "Are you—," he ends his sentence when his mother throws a glare his way. "I mean, alright. Goodnight, Mama."

Sharon gets up to leave the table and I stand to gather the plates and begin the dishes. Lincoln stands when I do and tries to tug his mother's plate from my grip, "You cooked, I'll do the dishes," he offers.

A part of me wants to be stubborn and refuse to let him pry the dish from my hands, but another part of me is thrilled that he's willing to do a few of the chores I've taken on in my time here. "Sure," I say, handing over the plate, "I'll go on to bed then, too."

"No you don't," he stops me, "Charlie wanted a movie night and until tomorrow, you're still here, so you'll join us."

I turn to face him, and while sometimes my height can be a nuisance, I like that I'm not too far away to make eye contact with him. "Just because I live here doesn't make me an around-the-clock nanny. Once you're home from work, I'm off the clock and you will not dictate my downtime."

His smile is one of menace and challenge, "Fine. Disappoint her. Be my guest."

Lincoln is playing dirty and pulling at my heartstrings with the little ray of sunshine that has made me happier this week than I have been in a long time. "Ugh, you're the worst. Fine. I will be right back, but I'm doing this for Charlie, not because you demanded it of me."

He smirks and I walk away to my room. Dick.

As I walk into the living room now comfortable in my pajama pants and an oversized sweatshirt so I could forego the bra, it's the perfect setup for a movie night. A large bowl of popcorn sits on the coffee table with drinks on either side. In front of the coffee table is a twin-sized air mattress with a tiny child bundled up in a rainbow blanket covered in flying ponies and unicorns sprawled out across it. Lincoln sits on the oversized gray sofa, looking incredibly uncomfortable. I opt to avoid sitting near him and go to sit crisscrossed on the floor next to Charlie.

"Umm, whatcha doing?" she asks as I take my place.

"I thought I'd sit down here next to you. Is that okay?"

Charlie furrows her brows and I stifle a giggle at how much it makes her look like her dad. She looks down at the hardwood floor that's covered by a thin rug, then she darts her eyes back up to me. "Umm, I think you would be more comfy on the couch. I would share my spot with you, but you are way too big."

Thanks, kid.

"I'm okay here on the floor," I insist. "What are we watching tonight?"

Instead of an answer, she shouts, "Daddy, play the movie!"

The beloved, grinchy holiday character has just begun stealing all the presents when a sharp pain shoots through my back. Charlie passed out a long time ago, and Lincoln is still staring straight ahead at the screen. I try to get up gracefully, but the pain has me gasping. I turn until I'm on all fours and then slowly walk my way up to standing.

"What the fuck was that?" Lincoln growls from the couch.

I glare at him in response, "I'm going to bed." When I go to take my next step, I whimper in pain and stop in my tracks. Lincoln immediately gets up and comes over to my side.

"What happened? What's wrong?"

"Nothing."

An unimpressed look graces his face when a whimper leaks out of me. "I must have pinched a nerve or something. I have a really sharp pain running through my lower back."

"Aren't you too young for back pain?"

"Aren't you too old to be a dick?" I retort.

Lincoln rolls his eyes at me. "Don't move."

Watching him walk in the direction of the kitchen, I mutter, "Don't tell me what to do." I attempt to shuffle my feet in the direction of my bedroom, but I've barely made it a foot before he's back with his hands full.

"Can you not do what you're fucking told?" he growls at me.

"Not when you're the one telling me to do it," I sass back at him.

Shaking his head, Lincoln stands beside me and wraps his arm around my waist, causing me to jump, which then causes me to let out a yelp.

"I'm only trying to help you to the bathroom. I grabbed the Epsom salts. I'll draw you a bath and then when you get out, I'll get you an ice pack. I also grabbed you some ibuprofen to take."

"I don't need all that Lincoln, I can take some medicine and go to bed. I'll be okay," I wince at the end of my declaration and when I look into his arctic gaze, I know he won't be taking no for an answer.

"Fine," I grumble and we continue our trek to the bathroom.

Lincoln does as he said and turns the water on, checking the temperature to make sure it's perfectly warm. He sprinkles some of the salts into the water and then uses his hand to mix in. As he dries his hand off with a towel, his eyes drag over my body, causing warmth to bloom inside me. "Why are you looking at me like that," I ask.

"Do you need help undressing?"

His question has me remembering exactly how talented he is at removing my clothes, and I decide it would be a very bad idea to allow him that opportunity again. Very bad because I very much want him to touch me. "No, no I can do it."

"Then show me," he insists.

"Excuse me?"

Lincoln shakes his head, looking exasperated, "I'm not leaving until I know you can get undressed and in that tub on your own. Show me that you can get your shirt off and I'll happily walk out of here."

I thickly swallow down the lust and hesitation that have built up inside me. Carefully, gently, and at the pace of a three-toed sloth, I pull at the hem of my shirt, attempting to lift it off my body, but the movement has me crying out in pain.

Lincoln wordlessly comes over to my rescue. He swats at my hands where they have a grip on my shirt, and I loosen them so he can take over. Ever so slowly, he begins to pull at my shirt, lifting it up over me. As he does, I feel his hand gently caress the side of my breast and I gasp while he mutters a low, guttural, "fuck."

When the fabric is over my head, the two of us lock eyes and I can see the same lust in him as I can feel rippling through my body. This man is an infuriating pain in my ass. And my body wants him. Bad.

The two of us stand there in silence as his hands move to the top of my pajama pants. I nod my confirmation and he begins to slide them down my body, taking my panties with them. His fingers graze my bare skin and I shiver at his touch. When I'm bare before him, I stand proudly with my curves on display. This man has shown me how much he loves my body and it gives me the confidence to keep his eye contact. I spread my legs slowly, allowing him to peek at what's between, feeling braver than I ever have. I want him to look. I want him to touch. I want him to taste.

Lincoln takes a step towards me, and I close my eyes in anticipation of his skin on mine, but when it doesn't come, I open them to see his retreating form leaving the bathroom. "I'm putting Charlie to bed," he hollers over his shoulder.

The bath felt amazing, but when Lincoln put me to bed and gently massaged the tender area, I could have orgasmed from that alone. He may be an ass, but it's one hell of one and my body knows what she wants. Sleep has evaded me, knowing that tomorrow brings the loss of this job I have already come to love so much.

I'll miss my talks with Sharon, though they're brief. I would love to be the one to help her heal. I will miss Charlie so damn much. That girl is sunshine in human form and it's insane how quickly I have fallen in love with the child. And I'll miss him. My grump.

I rack my brain for any way that I could possibly stay on in this position. In my week here I've barely managed to get Sharon out of her room. It would take some sort of emergency to get her out at this point. My body shoots up in bed and I wince at the dull pain lingering in my back, but the wince is quickly replaced with a smile.

I'm going to get Sharon out of this house.

And I'm going to keep my job.

Chapter Fifteen
Lincoln

I toss the towel to the side of my bed as I lay there naked and spent after having to take care of myself. Sierra's body was right there ready and waiting for me and fuck if I didn't want to give in and make my dick the happiest he's been in a week. Unfortunately for it, my hand was a poor substitute for her tight pussy.

What happened in the bathroom may have started out innocent, but my little brat made me falter way too quickly. Catching a glimpse of her glistening for me was damn near more than I could handle. It's a damn good thing she'll be gone tomorrow.

I'm jarred from the sinful thoughts of my naked nanny with a loud beeping and the automated word 'fire' repeating. What the fuck is going on?

I bolt out of bed and grab my boxer briefs from earlier, pulling them on quickly and rushing out my door to help the women in the house get out safely. Sierra has already got Charlie on her hip and I hear her shouting to Mama, "Come on Sharon, we need to exit the house."

"What's going on?" my mom asks.

"There's no time to explain," Sierra urges, "we need to get to safety."

Mama pads through the door in her slippers and nightgown, and Charlie and Sierra follow behind her, all three of the girls standing in the backyard. Safe. I go to follow them, but as I reach the door, I realize I don't have my phone and have no way to call the authorities. I turn to go back in the house and hear Sierra call after me, "Lincoln, what are you doing?"

"I'm going back in to grab my phone to call for help," I turn again, but am stopped when I feel a tug on my hand. I turn around and Sierra is standing there, looking not at all fazed by the situation we've found ourselves in during the middle of the night.

She smiles at me and a small giggle releases from her. Shit. Is she in shock?

"Sierra, this is serious. The fire department needs to come out here and I think you may need an ambulance." My words only have her laughing harder and panic begins to set in. I turn to rush back inside to call for help, but her grip tightens on me.

"Lincoln, no. It's okay. There's no fire," she explains, and I can't help but look at her bewildered. She motions to the house behind us, "Look, the house is perfectly fine. We're all perfectly fine."

I shake my head to try and clear it and see what she's pointing out. There's no flames or even smoke coming from my residence. "Then I need to go check the smoke alarm and see what caused it to go off."

Sierra's hand raises, confusing the fuck out of me. "Why are you raising your hand? What does that mean?"

"It was me, Lincoln. I caused the smoke alarm to go off."

The relief I felt moments ago knowing my family and home are safe and is quickly replaced with rage. "What the fuck were you thinking?" I ask Sierra through gritted teeth.

She smiles wide at me, her navy eyes sparkling in the moonlight, "I was thinking," Sierra waves her hand out, gesturing to where my mother is holding Charlie against her, looking at the lack of flames, "man, your mom sure looks good out of the house."

Well, shit.

"Janine, can you come to my office, please?"

"What do you need Janine for?" Keaton asks, sitting across my desk as we wait to attend the meeting regarding Caruso Enterprises and whatever make-believe issues they're concerned about now.

I roll my eyes at him, "Did you ever stop to think that maybe not everything under the sun is your fucking business?"

My older brother, and technically boss, raises his eyebrows at me, "It says Phisherman's Cybersecurity on this building. It's literally my fucking business."

Before I can retort, my human resources director knocks on my door. "You wanted to see me?"

I motion Janine to enter. "Come on in," I look at my brother, "and you get out."

He settles in his chair, "Nah, I think I'll stay." If it was any other employee in my office with us, I'd go ahead and punch his smug face, but doing it in front of Janine would mean a lot of paperwork and probably some stupid videos I would have to watch, so I decide it isn't worth it.

"I want to start by saying that I appreciate you helping me out and finding me who you feel was the best candidate for a nanny," I tug at the cuffs of my long-sleeve shirt. I hate these damn things, but it's my daily uniform to cover the ink that Corporate America seems to frown upon. Whoever decided you can't simultaneously look like a professional and a badass can fuck right off. "But I need you to reopen the search and begin considering other applicants, please."

Janine's face pinches and she looks between me and Keaton, "Is there an issue with Miss Thomas?"

"Yeah, Linc," Keaton adds, his lips twitching in amusement, "is there something wrong with your nanny?"

I clear my throat and proceed, knowing that getting her out of my house is the only feasible solution to the predicament I've landed myself in. My dick will be raw by the end of the week if I keep jacking off at the rate I have been since she's been in my space, parading that perfect fucking body of hers around, teasing me with that sinfully smart mouth of hers. "She's not who I need in the position," I explain matter-of-factly.

Keaton huffs, "You seemed to like her in a certain position."

Never missing a beat, Janine hones in on what Keaton just muttered. She presses her fingers at the bridge of her nose, closing her eyes and breathing in deeply. "If the Fisher men could stop sleeping with all of the company's new hires it would make my job so much easier."

"Technically Sierra is on my personal payroll," I clarify, causing the very flustered Janine to let out a groan and exit my office.

"Why are you looking to get rid of her? I thought she passed your little test? Seriously, that was a genius move on her part in an effort to get Mama out of the house."

I glare at him, "It wasn't genius. It was reckless and immature. That's another thing, she's too young. Too inexperienced."

"From the sound of things, you gave her plenty of experience."

I give my best death stare to my brother who is still perched in the chair, but when he makes eye contact with me, he simply shrugs. "I'm simply saying that from my view of things, it looks like you have a bit of a crush on the nanny. If that's the case, I think you should look into that."

"Not everyone gets the happy ending like you and Anna, Keat," I say weakly.

"You're right, not everyone does. But it doesn't mean that you can't." He stands, "I'm just saying, if she makes you happy, give it a chance."

"She doesn't make me happy, she makes me fucking insane," I protest, "she may be hot as hell, but she's a pain in my ass."

Keaton nods, "Well, let's go deal with our other pain in the ass. And hey, if things don't work out with Sierra, maybe you could always sleep with someone from Caruso Enterprises."

I reach for a pen on my desk and throw it in his direction, but the bastard dodges it.

Our senior analyst, Marty, is leading the meeting today. He's been droning on about the problems Caruso Enterprises claims they are continuing to have, and I've been daydreaming about the problem that sleeps on the other side of my wall. Last night Sierra walked by on her way to the bathroom, but stopped in my doorway. I was laying in bed, crunching the numbers for this month, and the temptress waltzed right in like she belonged there. My dick sure thought she did with the way her hips swayed as she moved. He reached out for her as I watched her pajama shorts creep up her thighs with her every step. Traitor.

"What's on your face?"

"They're called glasses," I answered, "You've never seen them before?"

"Not that look that damn good," she muttered, but I was able to catch it and the throbbing down south let me know he heard it, too.

Her eyes roamed over me, lustful waves of the ocean that I knew would drown me if I looked too long. Her tongue darted out over her bottom lip and I had to bite my own so a moan didn't spill from me. "I've got work to do, Sierra, so do you need something, or..."

My words must have made her nervous because she jumped at them, "Oh, yeah, um, well, I forgot. Sorry. Goodnight, Lincoln," and then she scurried off.

"Lincoln?" Marty asked, pulling me from my daydream. "Did you want us to go over the findings?"

"Sorry, the findings for what?" I ask, trying to hide the fact I wasn't paying one damn bit of attention, but I don't think it's fooling anyone.

"After hearing the most recent concerns from Caruso Enterprises, we opted for full penetration testing."

Thoughts of penetrating my nanny entered my brain. Fuck me. I clear my throat, "And what were the results?"

"Well our team found several vulnerabilities and, as you know, it's our job to fill those holes."

I shift uncomfortably in my seat and Keaton smirks at me, knowing exactly what, and more accurately who, I'm thinking about right now. Discreetly flipping him off, I lean forward on the long table that takes up the majority of the room, attempting to conceal anything that feels it may need to rise to the occasion. "What solutions do we need to build to assure them they're protected?" I may be the chief financial officer for our company, but I'm also pretty damn knowledgeable about what we do, so I take the lead as our chief information officer, too.

"We'll do another data backup and then harden the system by plugging up any of those open holes. We don't want just anybody to be able to penetrate them."

Who the fuck was in charge of coming up with terminology for my line of work? I'd like to have a word. "That all sounds good," I manage to grunt out, "let's make it happen."

Marty nods, "There's no position we won't tackle, sir."

I stand up and walk away from the conference room with the sounds of my brother's laughter behind me.

Chapter Sixteen
Sierra

My phone rings and I pick it up without looking, "Hello?"

"Another damn medical bill arrived today. Need you to take care of it."

Ugh, I really need to start screening my calls, "I haven't gotten paid yet and really don't have the extra money. How much is this one?"

"$300."

"Send me a picture of the bill and I will call and get it taken care of," I offer, though I'm not sure where the money is going to come from.

"No, Sierra, you'll send the money..." I hang up the phone abruptly, the sound of a screaming child catching my attention far greater than the greedy demands of my stepfather.

My mind races as I rush through the house in search of the source that produced the most devastatingly terrifying sound of my life. My heart beats rapidly in my chest and gruesome scenarios pop up in my head as I pass room after vacant room, unable to locate her.

What if she's somehow gotten tangled in her sheets, fallen from her bed, and broken her leg?

What if she got more gum in her hair?

What if something happened to Sharon?

When I reach her bedroom, Charlie is collapsed on the floor and my heart falls to it, as well. Tiny hands are tucked into her chest and when she turns to look at me, her beautiful cherub face is puffy, red and tear-stained with strands of her untamed dark hair sticking to it. She unclutches her hands and holds them out to me, showing me the tiny purple pony inside of them. The head of the horse is in one hand and the body in the other.

"She's dilapidated," Charlie sobs.

I have a hiccup of a moment to take in the brokenhearted little girl before she rams herself into my stomach, seeking comfort. "Oh Little Bit, I'm so sorry. But I think you mean decapitated."

She looks up at me, while still clinging to the trunk of my body for dear life. "Is that the word for when your head falls off?"

I nod. "Then yes, she's decapit-tit-tated."

Charlie's sobs begin to start again and I attempt to comfort her. "Can I take a look at her? Maybe it's something we can fix."

She hands over the spliced figure and I try to make sense of what exactly happened. "Umm, Charlie, I know it may be difficult, but can you tell me what happened here?"

"No," she replies meekly, "I mean, it was just a little twist."

"You twisted her head off?" I ask.

"Not a big twist! I didn't mean for it to come off. It was just a little twist. She was supposed to look behind her and see if the rest of the ponies were following."

I look down to her bedroom floor and see the army of tiny ponies set up in rows. "I see, well the good news is, I think I can maybe pop her head back in place."

"Is it going to hurt?" She sniffles, and my heart wants to burst from my chest at the absolute sweetness of this girl.

"Shouldn't hurt a bit," I smile at her, popping the head of the figure back on the body and making it whole once again. "See, good as new."

Charlie's hands squeeze me as tight as they can before letting go and snatching up the purple pony. "Thank you so much, Sierra. I love you!"

Three little words had me completely crumpling as I realized I feel the same about the child that I've been caring for the past week. I never thought I could feel so deeply for someone so soon, but she has absolutely wormed her way into my heart and the idea of ever leaving this sweet baby seems unfathomable. "I love you too, Little Bit."

As I turn to leave Charlie back to her army of pony figurines, Sharon is in the doorway, tears shining in her eyes. She simply nods at me and smiles before walking away, and I think I may have fallen in love with her, too.

"Thanks for supper," Lincoln says from behind me as I finish tidying up the kitchen before I head to bed for the evening.

"No problem at all, I enjoy cooking. Dishes, though?" I scrunch my nose up at him, "can't say that I feel the same."

He comes to stand beside me and takes one of the smiling scrubbers from the sink, "I'll do it, you can go on to bed."

"How about we do it together?" I ask, not realizing that the question would generate tension in the room. It's seriously the largest kitchen I have ever stepped foot in and I currently feel like I'm shoved in a box.

Lincoln snorts and begins circling his soapy sponge over one of the plates from tonight's meal. "So, um, you said you enjoy cooking?"

I smile, "Yeah, always have, really. I remember spending most nights with my mom in the kitchen and she would show me new recipes. There's something about starting from scratch and creating a dish that's truly delicious."

"What was your first dish?"

I start sorting through the fond and warm memories I have of my mother just like she would flip through her recipe box. My voice is quiet when I say, "Her spaghetti. I remember standing there at the stove, refusing to move because I knew the water in the pot would start boiling at any moment. It felt like I stood there for hours," I laugh lightly. "When the bubbles started rolling, I was so excited that I threw the noodles in and caused a splash. Water ended up everywhere! I tried to clean it up with a towel, but when I did, I ended up pushing the pot and water sloshed everywhere all over again. I wasn't thinking, you know, because I was eight-years-old, and I gripped the brim so I could steady it." I hold my left hand up so he can see the pads of my fingers. "You have to look closely, but you can tell that my ring finger has a little glossy spot that lingered long after the burn."

He cups my hand in his, pressing his thumb into my palm, then moving it closer to his face. His thumb glides up and circles the smooth skin. Then, in a move I wouldn't have expected in all of my days, Lincoln brings my hand to his lips and kisses the scarred space. It's gentle. It's sweet. It's so unlike him.

Lincoln drops my hand, panicked eyes finding mine for a second before he focuses them back on his task and continues washing and rinsing dishes without saying a word. The silence lingers too long and I take it upon myself to try and break the awkwardness. "Have you always enjoyed, um, owning a tech company?"

His chuckle sends a warmth through me that sends shivers to that spot between my legs. Bad coochie, we do not want our boss.

"Was the awkward silence getting to you, too?" I cringe at how easily he figured me out, but he continues, "Do you have any idea what I do?"

I bite my lip, shaking my head, causing him to chuckle again. I'm so glad the baggy sweatshirt I'm wearing is hiding the fact that he hardened my nipples with just a laugh.

"Not many people do, I suppose. Our company is in cybersecurity. Essentially we make sure that networks are secure and people can't infiltrate them to steal client information through phishing and malware. Stuff like that," he explains.

"So do you stop the hackers or are you the hackers?"

He smirks at me, "Maybe we do a little bit of both."

I want to ask him more. I want to do more. But the last of the dishes get loaded into the appliance my mom and I never could afford growing up, and I know my time with Lincoln is just as brief as all of our previous encounters. For the most part, it's been easy to cut myself off from him. He can be an absolute dick of mighty proportions. But tender moments like this one tonight, or the way I watch him take care of his mom and Charlie, well, it makes it hard to forget his touch and the fact that I would do absolutely anything this man asked of me.

Lincoln hangs the towel he's been using on the handle of the dishwasher. "Well, again, thanks for dinner."

"Thanks for helping with the dishes," I add.

As he walks away from the kitchen, I'm at war with myself on whether or not I should say more. 'Please come back and fuck me like there's no tomorrow' is probably not what I should go with, so I keep quiet and when Lincoln is out of sight, I head to my own bedroom. I have a date with my hand and thoughts of the sexy grump with a heart hidden under that rough exterior.

Chapter Seventeen
Lincoln

F uck, I came so close to kissing Sierra when we were in the kitchen tonight. It didn't help that when I walked in and saw her at the sink in those jeans that I swear she gets custom made to mold to her body, I thought I was going to explode then and there. She was swaying those sexy ass hips of hers to a song only she could hear and I wanted to take a bite out of her ass and make it my dessert.

It's official. Her being here is driving me insane.

Unfortunately, she's really fucking good at her job. Charlie is obsessed with her and wants Sierra to tuck her in at night just as often as she wants me to do it. She often asks for the both of us. They play with those ponies and work on her homework. I've even noticed that Charlie has been watching Sierra in the kitchen when she cooks, and I can't help but smile at how those scenes align with the story Sierra shared from her childhood.

The memory Sierra shared with me gave me a tender glimpse into her past. I know her mom meant so much to her and every now and then I can see the pain of losing her across her face. But I've managed to catch a few of her interactions with my own mother and can't help but notice that Mama is thriving, too.

When I came home from work the other day, they were on a walk. Sure, it was only to the end of the driveway, but that's the farthest away my mom has been from the house in over ten years. The only time she steps foot outside is to work in her garden. Passing that threshold was huge, and I know I have my nanny to thank for that.

Those moments where I catch a glimpse of the incredible woman Sierra is (you know, behind all the snark and sass she's directed towards me in the past couple of weeks) is what made me weak earlier. Pressing my lips to the scarred skin on her finger gave me a rush that had me trying to run away as fast as I could once I realized how close I was to crossing a line I shouldn't.

But those lips. Her eyes. That ass...

Undressing, I climb into bed and think of the woman who is sleeping on the other side of the wall behind my headboard. I dip my hand in my black boxer briefs and grip my hardened cock in my hands. This damn thing has been a bitch to hide every time she comes around. I stroke as I think back to the way it looked when I pushed my length through those full lips of hers. She took all of me seamlessly, like we perfectly align.

I continue to run my hand up and down the smooth skin, applying and releasing pressure as I imagine her pussy tightening around it. I lean my head back against the wooden frame, closing my eyes and picturing the cocktease who lives with me. My ears perk up as I hear muffled moans coming from the other side of the wall.

"Mmm, yes," I hear as the sound grows louder, causing my dick to stiffen that much more. "Yes, Lincoln, right there. Yes," the moans continue.

Holy fuck, the sound of her getting off while she's thinking of me has me leaking already. I use the additional lubricant as I strengthen my grip and stroke harder and faster to the sounds of Sierra.

"Yes, yes, yes."

Yes, fuck, yes.

"Lincoln, I'm coming."

Me, too, brat. Come with me.

A gloriously delicious moan spills from her lips as white cream spills from my cock.

Fuck, jerking off to her is the last thing I needed to happen tonight. This damn wall is not a big enough divide between us. As I clean myself up, I decide I need to talk to Janine first thing in the morning and see how she's coming along on finding more applicants for this job. The sooner I can get this nanny out of my house, the sooner things will be back to the way things were.

"You have a date tonight?" Camden asks.

I shake my head at both of my brothers who sit in the booth opposite me. Every Friday we come to Pizza Papa for lunch, and just about every Friday I have a new date lined up and tell them about the new prospect. Not today. Not anymore.

"Nah, I'm giving up on that," I admit, letting out a sigh and leaning back against the wooden backing.

"Tired of never getting past second base?" Cam teases, though until Sierra came along, he kinda had a point.

Keaton grins like a damn Cheshire cat, "Nah, he's out of the dating game because he finally found the one."

"What the fuck are you talking about?"

"Oh, only a certain nanny who seems to get under your skin. Tell me, has she gotten under your sheets since she's taken her new position?"

I look around the table for something to throw, but unfortunately come up short. "Would you stop it with that shit? There's nothing there."

"There was something there," he challenges.

"Well there won't ever be anything there again."

"And why is that?" Keaton asks.

I look at the two dumbasses across from me. It's got to be obvious right? But they both seem to be waiting for a genuine explanation.

"For starters, she works for me," I begin, but Camden interrupts.

"That doesn't matter. Anna works for Keaton and he sleeps with her."

Keaton has that dumbass grin on his face again, "Sure do. Twice today, actually."

Twice? The fuck? "You've been at work all day."

He leans back, putting his hands on the back of his head, extending his elbows and managing to hit Cam in the process. "Yeah, there's a thing about your wife being your sexy secretary."

I really wish our pizza was here so I had something to throw up. "Plus you've already slept with her, so you kinda burned that bridge."

I continue with my list, "She's also way too young. She's too involved with Charlie. She's an epic brat. Do you really want me to go on?"

"Yes, please continue with your list of all the reasons this woman is absolutely perfect for you," Cam smiles at me.

"Then how about we circle back to the most important one of all? I've given up on dating."

Keaton reaches across the table and grabs my phone before I can process what's happening. "What the fuck are you doing? Give that back."

I try to retrieve my phone, but Cam blocks me. "You too, baby bro? Since when did you join the ranks and become an asshole?" The two of them huddle over my device. "Fine, take my phone. You'll never figure out my passcode."

"You're really predictable, you know," Camden says. "Seriously, for a master hacker who owns a cybersecurity company, you should have a much stronger code than your daughter's birthdate."

"Whatever, I have nothing to hide."

Keaton's face lights up again and I really wish I had a parmesan cheese shaker to throw at his head. "No, but you do have a dating app that has lots of ladies who I bet would love to go out with you."

"Not interested," I all but growl out. I'm not sure what these two fuckers are up to, but I have no interest in going out with anyone. Ever. The idea of dating has me sulking while sending death glares in the direction of the imbeciles across from me. I've dated every variety of woman that's out there and the only one who has made me want to possibly consider a second date is the fucking bane of my existence.

She's all long legs. And thick thighs. And long, dark hair that I want to wrap around my hand. And midnight blue eyes that I could get lost in. And a smile that tugs at my heart.

She's got an ass that deserves a spanking. And a smart mouth that needs to learn a lesson.

See? Fucking nightmare.

Keaton flips my phone my way so I can see the screen. "Here. This one's a teacher who loves kids and enjoys the beach."

I snatch my phone from my brother's hand, but before I can close out of the app, I receive a notification. "You already asked her out?"

I click open the message and stare at the screen, seeing the message that I sent.

FatherAbraham: Hi, you're really pretty. Would you want to go to dinner with me tomorrow night?

"Seriously? So lame. You've lost your game since getting married."

Keaton shrugs, "What did she say?"

"She said she'd love to," I reluctantly admit, kinda shocked it was that easy.

Keaton clasps Camden on the shoulder, "Sounds like I've still got it, then."

Jillian delivers our pizza as Camden looks at me and says, "And sounds like you have a hot date tomorrow."

I look back at the picture of the woman I'm apparently going out with tomorrow. She's no Sierra, but maybe my brothers are on to something. Maybe the best way to get over my nanny is to get under someone else.

Chapter Eighteen
Sierra

"So how are things with the hottest grump in all of Kentucky?" Skyla asks as we slide into the booth at Pizza Papa.

"Definitely hot and definitely grumpy."

Anna snorts, "Sounds about right. I don't know how Keaton and Camden can both be the sweetest human beings on the planet and then be brothers with Mr. Frowny Face."

"Sometimes the brothers can be too sweet," Skyla mutters.

"What do you mean by that?" Anna asks.

Skyla shakes her head, "Oh, just that you and Keaton are so sickeningly sweet in love."

Anna smiles dreamily, "Well, I can't disagree with you there."

A pang of jealousy shoots through me as I look at her, wanting what she and her husband have. Losing my mom left me so lonely and now the thing I want most is a family.

A young girl with a blonde ponytail comes bouncing up to our table. "Sierra, this is Jillian, the best server in the place," Anna introduces.

"Oh, we've met," the bubbly teen says, "you were here on a date with Mr. Fisher, right?"

Anna and Skyla's eyes shine brightly at me, clearly wanting me to divulge details about the night I spent with him. "Umm, yeah, that was me."

"I thought so, I've never seen him on a date with anyone here in town, so the two of you are kind of a big deal. Are you excited about the one you're going on tomorrow?"

I look up at the girl with what I'm sure is a bewildered expression on my face, "I'm sorry, what?"

Jillian returns a mirrored look, "Umm, Mr. Fisher mentioned he would be going on a date tomorrow and I assumed that since you were here with Mrs. Fisher, that it was you he would be going on a date with."

The girls who invited me to lunch have changed their uplifted eyebrows from the intrigue of finding out sexy details to the downturn of them, genuinely confused about what's going on.

Well that makes three of us.

"I am so, so sorry," Jillian says. "I didn't mean to overstep."

"Oh you have nothing to apologize for, sweet girl. In fact, I am excited about my date tomorrow."

"You are?" Skyla and Anna ask in unison.

I nod, "Oh yes, but unfortunately for him, it won't be with Mr. Fisher. You see, I found that he came up short in some areas. No, instead I have a mighty fine man taking me out tomorrow. I think he may even be the one."

"That's so nice to hear, Sierra. I really am sorry if I stepped on your toes and misspoke. I'll be right back with your drinks," Jillian says, retreating a lot faster than she came.

Skyla narrows her eyes at me, "Okay, spill. Who is this 'mighty fine man' that's taking you out tomorrow?"

"Yes," Anna adds, "the guy who might just be the one?"

"Well, I don't know yet," I admit, pulling the dating app I've ignored the last couple of weeks up on my phone, "but I'm about to find out."

"And then Miss Hynes said since it was raining, that we get to stay inside and watch a movie. The whole class cheered!"

I had picked up Charlie after grabbing a late lunch with the girls and we were just now pulling into the driveway because, well, she asked for ice cream and what am I gonna do? Say no?

"I'm so glad you had a great day at school, Little Bit. How about we go inside and I wipe that chocolate off your face before your dad sees it. Then you can have some time to play in your room before dinner since it's the weekend and you don't have any homework."

Charlie beams at me and even though I'm beyond frustrated at the man she unfortunately shares half her DNA with, I can't help but return the smile back at the child I love so much.

"Ugh," I exclaim, throwing myself into the impeccable leather chair because of course the most frustrating man on the planet has great fucking taste.

Yes, I'm sulking.

Yes, I know it's immature.

No, I don't give a shit.

"Something the matter, dear?"

I nearly skyrocket out of the chair as I clutch my chest, gasping for air. "Sharon, shit, you scared me. Also, sorry I said shit. Twice."

She laughs, "You've heard the boys I raised. A little shit doesn't bother me." She eyes me with her mom stare and I feel like she can see inside my soul. "But it feels like maybe you have some shit bothering you?"

"Umm, it's nothing," I insist, though by the way she's looking at me I'm not doing a very good job of selling it.

I look at her. And she looks at me. And I look at her. And she looks at me. Ugh, fine. "Well, something has happened and it boils down to the fact that I need to find a date for tomorrow night."

Sharon's eyes light up. "Well a gorgeous thing like yourself, I'm sure we can find you someone in no time. Now, do you have one of those doohickey things on your phone to help you find a nice man?"

I snort, "An app? Yes. One with a nice man? Doubtful."

Sharon waves her hand in the air, "Pull it up and let me see. I'll find you somebody who will do the job."

My eyebrows furrow in confusion, "What job?"

She giggles a high-pitched sound I've never heard come out of her mouth, "Oh you know, just the job of taking you out on a nice date. Now come sit next to me and we'll scroll."

Slowly, I move myself over to the couch and let the woman I'm supposed to help heal work her magic on my love life.

She scrolls my phone, swiping furiously, and muttering the word no nearly just as fast. Suddenly she stops and stares at me. "Dear, can you explain something to me?"

Please don't ask me about your son. Please. "Hmm?"

"Why do so many of these men feel the need to pose with a fish?"

A burst of laughter spills from my lips. "Nobody knows, Sharon. Nobody knows."

She continues to scroll for what feels like forever when finally a slightly older man fills the screen. He's wearing a suit and everything about him screams expensive. If a man like that has to resort to dating apps, there's truly no hope for the rest of us.

"How about him? He seems nice. Oh, and look," she points to the screen, "he likes dogs."

I shake my head, "I don't have a dog, Sharon."

"Nice men like dogs, Sierra. It's a fact." She hits the message button at the top of the screen and begins typing something out, keeping the screen hidden from me.

"And send. Now what?" She asks, looking quite pleased with herself.

"Now we wait," I say.

Sharon sits back, a content smile on her face and it hurts my heart to know this woman could be experiencing so much more joy if she allowed herself.

"You know, Sharon, people your age are on these dating sites, too."

"Good for them, dear."

"I could help you set up an account if you'd like to meet someone."

"I've already met the love of my life. Nobody else will ever compare."

"You don't have to look for love," I suggest, "they have these apps for people who only want to make friends. Or get out of the house. Have something to do."

Sharon snorts, "I have three sons, a granddaughter, and a meddling nanny. I have plenty to do."

I try another approach, "Some days I miss my mom so much I wish I could simply shut out the world. She was absolutely everything to me and when she was gone, it felt like I lost a part of myself, as well." Sharon releases a shuddered breath, but I continue. "On those especially dark days, the ones where I lock myself in my room, hide under my covers and cry until I can barely breathe, I think about what she might say to me if she saw me that way. We talked about what my life would look like without her in it, and not once did we ever say it would be in the darkness. So I pull myself out of it, and live the life I know she wanted for me."

I put my hand on hers, expecting her to pull away, but she doesn't. "Do you not think your husband would want you to pull yourself out of the darkness, too?"

We sit there in silence for several minutes as she refuses to answer my question and instead stares at a screen watching a show about doctors that I think takes place during the Korean war. I was hoping my question would inspire her. Empower her. Motivate her. Instead, I fear I just made her close herself off to me. Some psychologist I am.

When her show ends and we still haven't received a response on my phone, I expect her to get up and leave the room. "I don't know what he would have wanted," she whispers and clutches my hand tightly. "When Russell passed away, we were still so young. We hadn't thought to discuss what a future would look like without one of us in it. It doesn't feel right to be in a world where he's not here with me. Everything out there is so big. So loud. I'm constantly reminded that he's gone. The looks of pity that the people in town would give me. The words they would say, not to be hateful, but it would still cut into me like a dagger because they were words that let me know the love of my life wasn't with me anymore."

Tears begin to slowly fall down her cheeks, but she doesn't stop. "In this house, I can feel him. He lives within these walls with the memories my boys and I keep of him. Why would I ever want to walk away from him? Why would I ever want to be without him again?"

A chime from my phone breaks the heavy confession Sharon just shared with me. She wipes her face, then holds up the phone to me with a smile. "You have a date tomorrow night, my dear, with a very handsome man. In fact, he is so handsome, I'd say he would make just about any other man absolutely jealous." A sly smirk spreads on her face.

I smile back at her, mouthing the words thank you. Sharon nods and stands, heading back in the direction of her bedroom. Before she reaches the hallway, she turns back to me.

"Sierra, I need you to do something for me."

I look at Sharon, "What's that?"

She smiles at me and with a wink says, "Give my son hell."

Chapter Nineteen
Lincoln

The November air is crisp and I'm thankful for the cooler days and this Saturday morning off from work. I'm sipping on my coffee while watching Charlie swing in our backyard when I hear the sliding door behind me inch open. Sierra bounces out in some red one piece jumpsuit thing that does wonders for that luscious ass of hers.

"Charlie seems to be having fun," she says, starting up a conversation. I grunt in reply, shifting so she doesn't catch what she's doing to my dick.

Sauntering up beside me, she picks up my mug of coffee and breathes in the aroma of the freshly ground beans. "The coffee you make always smells so good," she moans, not helping my current situation any. "Mind if I take a little sip?"

Before I can protest, Sierra has my coffee mug between those supple lips of hers, swallowing down a taste and continuing that moaning sound that's gonna have me busting through the seam of the jeans I'm wearing today. When she finishes her drink, she licks up the side of the mug to wipe away the bit that spilled over the edge, and I so badly wish that tongue of hers was running up my shaft.

"What the fuck are you doing?" I grit out quietly, so that Charlie doesn't overhear.

Sierra sits my mug back down, then cocks her head at me. "I don't know what you're talking about," she leans in closer to me, "daddy."

"Sierra, cut the shit. What is going on?"

She rolls her eyes and my hand twitches to smack that ass of hers before I bury my dick inside of it. "I am only teasing you, geez. Push that vein back into your forehead."

She lies down on the chaise to the right of me, stretching her fucking beautiful body in a way that I can't peel my eyes from her and sighs, "Oh, I just love Saturdays."

When I don't say anything she continues, "I love them because I get the night off. I can go and do whatever I want knowing that you're here to take care of your mom and Charlie. Well tonight it's not so much a do whatever I want as it is a do whomever I want," she giggles.

"What the fuck do you mean by that?"

"I have a date."

A date? Who with? I forbid it. No dates for Sierra. Nobody else is allowed to touch her curves and taste those lips of hers. If I can't have her, then nobody can.

Yeah, I heard the Neanderthal lying underneath, but if any man so much as touches that curvaceous body of hers, I might get a bit stabby. As good of an attorney as Cam may be, I don't know that even he could get me out of that situation. So to avoid homicidal rage and my little girl growing up without a mother and a father,

Sierra will just have to stay here and not go out with whatever loser has a death wish tonight.

"Well, you're gonna have to cancel it."

"Hmm," she puts a finger to her lips, "I really don't think I do."

I chuckle, but there's no humor in it. "You see, you can't have a date tonight, because I have a date tonight. I need someone to watch Charlie."

She dramatically pouts those big lips of hers at me. "That sounds like a you problem. I believe getting off on the weekends was in my contract."

"Being off on the weekends?"

"What was that?" she asks, shading her eyes from the sun to look over at me.

"You said getting off on the weekends. Was that a slip of the tongue?"

That gorgeous smile of hers spreads across her face as she hops up, causing her tits to bounce in a very distracting way. "No, I very much meant that I will be getting off this weekend."

I jump up from my chair and loom over her, my fists clenched, my heart racing and that fucking vein in my forehead being so close to bursting and making this back porch look like a scene in a Quentin Tarantino film. "Behave," I say in a voice so deep it can barely be heard, "brat."

Sashaying past me, she stops when she reaches the door to go back inside, looking over her shoulder. "Oh, I plan on it, daddy. I plan on being a very, very good girl."

It's late when I enter the house and realizing Sierra's car wasn't parked in the driveway and that she's still out with some douchebag who doesn't deserve her has put me in a foul mood. So when my eyes connect with Anna's, whose were just about to roll to the back of her head as she's lying back on the couch and my brother is pumping his cock between her tits, well, it's the last thing I want to see.

"Are you fucking kidding me?"

Anna squeals and reaches for a blanket to cover her body, though this is the second time my eyes have seen almost every inch of it. Keaton plasters himself against her, "Keep your eyes off my wife's perfect tits."

"Then stop fucking her in front of me," I say, "Besides, I wasn't looking at your wife's perfect tits."

"Yeah? Then how do you know they're perfect?"

"I don't think they're perfect. You think they're perfect. And you like to tell that fact to literally anyone who will listen."

Keaton puffs up. "You don't think they're perfect? You have a problem with my wife's tits? Are they not good enough for you?"

"No, I don't have a problem with her tits. They're fine tits. Great tits. Perfect, even."

Keaton nods in agreement, then slows his reaction and looks up at me, his face twisted to where he looks both annoyed and constipated. "Well you can't have her tits."

"I don't want her tits!"

"Well why not? They're perfect. Everyone should want them."

Anna chimes in, "Could you both please stop talking about my tits?"

Keaton looks at his wife and smiles, "They really are perfect. Just like you, Baby."

"Thank you," she says sweetly, "but they're also covered in chocolate syrup, so could you please clean me up? Preferably not in front of your brother?"

What the fuck is up with these two and syrup?

Keaton looks back over at me to demand I leave.

"I'm gonna have to burn the couch now," I complain, as I walk into the kitchen to give them time to clean up.

"Was Charlie good for y'all?" I ask Keaton and Anna after they've wiped up the sticky residue from their canoodling and invited me back into my own goddamn living room. Thankfully my older brother and sister-in-law were cool with coming over and hanging out with Mama and Charlie for the night while Sierra and I went on our dates. Though, they could have saved their extracurricular activities for their own house.

"She was a doll," Anna says, smiling, and wrapping her arm in Keaton's.

My brother snorts, "I wouldn't say that exactly."

"What did she do?" I groan.

"She asked me why I had nipples."

The fuck? "What did you tell her?"

"I told her I don't know why I have nipples. That there's a reason for women to have nipples, but I can't for the life of me think of one good reason why men have nipples. So then she asked me if my nipples could do any tricks. I tried, man, I really did. But I couldn't even make them move on their own, or get them to harden. They're lame. They serve no purpose. Seriously, what is the point of us having these things?"

"But," Anna says, "Other than her curiosity for nipple knowledge, it was really a great night. We put her to bed and haven't heard from her since. Tell us about your date."

I finally managed to go out with a woman who checked off so many of my boxes, but the whole time she sat at the table in that restaurant in Laurel, my mind replayed the scene in the bathroom where I first had the pleasure of tasting my nanny.

When our night came to an end and I walked her to her car, I did something I haven't done in years. I asked this woman on a second date.

And she fucking turned me down. "Don't get me wrong, you were a true gentleman tonight and you're hotter than any man I've ever seen before, but I get the feeling you were thinking of someone else tonight when you were with me."

I run a hand down my face as I relive the embarrassment of being called out for having dirty thoughts of my nanny while on a date with another woman. A great woman. A woman that, by all means, should be somebody I pursue.

But she's not her.

"I don't know, guys. I thought maybe I could try going out again, but I really think I'm done."

Keaton wraps his arm around his wife. "Have you tried, I don't know, not being a dick?"

I glare at him. "You're welcome to leave my house any time now."

"Keat, stop teasing your brother. Maybe he isn't the problem. Maybe it's the women he's choosing."

"Hmm," he kisses the top of her head, "you're so smart. I think it's definitely the women. He just keeps going out with the wrong ones."

Anna nods, "Yes, he really should simply go out with the right one and get it over with."

"Wouldn't that be nice?" I ask. "But that would mean that the right one would have to walk into my life."

"I think she'll be walking through your front door any moment now," Anna says with a soft smile.

I think about Sierra and hope that her date turned out to be the douche canoe I imagine he was. That she slumps into the house defeated and depressed. I hope she realizes that there's only one man who can satisfy her the way she needs.

And that man is me.

Chapter Twenty
Sierra

I circle back around downtown taking in the absolute adorableness of the town of Cheatham. The gazebo sits right in the middle of the square and as I take the traffic circle, I'm thankful for the fairy lights that illuminate it so I'm able to see the precious swags of foliage they've draped around the sides.

Taking the next right, I head back in the direction of the farmhouse I've been living in the past several weeks. The last time I drove past it, Keaton's truck was still there instead of Lincoln's Bronco, so I made another round through town. There was no way I was about to give him the satisfaction of showing back up at the house first.

My date tonight had to have generated an image from AI. I swear it's the worst because he looked nothing like the dashing silver fox from his profile. Seated at a high top table in Kalli's Corral, I waited anxiously for him to show up. I ended up getting lost in the music of the band that was playing and jumped when I heard a squeaky voice ask if I was Sierra. When I turned to see a man who was either pushing sixty, or had lived an incredibly hard life, and noticed his smile in my direction lacked a considerable amount of teeth, well, I'm slightly ashamed to say that I started speaking to him in gibberish as though I didn't speak his language.

It's not that I hold any ill will towards older men or those with dental deficiencies, but the truth is the actual man from the enhanced profile picture could have shown up and I likely would have still reacted the same way. The only man I wanted to see wading through the dancing crowd was the father of a spunky six-year-old who holds my heart. The man who appeared to be slightly jealous about me going out. My Mr. Fisher.

Instead, I happened to notice another Mr. Fisher who was looking around like he was in search of someone. Camden was seated at the bar, a beer seemingly forgotten in front of him. I thought about going up and chatting with him so I didn't feel so alone, but panic set in at the thought that he may have witnessed my exchange with the man who was supposed to be my date. I quickly gathered my purse and snuck out of the bar undetected.

Passing the Phisherman's Cybersecurity building doesn't help me forget these ridiculous feelings about my boss. As if the man couldn't just be the sexiest thing this side of the Appalachians, he also has to go and be a big-time successful cyber dude. Listening to his geek speak the other night when he was explaining what he does for a living shouldn't have gotten me all hot and bothered, but it did. It really, really did.

The house isn't too far from the company, making it convenient for Lincoln on his daily commute, but it's ramping up the nerves building in my belly as I get closer to the driveway. The driveway where Lincoln's Bronco is now parked.

As I pull in and park beside him, I flip the visor down and check myself in the mirror. Exactly as how I left the house earlier, my lipstick is perfectly in place, so I smudge it a bit and muss my hair up to give off a freshly fucked look. After a little mental pep talk to remind myself that I'm a badass bitch and Lincoln can eat his heart out, I push up my tits and get out of my car and head inside.

The living room is dark as I step into the house. Glancing down at my mother's watch, I notice that it's slightly past midnight, so I assume everyone is already in their rooms and fast asleep. I place my jacket in the coat closet, because it's finally cool enough outside to need one, and begin to tiptoe to my own bedroom, ready for this sham of an evening to be over.

"You're home awfully late."

His deep voice has me frozen in my tracks and, I'm not ashamed to say, slightly turned on. I turn around to see Lincoln stepping in from the kitchen and I try not to drool at the sight of how handsome he looks.

Standing in his bare feet — why the fuck is that a thing that turns me on — gray sweatpants sit low across his waistline, showing off the tantalizing sharp V that fades into the fabric. The fabric that very nicely outlines the biggest thing I've ever had the pleasure of having inside of me.

My tongue flicks out over my lips as I see that his ink is on full display since his top half is bare, reminding me of the night we met. Those Morning Glory vines snake up his muscular arms and I reach out to grab the sofa when my knees threaten to give out when he crosses them, making the biceps bulge that much more.

If I were a dude, I'd have quite the bulge right now, too.

He's cleaned up the scruff on his face to make sure it's neatly trimmed, but still prevalent. And those beautiful blue eyes that remind me of the first frost of the season are staring at me like he can see inside my soul.

I clear my throat, "I wasn't aware I had a curfew."

Lincoln steps closer to me, close enough to pick up some of the messy brown strands of my hair. "And I wasn't aware you'd be home tonight. Tell me, Sierra," he raises my hair to his nose and inhales, sending a shiver through me. Then he leans down slightly so he can whisper in my ear, "were you a good girl like you promised?"

My breath catches, but then I remind myself of the little chat I had in the car. You're a badass bitch.

"Wouldn't you like to know?" My question comes out way more breathy than I planned and I squeeze my thighs together to hide the invisible lady boner his ripped torso erected.

"Yeah," he says as he stands close to me. Way too close. So close that if I close my lips they would probably brush up against his. "I really would."

"I was, um, I," words have evaded me. Seriously, what language do I speak? I can't seem to draw any from my vocabulary right now.

His thumb brushes over the lipstick I smudged myself, wiping my face clean of it. He inspects it before looking back at me. "Messy hair. Smudged lipstick. It looks like you were a naughty girl, Sierra. And do you know what happens to naughty girls?"

I slowly shake my head.

"They get punished."

Fuck. Me.

"Are you going to spank me?" I ask, somehow finding my voice again, but Lincoln chuckles at my question and sends a ripple of desire over me so hard, my nipples harden.

"Spanking you isn't a punishment for either of us," he says, "but I think I know one that will have you crying out and begging for mercy."

He runs his hand down my side until he reaches the hem of my dress. Slipping his hand underneath, he runs his thumb across the front of my panties. "Just what I thought," he says in that dark voice of his, "fucking soaked."

"Lincoln, please."

"Please what, brat?"

Umm, anything? Kiss me. Fuck me. Breed me until we fill the farmhouse with little blue-eyed babies that growl and bake. "Touch me," I beg. "Fuck me."

"Hmm," he hums against my lips, "go fuck yourself."

He pulls his hand out from under my dress and begins to walk off towards his bedroom.

"You asshole!"

Jason

i need the money sierra

Sierra

I will call them and pay it over the phone. Don't worry.

Jason

u think i trust u to do that

Jason

hell no

Jason

send the money to me

Sierra

I promise I will call them and take care of it.

Jason

ull fucking send me the money u fat bitch or ill come and get it from u

Jason

> just wait til that rich motherfucker ur
> working for finds out what a piece of trash u
> really are

Once again, it's three fucking forty-seven in the morning and I'm wide awake after sleeping like absolute shit. When I stormed into my room after Lincoln's fucking edging session, I had a message from Jason. I really hate that I give that man any thoughts at all, let alone my money, but I worry about what he would do in retaliation if he didn't get what he asked for.

Like always, he's demanding money to cover my mom's bills, but I don't understand why he is so adamant about me sending the money directly to him. Then he implied that he knows where I am. He knows who I work for.

The thought of Jason showing up here at Lincoln's house and causing a scene has me shuddering. How would Lincoln react to that situation? My mind takes off in a fantasy of the tatted daddy facing off against the asshole who I would never see as a father figure. Lincoln would cuss him out, probably with an impressive number of f-bombs. Seriously, if this ever goes down, I should probably call Guiness because I'm sure it would be a world record. Then he would punch Jason in his stupid dick so hard it gets shoved up his throat.

I'm not even sure that's anatomically possible, but this is my fantasy, so I'm going with it.

Lincoln would slam the door in his face, then turn around to me. He'd be all grumpy and muscly and sexy. Like Shrek. Or the Hulk. Green's my favorite color. Sue me.

He would take me in his arms and say, "I never want to see or hear from that man again, Sierra. You're mine and nobody gets to be a dick to you like that except me."

Yeah, that's the kind of shit that does it for me. In fact, it does it so well that I am practically leaking between my legs. I lean over and reach for the vibrator in my nightstand drawer. If I'm lucky, I can tire myself out with an orgasm or two and maybe get a few hours of sleep.

I turn on my battery boyfriend and press it against my clit, instantly sending chills throughout my body. I rub the wand so that vibrations begin shocking my core, and thoughts of the asshole who left me needy and wanting earlier is what brings me to my first orgasm of the night.

Chapter Twenty-One
Lincoln

It's four in the fucking morning and something in this house is buzzing.

I've slept like shit since I was a dumbass and taunted Sierra the way I did, only causing me to ache so hard I could barely stand the pain by the time I made it back to my room. My hand gave no relief, knowing her pussy was eagerly willing and right there. If I had asked, she would have said yes, I have no doubt.

But giving into my desires is what got me into this mess in the first place. No good can come from sleeping with my 23-year-old nanny. Again.

The buzzing sound grows louder and curiosity wins. I get out of bed, pulling my boxer briefs on since I've been sleeping naked like a fucking creep since the day Sierra moved in. I step out of my room and listen for where the sound is coming from.

Two steps. It took two steps and I'm outside Sierra's door where the buzzing is much louder than it was in my room. She must be holding a pillow over it to soften the sound, or I would have heard it through the walls like I heard her the other night.

I'm at war with myself trying to decide what to do. I could go in and help her out. I could go back to bed and try to get some sleep.

I could saw off my dick so that I don't have to be tempted by the naughty nanny any longer. Yeah, that's a bit dramatic. There's no way I'm sawing off my dick.

I decide to twist the doorknob and see if it's unlocked. When I hear the sound of a click, I push the door open, not ready, but at the same time so fucking ready, to see what's on the other side.

As I step into the room, Sierra is arched with her back off the bed, her long legs spread wide. One hand is holding an impressive looking vibrator to her clit and the other presses a pillow down on top of it to muffle the sound.

When her back descends to the bed, her eyes lock on mine. She's staring at me, no shame in what she's doing, and it's sexy as hell.

"Did you come to watch or did you come to help?"

I gulp, not knowing the answer to her question. I should definitely not touch her. I should turn the fuck around and pretend I didn't see her beautifully pink pussy practically dripping and begging for my cock to fill it. Yup, it's decided.

I'm horrible at taking my own advice.

I walk over to the bed, my cock creeping out of my underwear, growing harder the closer I get to her. She's displayed so beautifully for me, and I can't wait to help make her shatter.

I begin to crawl up the end of the bed, a lion stalking its prey. I glide my hands over her legs, up to the apex and the wand that continues to buzz. "May I?" I ask, gripping the vibrator.

She nods and I relish in the fact that she trusts me to give her pleasure. I run the machine through her wetness. "Has this already helped you to come?"

Again, Sierra nods. She's so fucking cute. "Well then," I say, removing the vibrator from her cunt and turning it off, "it's my turn now."

I position myself between her knees, spreading them to open her wider for me. Her pussy is pure perfection. I lean down, blowing a breath over it so that she reacts to the chill. And react, she does. I love how receptive she is to my touch.

"Tell me, Sierra, do you want my mouth on you?" I ask, so close to her core that if I stick out my tongue it would be coated in her flavor.

She whimpers before begging and it makes my cock fucking throb, "Yes, Lincoln, please. Please put your mouth on me."

I lean in closer, once again blowing my breath over her naked pussy until she's shuddering and crying out. "Only good girls get to have my mouth on them Sierra, brats like you take whatever I'm willing to give."

Taking two fingers, I thrust them inside of her, eliciting throaty moans from her. "God, Lincoln, yes."

I continue pumping into her, curving upward so they hit that spot I know will make her come undone. "Oh no, Lincoln, you have to stop."

"There's no way I'm stopping."

"It's too much. I'm going to — ahh!'

Sierra's body lifts upward like she's possessed but in a really hot fucking way. I'm surprised her head isn't twisting in the opposite direction, but instead it's blissed out, her mouth open and eyelids fluttering. And gushing out of her is the sweetest liquid, coating my fingers, my hand, and well, everything.

As her body begins to relax, I pull my fingers from her and hold up my hand. The moonlight streaming in through the window displays the beautiful glistening liquid that I coaxed out of her.

"Did I just?"

"Yeah, you just."

She groans, "That's so embarrassing."

I look at her with furrowed eyebrows, but instead of annoyance like usual, it's a look of confusion. "I think you said hot wrong, because this," I slowly lick her pleasure off of me, "this is one of the greatest fucking things that has happened to me."

"Happened to you? I'm pretty sure I'm the one who squirted."

"Yeah. All over me. So this happened to me. Don't ruin this, brat."

"Ruin what exactly? Your perfect night with your perfect date?"

I smirk, pleased to hear her tone dripping with jealousy and decide to add to it. "It was a perfect date. She's beautiful, smart, my age, and do you know the best part?" I've managed to pin Sierra's hands to the bed and climb up her body, so that I'm practically hovering over her chest. "She doesn't have a smartass mouth."

She scoffs, "You like my smart mouth."

"Yeah," I say, brushing my finger over her lips, "I really do. Now let's put it to good use."

Her tongue darts out and she nods, giving me the permission to shove my dick in between those perfect lips of hers. I rock back and forth above her, pumping myself in and out and trying to hold myself back from coming down her throat sooner than I want. "Fuck, Sierra, your mouth was made to take my cock."

Her moan shoots vibrations down my shaft and my body begins to shake above her as she continues licking and sucking like I'm her favorite flavor of candy. "I'm close, if you don't stop I'm going to come down your throat."

She doesn't stop. In fact, somehow this beautiful woman giving me the greatest pleasure I've ever experienced in my life transforms into a fucking vacuum cleaner, sucking my cock like it's her fucking job and she wants a gold star.

"Sierra, stop, I can't hold back," I warn her, but instead of releasing me from her suction, she raises her hands and gently squeezes my balls. I can't stop myself from exploding into her mouth and she consumes every single drop of me like the champ she is.

When the two of us are finally spent, I roll off of her, trying to catch my breath as I look up at the ceiling Camden stared up at throughout his childhood. I think about him and Keaton and the shit they'll give me for hooking back up with Sierra. The problem is, now that I have, I don't know that I can stop.

"Nobody can know about this," I say after both of our breathing has regulated and the room has gone silent again.

"Fine by me" she says, sounding only slightly offended.

I look over at her, but she's staring up at the ceiling. "Seriously, you're the best I've ever been with and I don't want to stop, but nobody can know about the two of us."

She rolls her eyes, "You're the one who started this. Why did you even come into my room anyway?"

"Your buzzing woke me up," I eye the culprit laying lifeless beside her bed.

Sierra looks at me sheepishly, "You could hear that?"

I nod. "Yup. So I thought I'd investigate. I sure as hell didn't expect to see the nanny sprawled out in desperate need of a finger bang and a blow job."

She rolls her eyes and my hand twitches, "I wasn't in desperate need."

"Could have fooled me."

"You know what?" she huffs. "You did the job, so now you can leave. Just go back to your room. You can rest assured there will be no more buzzing."

Rolling off the bed, I stand and walk over to the vibrator, picking it up. "There won't be any more buzzing. Because this is going with me."

She eyes me angrily, "It absolutely is not."

"From now on," I say, feeling my chest vibrate with how low my voice is, "if you need relief, you come to me. You come for me. Only me."

She sits up on the bed and places her hands on her wide hips. Her very naked hips. And it makes me incredibly aware that my dick is still standing at attention. "I will do no such thing."

I shrug, "Then I guess you won't come at all."

As I walk out of the room, something hits me in the back. I bend down to retrieve the pillow she threw. "And I'm taking this, too."

Chapter Twenty-Two

Sierra

I t has been weeks of delicious torture as we enter the holiday season. Every night I'm either in Lincoln's room or he's in mine making good on his threat that I come only for him. And my god how I do. Every time. Multiple times.

Regardless of how heated our evenings get, he hasn't crossed the line and slept with me again. My core aches to feel the stretch of him again, but I understand that if the two of us have sex, it crosses a line that we may not be able to come back from.

Throughout the day, I've been spending every moment I can trying to forget the charming, but grumpy, jerk who somehow wrings out all the pleasure in my body all too well. But as I step into the kitchen and see multiple piles spread out around it, I can't help but realize I'm going to lose that battle today.

Tubes of toothpaste and toothbrushes, deodorant, rolls of quarters, protein bars, and more are being placed in a large zipper bag by my favorite little girl, who beams up at her dad who returns the sweet smile.

"What's going on here?" I question.

"It's blessing bag day!" Charlie exclaims.

I laugh at her excitement, "Wow! What exactly are blessing bags?"

"Every year, Charlie and I fill these bags up with some essentials and things to help those who may not be as fortunate as we are," Lincoln explains. "She mentioned that you were supposed to take her out today for some shopping, so I thought you could take what we have made so far this morning with you and pass them out."

My heart grows for the growly man at his annual act of kindness. "And you do this every year?"

"Yup!" Charlie says proudly, "We also go to the soup kitchen in the city and give food to people. Did you know that they have more than just soup there?"

I smile at her astonishment, "You don't say?"

"This summer they had barbecue sandwiches, corn on the cob, watermelon and coleslaw. I helped make the sandwiches." Her little chest puffs out and somehow my smile grows even larger.

"Wow, that's a very big girl thing to do. I'm sure you did an excellent job." She nods emphatically as I come to stand next to Lincoln. "That's quite the spread for a soup kitchen," I whisper to the man watching his daughter.

Lincoln clears his throat, "My brothers and I pitch in and try to make things better where we can. It's no big deal."

"It is, though, Lincoln. It's a very big deal." My words are soft as I look up at him and he turns to look back at me. He holds his eye contact, though it grows heated, and then flicks his tongue over his bottom lip. It's taking everything in me not to press my lips to his in this moment.

"Are you two going to kiss?" Charlie asks, shaking both myself and Lincoln from the moment. "It won't gross me out if you two want to kiss."

Lincoln steps away from me and it feels like someone opened the door and let in the cool breeze from outside.

"Of course not, Little Bit. I save all my kisses for you." He lifts his daughter from the chair she's perched in and starts peppering her with love as she squirms in his arms. I step away from the sweet scene to give them their moment and to remind myself that this life with them is only temporary. It won't be too long until Lincoln Fisher decides I'm no longer needed here in his home and the family that feels all too much like it's become my own will begin to forget me.

I'm startled by a hand on my shoulder and when I turn around, Sharon is there with a look of understanding on her face. "They need you, you know? We all do."

"But one day you won't," I say sadly.

"I'm beginning to heal, thanks to you," she says with a soft smile, "I've noticed it and so have my boys. But you're healing those two in there, too. You're giving them both exactly what they need."

"And what's that?" I ask, choking back tears.

"Love."

"Look at these!" Charlie rushes over to me with a pretty jar of cherries soaked in bourbon. A very breakable jar that I quickly take from her.

Confused, I ask, "Do you like cherries?"

"Yeah, but these are for Skyla. She loves them! She has the prettiest pink dress with them and then a swimsuit with them and she wears a necklace with them. They're her favorite."

Her smile is contagious and I add the jar to the shopping basket I'm holding in the crook of my arm. "Well then, let's get her these cherries and maybe we can find something else to go with it."

Charlie beams up at me as we continue our journey through the store that has everything from clothing to jewelry to home goods to toys. It's a hodgepodge of a place and normally it gets my anxiety ticking, especially the long line at the register, but somehow with Charlie it doesn't bother me this time. It feels right.

We finish getting a few more things for some of her family members and I kindly decline the red piece of lingerie she chose for me as we head to the counter. I pass over the black credit card Lincoln handed us to pay for everything while we were out today. Though I tried to argue about taking it, he insisted, really opening my eyes to how much money the man has. It's yet another discrepancy between the two of us and another reason this fantasy I've built up will never come to be.

"I have one more stop for us to make and then we will head home. Does that sound good, Little Bit?"

Charlie giggles in the backseat, "What's so funny?"

"You and Daddy both call me Little Bit and I don't think you know it."

I ponder her statement. "I guess I heard him call you that and started saying it myself."

"Nope. You called me Little Bit the first day we met," she corrects.

I frown, not remembering the detail that seems to have clearly stuck out in her mind. "I can stop calling you that if you want."

"Why would I want that?"

"Well, it's a special name between you and your dad. Special names should be shared with special people in your life."

"Then keep calling me it, because you're one of the specialist people in my life."

I keep my smile hidden from her as I continue the rest of the way to our destination. If only she knew that she was one of the most special people in my life, too.

As we arrive at the farm, Charlie begins asking millions of questions. Where are the reindeer? Do we get to pet the reindeer? What do the reindeer eat? Do they eat little girls? Why are the reindeer fenced in when they can fly?

We laugh and hold hands as we go around to the different areas of the reindeer farm, taking in all the different animals they have. An older woman comes and stands next to us as we listen to the man holding up an antler and explaining that male reindeer shed their antlers in the fall and early winter, while female reindeer keep their antlers until after winter passes, so that must mean Santa's sleigh is pulled by an all-female team.

"Makes sense," Charlie mutters.

"You're damn right," I nod in solidarity.

The woman looks between the two of us and smiles at me, "You and your daughter are so beautiful and precious. Keep making these memories together." She sighs heavily and I try to correct her, but she walks away as Charlie pulls me in the opposite direction.

"Where are you taking me?" I laugh as the small, but mighty girl, finally releases my hand. She's managed to drag me inside a metal sided building and in a corner comes a deep, "Ho! Ho! Ho!"

"Are you ready to see Santa?" I ask and eyes identical to her father's light up.

We stand in line silently, something that rarely happens with my sweet girl. She eagerly keeps watching as the number of people in front of us decreases, and when it's her turn, she's directed to take her place as I stand to the side to snap some pictures with my phone.

I look on as Charlie nestles herself onto the lap of the man dressed in a bright red suit and sporting an impressive gray beard. She hugs him, excited for their exchange and my heart blossoms at how much I love this little girl. At how much I love the whole family, if I'm being honest with myself.

"How was your chat with Santa? Did you tell him everything you wanted this year?"

She shakes her little head, smiling, "Nope. I told him thank you for bringing me my Christmas gift early this year."

Confused, I look at her, "What gift did he give you early?"

Charlie hugs me tightly before looking back up at me and smiling with that gap where she lost one of her front teeth last week. "A mom."

Chapter Twenty-Three
Lincoln

"Christmas will be here before you know it. Have you got all your shopping finished?" Mama asks as she fixes her Christmas village display. She hasn't gotten it out in the past couple of years and it brings a smile to my face as I see her, the real her, coming out more and more each day. I can begrudgingly admit that I have Sierra to thank for that.

I shake my head, "I think I finish up with Charlie and then she adds something else to her list."

"You know you don't have to buy that child every single thing she asks for, right?" Mama chides.

"I don't make all this money to deprive my baby girl," I explain and she shakes her head at me.

A few minutes pass and when Mama has finished fixing the village so that every piece of the buffet is covered in fake snow and all the pieces are to her liking, she joins me at the table. "And what about everyone else? Charlie isn't the only one you're shopping for, is she?"

I smile at her, "I made sure to get you something, too, Mama."

"While I deeply appreciate that, don't you think there's another woman you should be purchasing something for?"

I think for a moment, "I went in with Camden and we got something for Keaton and Anna together, if that's what you mean."

"Something for a woman who seems to be a bit special to you?" she presses, and I realize now that she means the other woman living in our household. The woman who came on my tongue last night, and the night before that, and, well, the night before that.

My face drops as I realize Christmas Eve is tomorrow and not once did I consider getting Sierra a gift. I had planned on simply giving her a Christmas bonus like I do with the employees at my company. When I tell my mom as such, her face drops. "You think she'd want an actual gift?"

"It just seems like the two of you have been spending a lot of time together and that you would perhaps know her well enough to get her something a little more personal." I shoot her a questioning look and she huffs at me, "I may be old, but I do have eyes. I can see the way you stare at that girl. And the way she stares back at you."

I lean over the table, resting my forehead to my crossed arms. "I don't know what I'm doing, Mama."

I hear the chair legs scraping the tiled floor and feel my mom's hands run over my barely there hair in the back. "You're falling, baby. Ain't it great?"

Our ragged breaths are the only sounds in the room as Sierra and I both come down from our orgasms. Tonight, we contorted our bodies into the trusty sixty-nine position and I devoured her delectable pussy as she sucked my cock like it was her life source.

I crave to be buried inside of her, but I can't bring myself to cross that line. Especially after my mom told me exactly how I was feeling. I'm falling for Sierra Thomas.

The woman who lives rent-free in my house and in my mind must be feeling awkward in the lack of communication, so she speaks up. "Are you excited about all of your family coming over tomorrow?"

Now that Anna and Keaton are together, they want to spend Christmas day with one another, so everyone will come over tomorrow night for Christmas Eve. We will spend the evening eating, decorating cookies and sharing our gifts amongst one another.

I shrug nonchalantly, "I guess. It's always fun to see Charlie so excited."

Sierra hums, "You're really blessed to have your family, Lincoln."

I look over, catching the sadness on her face. "I know you lost your mother this year, but you don't have family you should be spending tomorrow with instead?"

"I kinda thought you guys were my family now," she admits quietly. A blissful silence takes hold of me, but she must misinterpret it and tries to take the words back. "I mean, not that you're my family, but I don't have a family of my own anymore, so I meant that yours is the only family that I would be with. But if you don't want me here tomorrow, I can go find something else to do. I don't want to impose or anything."

Reaching over I put a finger to her lips. "Calm down, Sierra. You're not going anywhere. And you're right, you are our family now." Her lips are so soft against my skin and I can't help but take advantage of the moment and lean in to brush my own against them. She deepens the kiss and I'm as hard now as I was earlier. This woman is making me come undone and I don't know how the fuck to feel about it.

I pull back and run my hand over my close cut, cursing myself for not growing it out so I could tug at the strands. Charlie used to pull my hair when she was a baby and it hurt like hell, so I cut it short and have kept it that way since. When I look back over at Sierra, her features are screwed up in a defeated expression.

I hate that our relationship has been fire and ice and that I'm not big enough to tell her how I truly feel, or at least, how I think I'm beginning to feel, but there's too much at stake.

I lost my dad.

I lost Nicole.

I lost my mom.

Each loss killed a part of me inside and to think that I could potentially lose someone as incredible as Sierra and risk Charlie getting hurt like that in the process is too much to bear.

"I should probably get back to my room," I say and Sierra nods her confirmation, turning away from me and snuggling under the covers.

Feeling as defeated as she looks, I head back to my room. Alone. Again.

Chapter Twenty-Four
Sierra

This is my first Christmas without my mom and I expected to spend it wallowing and in tears, absolutely miserable with the emptiness and loneliness from not having her here. Instead, the Fisher Family was incredible and welcomed me as though I was one of their own. I don't know if Lincoln told them to treat me like family, but everyone acted as though I've been part of the family for years.

While there is still a huge chunk of my heart missing with the absence of my mom, I had one of the best holidays of my life. Watching Charlie light up with every gift she opened was absolutely magical. The laughter of Lincoln's family was the cozy comfort I needed. But now it's just the two of us as we finish piling the gifts from Santa under the tree for Charlie to wake up to in the morning.

It's been a comfortable silence as we've navigated around one another, but as the job finishes, we both collapse onto opposite ends of the couch, exhausted but with adrenaline coursing through us. I steal glances at Lincoln as he scrolls through the checklist on his phone, making sure every one of Charlie's gifts is accounted for. I worry the watch at my wrist, wincing as it pinches my skin. The confession about the Christmas wish Charlie shared with me has been on the tip of my tongue these past few days and now that we're sitting here in silence, it wants to bubble up out of me.

"Lincoln," I say at the same time he says my name. We look at each other sheepishly, but I bite my words back so he has the floor to speak.

From behind his back, Lincoln pulls out a small ring-shaped box, and my heart begins to flutter. The red foil wrapping glistens in the dim light from the tree and the gold bow wrapped around it sparkles.

It's not. It can't be. That's ridiculous.

"We typically wait until we're with the whole family to open our gifts, but I thought maybe I could give you this one when it was just the two of us."

"Lincoln, this is too much," I begin to say, but he shakes his head, cutting me off.

"Can you not argue with me for one fucking night and take the damn gift?"

I cut him a weak glare, but take the box from his extended hand and slowly unwrap the present. When I pull the velvet box from the package, my hands begin to tremble. Ever so slowly, I open it to reveal a single silver link. A link that is identical to the ones on my watch. I glance up, making contact with the glacial orbs of the man that takes my breath away.

"I've noticed you always wear that watch, but you also fuss with it. I thought maybe if we added an extra link to it, you could wear it more comfortably."

Tears fill my eyes as I realize he noticed. He noticed something about me and cared enough to bring comfort into my life. "It's perfect," I whisper.

"Here," he reaches out for my wrist and unclasps the watch, rubbing at the imprint left on my skin. He doesn't say anything, simply soothing the spot with his touch, then he focuses back on the task at hand. When he's added the link, he clasps the watch back on my wrist and smiles as he moves it around more freely.

"Thank you," my words come out soft and shaky, "for everything."

He smirks at me and I lean forward, hoping he'll capture my lips with his own, but instead he asks a question that has tears brimming once more. "This watch was your mom's, wasn't it?"

I nod as I'm flooded with memories of her.

"Tell me about her?"

"She was my everything." I look at him, slightly embarrassed, but find no judgment on his face. "I know that's probably pathetic to say about your parent, but it was always me and her against the world."

Lincoln scoots on the couch so that he's sitting a little closer to me now. "And your dad?"

I give a small shake of my head, "He took off when I was a baby. I couldn't tell you one single memory I have off the man."

"Sounds like Charlie's mom," Lincoln confesses, and it's the first I've heard about the woman who helped create the most wonderful little girl in the world.

"What happened there?" I asked, genuinely curious and hoping he doesn't shut down in this moment of confessions.

Lincoln sighs deeply, but to my surprise, answers my question. "The day she and Charlie were discharged from the hospital, I was ready to take them home. Had bought a ring and thought I'd do the right thing and make an honest woman out of her. Instead, I got Charlie tucked into the backseat and when I turned to help Nicole, she told me she wasn't coming with me. This small town life wasn't what she wanted. Cheatham was never enough for her. Neither was I. And neither was Charlie."

I can't begin to fathom a world in which someone can't love this town and this man who makes the world a brighter place. "And she never changed her mind? Never came back?"

"Nope," Lincoln says, popping the final consonant sound. "She terminated her parental rights, so Charlie is all mine. As far as I know, she's never stepped foot back into town. Not surprised," he snorts, "she hated this place with a passion."

"Why is that?"

"Told me she was destined for bigger and better things than what this town had to offer. She had it all here. A great job, loyal friends, a loving family. But it was never enough."

"That's sad," I admit. A vision of Charlie conjures in my mind and I smile at the brilliant beauty. "She had to have been beautiful, to make someone as stunning as Charlie."

Lincoln hums in agreement, and then fixes his eyes on mine. "But not near as gorgeous as you."

My eyes roll.

"I thought I made it clear that you don't fucking roll your eyes at me, brat," Lincoln growls. His typical bright blue eyes have darkened in desire and arousal builds inside me, and okay fine, maybe it's dribbled outside a little, too. I ache for his punishment. I crave his domination.

"Sorry, daddy," I whisper and just as we are about to meet one another, all of my fantasies vanish with the buzzing sound of my phone that lies between us.

Lincoln looks down at my screen first and when his eyes turn back up to mine, the look of want and desire have been replaced with anguish and fury.

Glancing down at the cushion, I can see my illuminated phone and the single message displayed.

Jason

When I look back at the man I was sharing a tender, but still intense, moment with, his rough exterior is back. "Lincoln," I try to say, but he abruptly stands, towering over me, and I lose my words.

"Go to bed, Sierra."

"Lincoln it isn't what you think," I say softly.

"Go. To. Bed," he grits out, and now the moment between us is definitely lost and I'm infuriated with his refusal to hear me out.

"Did you order me to bed like a child?"

He huffs, crossing his arms. "You're twenty-three. It's not far off."

Oh, no the fuck he didn't.

I rise to my feet to face off with him, thankful for my height at this moment. "And at twenty-three, I've managed to get a college degree. I found a job in my field earning a living wage that has good benefits. I've helped a wounded woman heal and a little girl thrive. All while grieving the loss of my own mother, whom I nursed and stayed with until the very end. Oh, and there's this giant asshole I have to put up with every single day."

Lincoln's jaw clenches, his hands form fists. "Sierra, I told you to go to bed." His words are soft, but firm and it only pisses me off that much more.

"And I'm telling you to go to hell." I storm off in the direction of my bedroom, not to do as he demanded, but to get away from him. To put distance between me and the arrogant asshole who goes from hot to cold in the blink of an eye. It's childish and I know it only fuels the way he threw my age in my face earlier, but I slam the door behind me, immediately cringing as I know Charlie and Sharon are in the house trying to sleep. I want to go out and apologize for being loud, but I absolutely refuse to give him the satisfaction of those words.

I sit down on my bed and look down at the message from the man who ruined my amazing moment earlier. The man who has ruined every aspect of my life since he came into it.

Jason

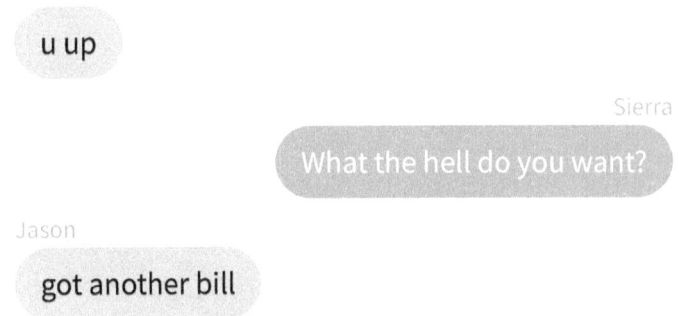

u up

Sierra

What the hell do you want?

Jason

got another bill

Where the hell are all of these medical bills coming from? It wasn't the best coverage ever, but Mom did have insurance. I also know for a fact she had met her deductible and she should have reached her out-of-pocket expenses.

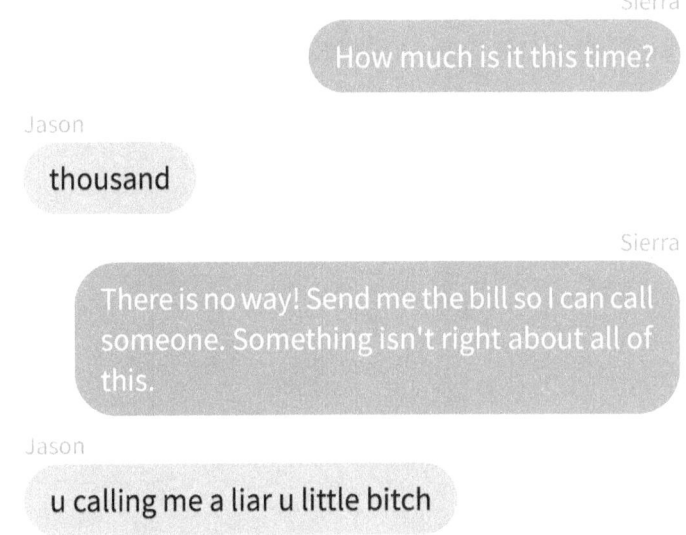

Sierra

How much is it this time?

Jason

thousand

Sierra

There is no way! Send me the bill so I can call someone. Something isn't right about all of this.

Jason

u calling me a liar u little bitch

I've seen Jason angry and it isn't pretty. While I don't think he ever physically touched my mom out of malice, I have seen him throw a few things around the house and he even punched a wall, leaving a fist-sized hole in the living room of their house.

Sierra

No, but I think the hospital has messed something up with the billing. I just want to talk to somebody because I feel like I'm being overcharged.

Jason

until u do that give me my money

Sierra

I can call them first thing after the holiday.

Jason

listen fatass i don't trust u to convince them ur right so ur gonna send me my money now so i dont have to get any calls and threats about late bills

Sierra

Jason, you won't get any calls. I will call as soon as the finance department is open. If they say I owe, I'll pay it, otherwise we won't have to worry about this anymore.

And you'll finally be out of my life for good, I don't add.

Jason

i dont believe u

Jason

send me my money tonight

Sierra

Jason, I don't have that kind of money right now.

Jason

im tired of talking to ur fat cunt send me my money tonight or i will show up at that rich tech guys door and make him give it to me

Sierra

You can't do that!

Jason

then find me my fucking money

Jason

im sure the rich fuck ur probably fucking has a thousand stashed somewhere

Jason

snatch it

Sierra

Stop. I'll get it to you.

I have no idea how I'm going to get the money to Jason, but I sure as hell am not going to steal it from Lincoln. Now that I think of it, how does Jason know where I am and who I work for? I try to rack my brain, thinking about a time I told him where I was going or about the new job that I landed, but I really don't think I ever did. In fact, there's nobody from back home who would have known where I had ended up.

The weight of tonight's drama has me barely able to keep my eyes open. I stand and stretch my body that's all tight with knots now before I make my way to the door so I can get ready for bed in the hallway bathroom.

As I open my door, Lincoln is standing there, his hand running over his short spikes of hair.

"Who the fuck is Jason?"

1 1 1 0 0 0 0 0 1 0 1 0 0 0 0 0 0 0 1 1 1 0 0
1 0 0 1 1 0 0 0 1 0 1 0 1 0 1 1 1 1 0 0 1 0 0
0 0 0 0 0 0 0 1 1 0 0 1 1 0 0 0 0 0 1 0 1 1
1 0 1 0 1 0 1 0 0 0 1 1 0 0 0 1 1 0 0 1 0 0
0 0 0   0 1 1 1   1 0 0 1   0 0 0 1 0 0 1 0
0 1 0   1 1 1 0   0 1 0 0   1 1 1 0 1   0 1

Chapter Twenty-Five
Lincoln

I think about her question. Why do I care?

"If you're fucking other people while also fucking me, I have the right to know."

She rolls her eyes, "Us occasionally going down on one another is not fucking."

What? "Um, yes it is."

Her eyebrows furrow and she looks at me with her mouth open like I'm the biggest idiot on the planet. "It is not the same, Lincoln."

"It's penetration. It counts."

"So you're telling me," she crosses her arms and pops out her hips, "that if I was a virgin and you fiddle-faddled me with your fingers, that I would no longer be a virgin?"

I scowl, "Well, yeah, I guess you still would be."

"So penetration isn't the definition of sex?"

"Penetration with penis then," I offer, feeling quite smug at how quickly I came up with that.

"So you're telling me," she repeats, shimmying her shoulders as she says it, "that if I was a virgin and I got down on my knees and sucked you off, that I would no longer be a virgin?"

I think for a moment, "You're trying to confuse me."

"You're confused, alright."

I shake my head as I realize she did a great job deflecting and getting me completely off topic, but I still need to know what's going on. "Who is he, Sierra?"

She motions for me to come into her room, so I follow her. She perches on the end of her bed, but I remain standing, arms crossed. I know I look like a dick right now, but I feel like she owes me some answers.

"Jason is my stepdad."

Can't say I expected that. "What kind of kinky shit are you into?"

"Eww! Gross, no. Oh, gross. I think I'm going to be sick." She begins making dramatic gagging sounds and it has me pulling her signature move and rolling my eyes.

"Fine, if you aren't fucking your stepdad, then please explain to me why he's sending you booty call texts in the middle of the night."

She looks off to the side and I can't quite make her expression. Guilt? Shame?

She mutters something that sounds an awful lot like monkey, but that doesn't make sense. "What?"

"Money," she says more clearly, still looking away from me. "He keeps saying these bills are coming in for my mom and he needs me to pay them. But it doesn't make sense."

"Have you asked to see them?"

"Oh gee, what a genius idea. I'm so glad you're here since I'm such a damn moron and never thought to ask for copies of them myself."

My cock twitches in response to her sharp tongue, but clearly there's an issue here we need to figure out, so I mentally tell it to calm the fuck down. "And?"

"And he says he doesn't have to show me. He demands I send the money directly to him."

"And you don't think that's pretty fucking suspicious?" I seethe, knowing she's being taken advantage of and knowing she's too damn smart to let that happen to her.

She glares at me, "Why do you even care? Just go, Lincoln."

Sierra tries to push past me, but I reach out to grab for her, clasping her fingers in mind. "I care, Sierra. Please, tell me what's going on."

Looking down at where our fingers are linked, she sighs deeply. "He threatens me. He threatens to take away my mom's things. And tonight," she gulps so hard I can hear the sound, "tonight he threatened you."

"What do you mean he threatened me?"

She pulls at her hands, then grabs her phone and pushes it into mine. "See for yourself."

I read through his messages to her and my blood begins to boil at the way he speaks to her. The way he shames her fucking flawless body. The way he demands her money and then demeans her when she asks questions. Good questions that she should be asking.

"I wasn't going to do it," she whispers, causing me to look up from the phone and see her cowering away from me.

"Do what?"

"I would never steal from you. No matter how badly I needed the money. I would swallow my pride and ask you for help before I would ever take from you." Tears begin to fall down her face and I can see the fear in her eyes. Not fear from the dick who has been stealing from her this entire time, but the fear that I wouldn't believe her.

I toss her phone to the side and sit on the bed beside her, pulling her into my arms. "I believe you, Sierra. I will always believe you."

"I'm gonna kill him," I say as I pace my office. My brothers are sitting in the leather lounge chairs, each with a glass of bourbon after another fucking exhausting meeting with Caruso Enterprises. Their bullshit was the last thing I needed after staying up and watching Sierra toss in her sleep the past couple of nights. She's supposed to be calling the hospital this morning to figure things out while I'm at work, and being tied up dealing with more grief from our biggest clients has my anxiety working overtime.

Cam pinches the bridge of his nose, "I really need the two of you to stop saying this shit in front of me."

"He's threatening her, Cam. He's stealing from her. He tried to convince her to steal from me. What can we do?"

Cam sighs and leans back in his chair, "I mean it's fraud. It's theft by deception. And unfortunately it happens every millisecond of every day. I'd like to say there's a lot of options and there are ways she can get her money back, but she has to prove that he didn't use the money for what he claimed and that he ended up keeping the money for himself."

"She's supposed to be calling the hospital and confirming things this morning." I pick my phone up off my desk and see I have no missed calls or new messages. "Still nothing."

"Do you know how much money he ended up taking?"

I shake my head, "He asked for a thousand this last time and from her reply, that sounds like the most he's ever asked for."

Cam releases a breath, "If it's not that much money, then it's a small claims case. It could only mean a misdemeanor for him."

Well that's not the fucking answer I want to hear. "That's not good enough. I want him to hurt. I want him to suffer. He's been taking advantage of her and using her mother against her as she's been grieving her loss. It's not okay."

"We'll do whatever we can to help her out," Keaton says, "You know, it would probably help if we knew a guy that could hack into this guy's bank account and see if he's been pocketing the funds."

I snort, "Umm, I can do that."

Keaton rolls his eyes as Camden stands up to leave. "The two of you have to stop saying shit like that in front of me, too."

Chapter Twenty-Six
Sierra

I knew Jason was an absolute piece of shit the day I met him, and a simple phone call to the hospital just confirmed my suspicions. The bills have been paid in full for months and they confirmed nothing has been mailed to my mom's house since the spring.

The past few days have been torture as the holidays led into the weekend and I had to wait for the offices to open back up before I could get in touch with someone about what's been going on. After dropping Charlie off at school this morning, running a few errands around town, coming back and doing some laundry and other household chores I try to keep up with, it was mid-morning before I could make the call. Then, of course, I had to wait on hold for what felt like half a century before I could be directed to the person who could help me find some answers.

Lincoln has been as impatient as I have been about the whole situation, so I pick my phone up to type out a message with an update. Before I can even begin, there's a knock at the front door and I make my way across the house to see who it could be, not for one second expecting the gorgeous brunette on the other side.

"Umm, hi, can I help you?"

She whips her large black sunglasses that would make anyone else look like a bug, but somehow enhance her high cheekbones, off her face and plasters on one of the most perfect smiles I've ever seen before. Her pushup bra is working wonders for her in that red sweater she has on and pushing up the girls even higher than mine, though I'm probably younger than her by a decade. "Oh, hi there sweetie, I'm here to see Lincoln. Is he in?"

"No," I say confused about why he wouldn't have mentioned that someone was stopping by. "May I ask what it is that's bringing you by?"

"Oh, I'm sorry," she licks her bottom lip before biting it and sending a wink my way, "that's personal."

An uneasy pressure starts to build in my chest, but before I can even begin thinking of what to say next to this woman, the sound of yelling from behind me has me startled.

"You get the hell off my property you Jezebel!"

The woman on the porch shakes her head and rolls her eyes, "Oh, Sharon, always so dramatic. I don't need to speak with you. I have business with Lincoln."

"Like hell you do. Get your fucking fake ass off my fucking beautiful porch and you stay the fuck away from my family."

I'm stunned, blinking at the small woman with the big mouth and colorful words I've never heard from her and clearly understand now how the language was passed down to her boys.

"Just tell him I stopped by. I'm sure he will be more than happy to know I'm back in town."

"Why? So you can ask him for more money? Ask him to knock you up so you can leave another child behind like you had no part of their making?"

I gasp at the accusation and look once again at the woman in front of me, the woman who has turned from drop-dead gorgeous to the ugliest person on the planet. "Nicole?"

"Guilty," she smiles at me. "And don't let this old biddy tell stories on me. I'm really nice when I want to be. Especially to the help."

She winks at me again and a sudden surge of defensiveness takes over. For Sharon. For Lincoln. For Charlie. For my family. "The help? What makes you think that's all I am?"

"Oh sweetie, well, you're not exactly Lincoln's type now are you? Lincoln's hot and, well," she motions to my body, "you're not."

"I'll have you know my son is crazy about this woman right here. We all are. I love her. Charlie loves her. And if my son can get his head out of his ass and let another woman in his heart after the hell you put him through, he'd realize he loves her too."

I stare at Sharon, who has made her way through the door and continues to walk, backing Nicole off the porch.

"Wow," Nicole says with disdain, "actually stepping foot outside the house now, Sharon? Didn't know you had it in you."

"I'd walk through hell and back if it means keeping you away from my son and granddaughter. Now you're not welcome here, Nicole. Leave."

Nicole throws her hands up, "I'm going, I'm going." She looks back up to the doorway where I'm still standing in shock and does a little wave. "Please let Linc know I showed up today. I really do think he'll be eager to hear what I need to tell him."

Sharon continues barking insults at Nicole as she gets into her shiny red sports car. When Nicole finally pulls the vehicle out of the driveway, Sharon makes her way back to me, reaching up to take my face in her hands so she can focus it on her.

"You don't listen to a word that devil woman says, you hear me? You are the best thing that has happened to him."

I scoff at what she implies, and she shakes my head again for good measure. "Don't you let her sharp tongue make you think otherwise. You and my son have something between the two of you that's special and while he can be a dumbass for sure, he's too smart to go back to her. Especially with you here."

"Sharon, I don't know what you think is happening, but I promise it's nothing more than me being here for you and Charlie. Lincoln's my boss. That's all."

She crosses her arms in front of her, "This house is solid, but the walls ain't that thick. You think I don't hear what the two of you are up to every night?"

"It's not every night," I mutter and she cuts her eyes at me like I'm lying to her. "Besides, that's just the two of us giving each other what we need physically. Relationships deserve more than that. He deserves more than that."

"And you do, too," she reminds me.

I nod my head agreeing with her, because my mom didn't get to live on this earth long enough to do all the things she wanted, but she did get to live long enough to teach me to believe in myself and know my worth. "Yes, ma'am."

"What time is it?" she asks, nodding towards the watch I always wear. The watch that no longer pinches my skin and fits me better now since Lincoln gave me his thoughtful gift.

"Almost noon," I answer her, wondering where she's going with this.

Sharon nods, "Well, that should give us plenty of time."

"For what?"

"To go grab lunch and then pick up Charlie from school."

I smile at her, "What would you like me to fix us for lunch?"

"Oh, I was thinking we could go down to Crumb and Get It and get us some sandwiches," she suggests.

The idea of their turkey sandwich with those awesome pickles does sound good, so I find myself nodding. "I can call in the order and go grab it for us."

"No need. We're going."

I'm baffled at what Sharon is suggesting and certain I'm not hearing correct. "Did you say you want to go with me?"

"Isn't that what you've been trying to do since you got here? Get me out of the house?"

"I mean, yeah, I just didn't actually expect for it to happen," I blurt.

Sharon smiles at me, "Well it looks like today is full of surprises. Let's go."

I manage to find a spot right in front of the little café and snag us an outdoor table seated directly beside one of those standing heaters. It's still a little cool, but Sharon and I are bundled up and I have a feeling that even with her newfound bravery, being around too many people could trigger her and cause us to have an abrupt return home. We had just placed our orders and sat down when Skyla, Anna, and a woman I haven't met yet come walking our way, tears streaming down Anna's face.

"Oh, Sharon, this is wonderful! I am so, so proud of you," Anna sobs as she hugs her mother-in-law.

Skyla nudges me with her elbow and whispers, "How in the world did you manage this?"

"It was her idea," I admit, watching Anna and Sharon with a smile.

"Daddy Lincoln is going to be very impressed," Skyla winks at me and I bite my lip at the idea. Riling that man up is a lot of fun and when things get heated between us, it's, well, hot. But the idea of being his good girl sounds really nice, too. "Speaking of Daddy Lincoln, this is Amanda. She's his assistant."

I turn a crimson shade at the idea of her going back to the office and telling her that I practically went into heat thinking about the man being proud of me. She smiles and reaches her hand out and I take it. "Don't worry. I won't tell Daddy Lincoln about his nickname."

I glance over to see Sharon waving her hands around. "Stop all this fussing and you three join us. Or is it too cool for you out here? I don't want to risk anything happening."

Anna puts her finger to her lips and I wonder what all that is about. "It's not too cool out here at all. We're bundled up pretty well and this heater is toasty. I would love to join my mother-in-law for lunch." Anna looks over to where Skyla and I are standing, "and my friends, too, of course."

"Oh that was delicious," Sharon announces sometime after we've all finished our meals without so much as a crumb in sight. "Somehow I believe it tastes better with the crisp air blowing in your face."

I laugh, but have to agree. "I'm so full now, though. And we have some time before we need to pick up Charlie. Would you want to go for a walk?"

Sharon nods eagerly, "I really think I would!" She looks over at our three unexpected, but welcome guests. "Would you want to join us?"

Amanda is the first to speak, "I would love to, Ms. Fisher, but your son is expecting me back in the office."

"And your other son is expecting me back, too," Anna says with a smile. "Honestly surprised he hasn't sent a search party out yet since I'm a little past when I told him I'd be returning."

Sharon shakes her head and carries on about having to fuss at her boys for working their employees too hard, but Amanda and Anna are all smiles as they head back to work.

"I'm actually walking over to the bed and breakfast," Skyla says, "so if the offer still stands, I'd love to join you two."

As we walk towards the courtyard, we pass the other little shops on the street and I realize how much I love this little town of Cheatham. I'm from a small town, too, but it doesn't quite have the charm of this place. Little stores boasting local and Kentucky

Proud products are still displaying their holiday décor. The local radio station is blasting out an interview with the town mayor. A small white church sits on the corner. I look both ways to cross the street as I make my way over to the gazebo, chatting with Skyla about this, that and everything. When the two of us step into the gazebo, I look around and notice I'm missing a very important member of our party.

"Shit, Sky, where's Sharon?" I ask, in complete panic. Then I hear a scream that shatters my soul.

Chapter
Twenty-Seven
Lincoln

"We'd like to send someone out and talk this over face to face," Giovanni Caruso tells me and my staff on our conference call. "As you may have noticed already, our casinos and resorts may be high-tech and ahead of the times, but we run our operations a little more old-fashioned."

I clench the pen in my hand and look over at my older brother to take lead on this. "We look forward to seeing you soon. My assistant will reach out to make arrangements."

When he ends the call I can't hold back much longer, "Are you fucking serious? You really want them coming out here and making even more demands?"

"No," Keaton says calmly, knowing I'm ready to explode at any moment, "I don't want them here at all, but they are our biggest clients and if coming in and explaining their view on things is what makes them happy, then we're going to appease that."

I grumble as I leave his office to retreat to my own, almost running over Amanda in the process. "Shit, sorry."

"Where are you off to in such a hurry?" she asks.

"Just away, I need a moment." I continue walking to my safe haven, the place where I can sink behind my desk in my fancy and expensive leather chair that is somehow one of my more practical purchases. I'm almost there when Amanda's next words have me stopping in my tracks.

"It was so nice having lunch with your mom."

My mom? The woman who has refused to leave our home for a decade? The woman who has a panic attack thinking about just riding in a vehicle with me anywhere? "Did you go out to the house?"

Amanda laughs, "Yeah, like you give me enough time for that." Seeing my frown, she continues, "She and Sierra were at Crumb and Get It. Anna and I were meeting Skyla there and ran into them. She looked good, Lincoln."

I try to process this new development, but before I have the opportunity to call Sierra, I see Anna and Keaton running my way. "We've gotta go," my older brother says to me as they head in the direction of the elevators, "something is up with Mama."

"Amanda was telling me about it. I can't believe Sierra did it."

"No Linc, something bad. Skyla called Anna and said to get over to the square now."

As we crowd onto the elevator, Anna fills me in with the limited details Skyla gave. "I swear guys," she says defeatedly, "she was smiling and everything seemed like it was going great when we left. I don't know what could have happened between then and now."

"We'll figure it out," Keaton says, kissing his wife's forehead.

I dial Sierra as we drive across town, needing answers now, but my calls continue to be forwarded to voicemail. "Fuck! Why isn't she answering?"

"She's probably tied up with Mama, Linc. We're just about there." I shoot a glare at my brother who is acting far too calm for my liking in this shitshow of a situation.

Once we're parked and exit Keaton's truck, townspeople we've grown up with our entire lives shoot us pitying glances as we make our way in the direction of the old Baptist church. The one Mama married our dad inside.

When we finally reach her, we see that Camden has already made it here first, thanks to his office being nearby. He looks our way and then speaks softly to Mama, "Hey look, Keaton and Lincoln are here. We're all here, Mama. All of us are here together."

"I thought I could do this. I thought I was better. I'm never gonna get better, baby. I'm broken." Listening to my mom sob as she struggles with her grief is enough to almost bring me to my knees. I search the area for Sierra and see her in Skyla's embrace. In any other circumstance, their height difference as they lean against one another would be comical, but when I meet Sierra's red eyes and pained expression, there's nothing funny about the situation we're currently in.

As much as I need to be here for my mom, I want to take Sierra in my arms and let her know none of this is her fault. That if anything, she's helped Mama heal enough to even get her this far, but the woman on the ground shaking while cradled in my brothers' arms has to be my focus right now. "Come on, Mama.

Let's get you home." I walk her over to Keaton's truck and get her settled between him and Anna.

"Cam," I holler at my younger brother, "I'm riding with you." I glance over long enough to see Sierra still being consoled by Skyla. I know I should probably go over and comfort her right now, but my priority at the moment is to get Mama home and out of the public eye while she has a meltdown. I'll have to take time later to consider why all I want to do is push Skyla to the side so that it's my arms wrapped around Sierra instead. It's my words whispering comfort into her ear. It's my lips pressing gentle kisses against her skin.

Yeah, best to think about that much, much later.

I find Sierra on the couch after I get Charlie tucked into bed. She and Skyla didn't show back up to the house until later, giving us time to get Mama settled and in her room, and also time for them to pick Charlie up from school. She's been avoiding me since then, but I'm done playing that game.

"Hey, can we talk?" I ask from behind her, causing her to jump from where she's seated.

Concern and remorse are all over her face, and I want to soothe them away. She wrings her hands and begins pacing the living room as she talks. "Lincoln, I am so sorry. I know you're probably furious with me, and I don't blame you. Sharon said she was ready and I should have thought about it and maybe even talked her out of it, but she was determined that we go out for lunch. She looked good, Lincoln. Lunch was good. Then we went for a walk and when I turned around to check in with her, she was just gone. That's when I heard the yell. I don't even know what set her off."

"The church," I say softly. "That was the church where she and my dad got married. I'd say the memory hit her and her grief overwhelmed her."

"I'm so sorry," Sierra says again, even though she doesn't have anything to be sorry for.

I cross to where she's pacing and stop her in her tracks, "You have nothing to be sorry for, Sierra. You didn't know. You couldn't have known."

Sierra burrows herself into my arms then wraps her own around my waist, embracing me in what has to be the sweetest hug of my life. We stand like that silently for several minutes, her face pressed against my chest, tears soaking into my shirt, and my hand running soothing strokes through her hair. The tender moment is broken when Sierra adorably, but grumpily mumbles, "I blame Nicole."

I chuckle at the random comment regarding my ex, unsure of where that came from. "Why do you blame her?"

She steps away from me, wiping her eyes and taking a few deep breaths to center herself again. "Umm, well, she stopped by the house today."

A rush of anger begins to ripple through me. "She what?"

Sierra takes a step back from my tone. "Yeah, she showed up out of the blue. Asked to see you, but I explained that you weren't home. Then your mom came out and said some things to her," she cringes, "I don't think your mom is Nicole's biggest fan."

I snort, "That's an understatement. Did Nicole say what she wanted? Why she was in town?"

She shakes her head, "No, she was adamant that she needed to speak to you and that I was just 'the help.'"

My face softens and I reach for her again, "Sierra you are more than that, you know?"

"I am?" she asks, her eyes glistening with unshed tears and what looks like it may be hope.

"You know you are," I tilt her chin in my direction and let my hand linger there as I debate whether or not to press my lips to hers. We're normally fire and ice, and if I kiss her in this moment, it will mean something entirely different. Before I can make up my mind on whether or not I should give into my desire, her whisper cuts through.

"She's pretty."

I snort, "Pretty terrible."

"I mean it, Lincoln, she's stunning. I can see why you fell for her. I guess I'm pretty far from your type, huh?"

"My type?" I say angrily, "My type? I'm so sick and tired of everyone asking me about my fucking type."

"Well, typically people have certain characteristics they're drawn to," she tries to explain.

"I'm so sick and fucking tired of being asked my type. People want to set me up and so they ask what's my type. People have friends and insist they are just my type," I growl and she flinches. "I never thought I had a damn type, but I guess I do. My type is you. And she can't just be a brat with perfect lips and a smart mouth. She can't just be close to my height so that I don't strain my neck when I reach down to kiss her. She can't just have the most mouthwatering curves that I can grab hold of when I thrust inside of her. She can't just have the deepest blue eyes that I can get lost in. She can't just have silky dark, chestnut hair that wraps around my hand so well. She has to have it all, because she has to be you. You're my type, Sierra. You're the only woman I want."

I don't give her a chance to process or respond as I plunge my lips to hers, taking in everything this incredible woman has to offer. And nothing ever felt more right.

Chapter Twenty-Eight
Sierra

I'm pretty sure Lincoln somehow confessed his feelings for me, but the way his lips are searching for my soul as he plunders my mouth has me in a different dimension and unable to be certain of anything.

Well that's not true, I am certain that his lips on mine is the most incredible feeling in the world. That the way his hands are cradling my curves is bringing me pleasure instead of insecurity. At this moment, I have no doubt that this man can completely ruin me and I'm ready to let him.

"I need you," he says between kisses, pulling me toward his bedroom, and my feet follow as though they know there's no other place I should be.

When we reach the bedroom, I begin tugging at his shirt, eager to get my eyes on his ink and my hands on his body. He helps me out by pulling the tight black tee over his head and then takes it upon himself to remove his sweatpants so I can explore. When he springs free, I can feel how much he really needs me against my thigh, and I don't want to wait any longer.

Gripping his cock, I drop to my knees, then plunge the smoothness of him inside my mouth. He's so big that he instantly begins to dip down my throat, but I refuse to not completely consume this man. His thrusts and moans have me rubbing my thighs together to get some relief of my own. "Touch yourself," he urges, and he doesn't have to tell me twice. I dip my hands under my waistband and begin to rub circles over my clit, causing myself to moan against his shaft.

"Yes, you're being such a good girl for me, Sierra. The way you look right now taking my cock is so fucking hot."

His words spur me on and I try to take more of him as I rub myself harder. "Does it feel good touching yourself like that? Or do you need more?"

I let my mouth pop off his dick long enough to beg for more and he instructs me to climb up on his bed. He yanks down the joggers I put on when I got home, and my panties along with them. "Spread those legs and let Daddy make you feel good."

A whimper escapes me, but I waste no time doing as I'm told. "Where has this good girl been all along?"

Lincoln teases me before swiping his tongue up my slit. "Mmm you even taste sweeter."

Words evade me as unknown sounds resonate from within while Lincoln laps up every drop from between my legs. When the both of us are finally sated, he aligns his cock up with my entrance.

I'm so ready to take him. It's been too long since I've felt his length inside of me and I feel like I'm going to combust. "Tell me you want this Sierra. Tell me you're ready."

I nod and thrust my hips in his direction, ready for him to enter. "I need words. Tell me you want this."

"I want this, Lincoln. I want you. Please," I beg him and before I can fully get the last word out I'm gasping as he fully enters me, burying himself to the hilt.

"Fuck, Sierra, you feel better than I remember." He takes a moment once he's fully seated and I use it to look at how breathtaking he is. Somehow the man of my dreams has been brought to life in the form of Lincoln Fisher.

I whimper as he begins thrusting, first from the pain of the stretch, but then at how good he feels. "Yes, Lincoln, you feel so good. Harder, please."

His hand comes up and wraps around my throat, squeezing with just the right amount of pressure to have me on the brink of full-out pleasure. He continues to pump inside of me, cursing as I clench my walls around him. "Fuck, brat, you're so damn tight. I could fuck you forever and never get enough."

But forever comes too soon as we both reach our climax, shouting one another's names, and me coming to the realization that I'm completely in love with this man.

Just as before, sex with Lincoln was incredible but this moment right after, when he helped clean me up and now we're in his bed holding one another and being in each other's company, it's beyond words.

"I really don't want to ruin this moment, but you're sure Nicole didn't give you any insight as to why she's in town?" Lincoln asks in the darkness.

I turn in his arms so that I'm perched up on his incredibly chiseled chest. I guess he uses that home gym of his more than I thought. "Lincoln, I promise she only asked for you. She said it was personal and wouldn't say anything else."

He grunts, "I'm surprised she didn't resort to name calling. She's good at that." I scrunch my nose up and I guess he can see the action with the little bit of light coming in through the window. "What the fuck did she say, Sierra?"

"It wasn't a big deal. I've been called much worse."

"What did she say?" he grits out.

"Well, your mom implied something and I guess it ruffled Nicole's feathers. She referred to me as the help and made it very clear to everyone that you and I are not on the same level when it comes to looks."

"That's bullshit. You're fucking gorgeous and I love your body." He squeezes me tighter, causing me to smile, and I press a kiss to the country of Australia on his chest.

"What was it Mama implied?"

I try to pull away, but Lincoln refuses to let me so much as budge. Sighing, I cave. "She said you were crazy about me. That she and Charlie love me." I leave out the part where she said Lincoln does too, he's just not ready to admit it. Those are words I crave to hear from his own lips one day, and I would rather him not feel like they were forced on him.

We lay there in silence long enough for me to grow anxious. Long enough for me to consider pulling away from the comfort of his arms and shamefully walking to my own room. Long enough for me to feel like a fool for hoping that this man could reciprocate my feelings. I begin to squirm in his arms so that I can begin my retreat, but Lincoln stops me.

"She's right," he says as he runs his fingers through my hair. "You mean so much to Charlie. I can see the love in her eyes when she looks at you. Same with my mom." He takes a deep breath, "I know I can be an ass. Nicole caused a lot of damage when she walked away six years ago, and the women that I've met haven't been what Charlie and I have needed. But you are."

"What?"

"You're what we need Sierra. You're what I need. And what I want. Mama was right. I am crazy about you, and as crazy as it sounds, I'd like to see where we can take this."

I pull back and stare into his eyes, the ones I know are beautiful pools of icy blue, though the shadows make it hard to tell at this moment. I'm too stunned to speak and he clears his throat.

"I mean, that's if you feel the same way. But if not, that's okay, too." I press my lips to his to shut him up and the kiss is strong, but gentle. He deepens it, bringing his hand to the back of my head and pulling me closer to him. I don't think I could ever be close enough to this man.

We break the kiss and a giggle escapes me, making me feel like the young girl I know I am compared to him. "I'm crazy about you, too."

He smiles and brushes my cheek. "I don't want to hide you, but I also don't want to get Charlie's hopes up. I'm also not entirely prepared for the shit my brothers are going to throw my way. Would you mind if we keep this between us for a bit?"

While the words sting a bit, I understand where he's coming from. I give him another kiss to confirm my agreement, and eventually fall asleep in the arms of the man who just admitted he's crazy about me.

Chapter Twenty-Nine
Lincoln

"What the hell is she doing here?" Camden asks over a slice of sausage and mushroom.

It's our typical Friday lunch at Pizza Papa and I've just informed my brothers about Nicole's impromptu return to our hometown.

"Didn't say. All I know is she told Sierra that she needed to speak with me. Pissed Mama off real good too, from what I hear."

Keaton snorts at that, "I heard she ran her off the property. Good for her."

Our server brings us some refills and we each grab another slice of pizza and eat before Camden speaks up again.

"So, are you gonna reach out to her?"

I run a hand down my face, "I don't fucking want to. I want nothing to do with the woman. But I guess I need to find out why she's here so I can get her the hell out."

"You think it's about Charlie?" Keaton asks, his tone hushed. I may be her father, but my brothers love her as their own and I have no doubt the three of us would protect her from anything Nicole has planned.

I shake my head, knowing Nicole has never wanted anything to do with the daughter we created. "I honestly don't know what she could want. The last time she showed up she asked for money. She's probably looking for another handout."

"I thought you didn't give her any," Keaton says with a stern tone, acting like the father we lost so many years ago.

"Of course I fucking didn't," I can hear my voice raise as my temper does the same.

Camden's tone is soft, "Umm, guys, I love a good fuck as much as the next guy, but we are in public, so maybe keep your voices down."

We laugh away the tension and continue eating our pizza until Keaton brings up another unpleasant topic of conversation.

"So the Carusos want to visit us, sooner rather than later. When do we want to get that on the books?"

I release an aggravated sigh, "I don't know why you're encouraging this. No other clients make the demands they do on us."

"And if they did, we would do our best to accommodate," he insists. "We have nothing to hide, so there's no reason to not allow them to come in and see how we run things here. We need to go ahead and schedule it because we leave for our trip the week after next."

"I'd rather do it before our trip so we're not stressed out when we're supposed to be soaking up the sunshine and relaxing."

"Is this something you need me to come in on?" Cam asks, and I look at Keaton for the answer.

He shrugs, "Couldn't hurt to have legal representation there. I don't expect there to be any issues, but it would be nice just in case they try to twist things for whatever reason."

I lean back in my booth and blow out a breath. "Nicole shows up. Caruso Enterprises is demanding a meeting. They say bad things come in threes. Can't wait to see what comes next."

Keaton smirks at me, "Maybe it will be that you realize you're falling for your nanny."

If only he knew...

"If you follow me this way, I'll take you to our conference room. We have some snacks and drinks set up for you. I'm sure it was a long flight from Vegas." Keaton is ever the gracious host. He's not simply the CEO of our company because he's the oldest, and the business was technically his idea. He's a really great face for our company and makes all of our clients feel special.

"Well, I had a great travel partner with me, so it wasn't terrible. And please, call me Dario." The youngest of the Caruso brothers glances over at his attorney, Jasmine Baker. She's known for her ferocity, and while fair, she's tough. But Dario looks at the known shark like she's a kitten he wants to cuddle.

Keaton beams, "My wife was so happy to hear that her best friend was going to be joining you so she could visit, though she was surprised to hear that she's working for your company."

Dario can't seem to take his eyes off of the woman hanging out at Anna's desk as a smile spreads on his face, "It's a new development." He shakes his head and returns his gaze to me and my brothers. His smile loses its hunger and shifts into a more friendly one, "So about these snacks?"

"So as you can see, we have made sure to take every precaution and cover every concern you and your brothers have addressed. Do you have any questions?" Keaton finishes up his pitch as Dario pops the last olive on his plate into his mouth. He then takes a sip of his bourbon, seemingly considering everything just outlined to him.

Placing the glass back down in front of him, Dario smiles at the three of us, "I think it all sounds great. We're very pleased with your company and your dedication to our demands. I know we aren't the easiest assholes to deal with."

A relieved chuckle leaves Keaton's mouth and my shoulders begin to relax. "That's a relief to hear," my older brother states, "I'm not gonna lie, when we heard one of you wanted to come out and see us, we were a bit worried it was to cut ties."

Dario stands, straightening his gray suit that's smartly paired with a plum undershirt. "Nah, if we wanted to fire you, Giovanni would have made the trip. But if you hear that Luca is on the way, well, then you may want to be worried." He winks at us and heads back over to the spread of food Amanda and Anna had prepared for our meeting. Picking up a bunch of bananas, he asks, "Do you mind if I take these with me? They're Jasmine's favorite."

"By all means, take whatever you'd like," Keaton says, his voice not nearly as tense as it once was.

Dario nods and walks out of the room, the three of us following. He makes a beeline over to where the ladies are still hanging out across from Keaton's office. He holds up the bananas, "Here Jaz, got your favorite."

When he passes the fruit to her, he brushes a kiss against her cheek and a blush comes to the cheeks of the woman I've admittedly been terrified of since the day we met. Jasmine is a shark and to see this reaction out of her is an interesting and new development, for sure.

"Mr. Caruso, I just invited Jasmine to join us for dinner tonight. Please say you can make it, as well." Anna smiles at him sweetly, but his eyes are locked on her friend.

"If Jaz wants to go, then we will be there," he says.

Interesting indeed.

Anna

The girls are back in town! Dinner at our place tonight!

Penny

Not all the girls :(

Anna

I'm so sorry, Pen. We miss you! When is your next break from school?

Penny

Not until April, but I'll try to come see you then. We are still planning our annual trip again, right?

Jasmine

I hope so. I need a vacation.

Anna

And this time Sierra can join us!

Sierra

> You want me to come?

Skyla

> Of course we do!

Sierra

> Well I'll have to check with my boss. He's kind of a hard ass.

Skyla

> But what a fine ass it is...

Anna

> Eww, Sky. That's my brother-in-law.

Skyla

> You can't hoard all the Fisher men, Anna Banana.

Penny

> That's right. Leave some of the good ones for the rest of us.

Anna

> Ok, fine. But I do believe from the glances I've seen, Lincoln may be off limits. Do you know anything about that, Sierra?

I bite my lip as I consider what I should reply. I know Lincoln said that what happened between us should stay between us, but I desperately need to talk to someone about it and this group of girls seems like the perfect crew.

"What are you concentrating on so hard over there?"

His deep voice has me jumping and clutching my phone to my chest. My startled demeanor causes him to furrow his brows and that vein of his is popping on his forehead. I want to soothe it away for him, by way of licking.

"Is it your stepdad? Is he threatening you again?"

I shake my head, "No, he's been surprisingly silent. It was Anna, actually. She invited me to dinner tonight."

"Oh, yeah, we can ride over together. I'll leave Charlie here with Mama tonight so it can be an adult get-together."

I'm stunned by his response. "You want to go together?"

"I want to do a lot of things together," he smiles at me, walking over and holding me at my waist. His eyes scan the room and when he sees nobody else with us, he leans in and lets his lips linger against mine. "A lot more than that," he says, pulling away.

I can feel the rush of heat to my cheeks, "I'd like that."

"Later tonight then," he winks at me, then walks off to greet his mom and daughter in the other room.

Tonight has been exactly what I needed. Anna made an awesome meal and we all dined and wined, but now the men are talking about work and some upcoming trip. Us girls are talking about the men.

"He really is my perfect person," Anna gushes, causing Jasmine to fake gag.

Anna playfully pushes her friend, "You'll understand when you find yours."

Jasmine snorts in response, "I would have to do something other than work all the time in order to find my perfect person."

"I'm not so sure about that," Skyla says, "there are surely some men you work with. Maybe even a tall, dark, Italian man who looks at you like you hold the key to his heart."

"He is definitely not my perfect person," Jasmine rolls her eyes. "And if we're talking about men with hearts in their eyes, whatever happened to that man at the bar, Sky?"

Skyla shakes her head and where she always seems to have a smile on her face, her spirit seems to dim a little. "Oh, I don't think that's going anywhere."

"Why not?" I ask.

She smiles at us, but it doesn't reach her eyes, and I wonder why she seems to be holding back with this man. "He's so nice. Too nice for me. I need someone a little less vanilla, if you know what I mean."

Suddenly a crash has us turning our eyes to Camden who dropped an entire bottle of bourbon over the bar in the back of the room. He looks up at us sheepishly from the mess he made, "I'm so sorry. Guess that's my cue to leave."

He abruptly turns and heads out the back into the dark of the night.

"That was odd," Anna said.

"Maybe someone's cat is stuck in the tree and Superman needs to swoop in and save the day," Jasmine suggests, causing us to giggle.

I stand up and head to the bar to clean up the mess he left behind, the girls following behind me.

"You don't have to do that," Anna says.

"Oh, I don't mind. I just hope Cam is okay."

"Do his slutty little glasses do something for you?" Jasmine teases.

Anna shakes her head, "No, I think Sierra is more into the tattooed daddy type."

Her comment has me stopping mid-wipe and staring at her. A knowing gleam sparkles in her eyes and I can feel my face pale. "I, I don't know what you're talking about," I manage to stutter out.

"Girl, the two of you are as subtle as fireworks at a funeral. He's been eye-fucking you all night. So tell me, is he a daddy in the bedroom, too?"

"Sierra," Lincoln's gruff voice makes a squeal squeak out of me. "It's time to go."

The ride back to the farmhouse has been tensely quiet. I can feel the anger radiating off of Lincoln and I'm afraid I've made a huge mistake. The whirlwind romance between us seems to be over as fast as it started.

"I didn't say anything to them," I whisper. "I didn't tell them about us. Anna merely made an assumption, but I didn't confirm it."

He remains quiet.

"What was all the talk tonight about a trip?" I change the subject.

"Every year my brothers and I go to our beach house in the Caribbean. Since school doesn't start back until a little later in January, we leave next week so Charlie can go."

"Oh? Does she not normally go?"

"She's been a few times," he explains, "but it's practically the only time I get to unwind and, as much as I love her and want to be with her, sometimes that's difficult to do with your kid around. Besides, this year Keaton will have Anna and she's bringing Skyla along."

I smile, "Oh, I'm sure Camden will love that."

Lincoln's grumpy look remains. "What do you mean by that?"

Men really are fucking oblivious.

"Nothing," I shake my head. "So, what about your mom?" I glance at the wall as though I can see Sharon tucked in her bed behind it. If there is anyone in this world who deserves a vacation, it would be her.

Lincoln sighs and it sounds like the weight of the world is on his shoulders. He shakes his head, "We've tried, but as you've noticed, she isn't one to leave the house, let alone the country. We even got her a passport just in case , but we haven't managed to talk her into it yet."

I nod, knowing that getting Sharon to agree to a trip that far away would take an act of God. "How long do you typically stay down there?"

"A couple of weeks." Lincoln's using his bedroom voice, the low, growly one that does things to me down below.

"So is that when I need to use my vacation days, too?" I really hope that isn't the case. Jason has drained me of all my extra funds to cover my mom's outstanding bills, so I wouldn't be able to travel anywhere. And if I'm being honest, being with the Fishers and here in Cheatham is the only place I want to be.

Lincoln's eyebrows furrow causing a line to form between them, his typical grumpy face. "What do you mean?"

Now it's my turn to look at him confused. "Since that's when you're taking your vacation, I just assumed you would want me to use my vacation days during that time, too. Or do you want me to stay at the house with your mom and look after her?"

He swallows, and I watch his Adam's apple bob. Why the hell is that sexy? "What makes you think you wouldn't go with us?"

I roll my eyes, "It's a family vacation, Lincoln."

"Yeah, and I thought I made it clear that you're family. I want you there, Sierra. With Charlie. With me."

The butterflies in my stomach take off at his confession. I want to be completely devoured by this man. I want his lips to crash down on mine. I want his hands to roam, and squeeze, and plunder. I want him to spread my legs and connect us in a way only he knows how. But then I remember how angry he was earlier at the idea of someone knowing what was happening between us.

"You seemed really upset earlier at the idea of someone knowing that something was going on between us."

He huffs out a long sigh as he pulls into the driveway, "I overreacted. I have no doubt that you kept your word."

"No doubts," I whisper.

When he puts the Bronco in park and cuts the engine, I go to open my door, but he pulls at my shoulder to stop me.

"Wait," Lincoln says, his brows furrowing. "You do have a passport right?"

"Yeah, I do. But I'm sure if I didn't, you would find a way to get me one," I tease.

Lincoln snorts, "I can do many things, Sierra, but even I can't rush the government."

Chapter Thirty-One
Lincoln

"**W**here have you brought us? We still have to go through security and then get to the gate to board. If we miss our flight, I'm gonna be so fucking pissed at you."

I smile at my brother who is all worked up. His fear of flying has his anxiety at an all-time high right now and it makes my day to see the always cool, calm, and collected Keaton freak out. "Trust me. We're exactly where we are supposed to be."

Keaton snorts as I lead the way as my family follows me through the tinted glass doors. We're all headed to the Caribbean for a much-needed week away. Well, everyone but my mother. She somehow convinced me she would be just fine home alone and if I asked her one more time, she would go into heavy detail about the day I was conceived. A shudder runs through me at the thought as I walk my way up to the blonde receptionist sitting behind a desk. I nod to her, having already called ahead to let her know we were on our way.

"They're ready for you, Mr. Fisher," she greets me. "If you'll have everyone leave their luggage here, we will take care of it for you. Have a safe flight,"

"Seriously, what the fuck is going on?" Keaton asks, and I reply with nothing but a chuckle, until he grabs my arm in a demand for answers.

I release myself from his grip and stand tall so I can remind him that while he may be older, between the three of us, he's the "little" brother. "We're flying private, asshole. This is the private side of the airport."

He visibly relaxes and after everybody has checked their baggage with the receptionist, we continue making our way to the edge of the tarmac. This side of the airport is so different than what I've been used to, and it makes me question why we haven't been flying private all this time. Nobody is rushing past you as they're late to their gates. There is no rolling sound of luggage, chattering passengers, or walkways that stretch on for miles.

We pass a cluster of oversized arm chairs in a lounge featuring a large television and what appears to be a coffee bar, but before too long, another airport attendant greets us at a doorway. "Good morning, Mr. Fisher. Is everyone here and ready to board?"

I look around to make sure my family is all here and accounted for, taking note that my daughter is in the arms of Sierra. She catches my eye and gives me a soft smile, but I'm able to catch the movement of my lips turning up and quickly look back at the man who had asked me a question. "Yes, we're all here."

"Very well, sir. I will walk you out to your plane, and then you may board."

When we purchased the plane, only Camden and I were present and had laid eyes on it. Our other purchasing partner has not yet seen what they invested in. The fuselage is split cleanly in two, with the top half of a beautiful, bright shade of blue, and the bottom half immaculately white.

"She's a beautiful vessel, sir, you bought a solid piece of machinery," the attendant whose name I never caught says to me. Keaton stiffens beside me and stops in his tracks.

"You bought a fucking plane?" My older brother asks, staring at the private airliner we're about to board that will take us to the Caribbean. His eyes scan over the navy letters painted in the lighter blue that display the name of the plane, and I can't help the shit-eating grin that spreads across my face. "And you fucking named it Fear Force One?"

A chuckle escapes me, "We bought a fucking plane, brother."

"You and Cam?" He asks for clarification.

"Nope," I look over at my sister-in-law who is wringing her hands in anxiety.

Keaton looks at his wife in disbelief, "You were in on this?"

"Well, I just thought that if you were going to freak out on a plane again, you would prefer to do it in private. So when your brothers asked me about it, well, it sounded like a good idea. Are you mad at me?"

My older brother shakes his head and walks over to his wife, "Never, Baby. Thank you for being so sweet." He kisses her and I look away, but my eyes catch on Sierra who I notice is staring at them longingly like she wants nothing more than what the two of them share publicly.

Keaton and Anna break their kiss and he looks my way again, "But I'm fucking pissed at you."

The plane ride was uneventful, much to Keaton's pleasure, but to my dismay since I owe Camden a hundred bucks thanks to the lack of a panic attack occurring. I like my sister-in-law, but she's costing me money and causing me to lose bets.

Now we've arrived at our beach house and none of us thought to account for people and rooms prior to the trip. Keaton pushes through the front door. "I don't give a fuck where the rest of you sleep, Anna and I are in my room."

"That's not very nice, Uncle Keat! That's why Uncle Cam is my favorite."

"Does that mean you're rooming with me?" Camden asks my daughter, who nods emphatically. "Then hop on and let's head that way." He bends his 6'5" frame down to the ground so my daughter can climb on his back and then they're headed in the same direction as Keaton since their bedrooms are in the same hall.

The house has four bedrooms total, two on each side of the living space and kitchen. My room is located next to our spare, the one that Charlie sometimes takes, but is otherwise open in case Mama ever decides to make the trip with us. Skyla, Sierra, and I remain standing in the open space, Skyla looking down the hallway after Charlie and Camden, and Sierra looking up at me.

"So where should I sleep?" Sierra asks, and what a loaded fucking question that is. I want her in my room with me. In my bed next to me. Under me. On top of me. But there's no way we can keep things under wraps if she and I share a room this week.

I nod down the hallway with the two remaining rooms, "Our rooms are this way. Follow me."

I walk the girls to the bedrooms right next to one another and jerk my head to the one furthest down the hallway. "This one is mine, so that leaves this room..." I trail off, not wanting to push the dagger in any farther that I'm treating Sierra like she's a dirty little secret.

When I look over both girls are wearing defeated expressions. Without a word, they walk into their room and shut the door behind them.

"We have dinner reservations at seven," I say through the door, but am only answered with silence. "It's a fancy place, so dress for the occasion."

I stand outside the door for a few more moments, hoping Sierra sneaks out and comes into my room with me, but the longer I stand there, the more I feel like a fool. I head into my room and collapse on the bed.

It's gonna be a long fucking week.

1 1 1 1 0 0 0 0 1 0 1 0 0 0 0 0 0 0 1 1 1 0 0
1 1 0 0 1 1 0 0 0 1 0 1 0 1 0 1 1 1 1 0 0 1 0 0
0 0 0 0 0 0 0 0 1 1 0 0 1 1 0 0 0 0 0 1 0 1 1
1 0 1 0 1 0 1 0 0 0 1 1 0 0 0 1 1 0 0 1 0 0
0 0 0 0 1 1 1 1 0 0 1 0 0 1 0 0 0 1 0 0 1 0
0 1 0 1 1 1 0 0 1 0 0 1 1 1 0 1 0 1

Chapter Thirty-Two
Sierra

"**S**o dress for the occasion," I mimic on the other side of the door. Skyla gives me an amused look.

"Is Daddy being a dick?"

"Always," I answer, though I know it isn't true. This past week he's been attentive and kind both in and out of the bedroom. It's been different. Weird. Wonderful.

Skyla jumps off the bed and onto her feet, then flings my suitcase on top of the bed. For a petite thing she can apparently pack a punch. "Then let's look at what you brought so that we can bring Daddy to his knees."

She begins rifling through my suitcase chaotically. Normally I place my items neatly in drawers as I would when I'm at home, but Skyla is all chaos as she flings panties to one side and swimsuits to the other.

"I don't believe it," she says amazed once she's reached the bottom of the luggage. "You came on a weeklong trip to the Caribbean and didn't bring a single toy along for the journey? Not a single rabid rabbit? No bean flickers? No clit commanders? There's not one massaging machine? No booty buttons? Or a buzz buddy?"

I swallow down the truth. That all my toys are with Lincoln. All of them confiscated for my bratty mouth and for him to ream his own pleasure out of me. Instead of admitting that the man on the other side of this room dictates my pleasure, I smile weakly and shrug.

"Well, if you don't have a battery boyfriend, then we need to get dolled up so you can fuck the real thing. You'll want these," she tosses a pair of panties at me, "and then this dress will do."

I hold the dress up against my body, "I'm not sure about this. I put it in my bag in case I have enough drinks to make me brave enough to wear it, but since I'm sober, maybe we should pick one of my other options."

Skyla crosses her arms, "I'll make a pitcher of margaritas if it will help, but you're wearing the damn thing. Now put it on."

"Daddy won't be able to take his eyes off of you tonight," Skyla says with a wink as she applies the last of my mascara.

I stand up from the edge of the tub and look at myself in the bathroom mirror. This dress cuts off right at my knees, accentuating my long, albeit chunky, legs. The halter top prohibits me from wearing a bra, but it showcases my breasts perfectly. The deep plum color compliments my complexion beautifully. I smile at the woman in the mirror because Skyla is right, Lincoln is going to love this on me.

Eat your heart out, Daddy.

The plane ride took a lot out on all of us and I believe everyone stayed in their rooms, napping the day away until it was time for dinner. At least, that's what I would have done if Skyla hadn't demanded I take an everything shower and pluck every stray hair off my face. When we reach the living room, everyone else is already there, dressed and ready for dinner.

Lincoln's back is to me as I watch the sweet moment he's having with Charlie, twirling her around so that the pink, sparkly dress she wears flares out. As she spins, she spots me.

"Whoa, Sierra. You look like an angel," she gasps.

Lincoln turns then and I have to gulp down the saliva that builds in my mouth at how exhilaratingly handsome he is. A pale blue shirt that matches his eyes perfectly is tucked into a pair of khakis that hug him so well, but it's the look on his face that has me near panting status.

Right here, in front of his family, his eyes roam over me and there's no denying the desire lying within them. His tongue darts out and coats his bottom lip, leaving a sheen that I so desperately want to feel.

"Tell her, Dad." I'm snapped from my stare as Charlie speaks and tugs on her dad's arm. "Tell her how beautiful she looks."

Lincoln clears his throat, "You, umm, you look nice Sierra."

"Dad!" Charlie chastises, "she looks fucking hot."

"Charlene Elizabeth! You do not say those words."

"Then you should say them. I mean look at her," Charlie waves her hand in my direction and I bite my lip to keep from laughing.

"Just go get in the car," Lincoln says to his daughter, who leads the way out of the house.

The restaurant is incredibly nice, much nicer than the place in Laurel where I first met Lincoln Fisher. We've all been laughing and chatting. Well, all of us but Lincoln. All night long he's had a pained expression on his face, barely murmuring a handful of words. He's back to the grump I came to work for.

Skyla has been sitting between me and Anna, but now that Anna and Keaton only seem to have eyes for one another, she's tugging on me. "Let's go dance, Sierra. There are a couple of hotties out there on the floor."

Lincoln stiffens in his seat across from me and when I look up at him, he gives a subtle shake of his head.

Fuck. Him.

"I'd love to dance. I'll take the blonde."

We make our way over to the dance floor and begin dancing with one another as we strike up a conversation with the two men who are here on their honeymoon.

"My girl here needs a man to stake his claim," Skyla says to them, nodding in my direction. "Are you boys willing to help us out?"

"Make a man jealous? Sis, say less," the blonde one says as he comes to stand behind me and begin swaying his hips. His husband stands at my front, mimicking the movements.

We laugh as Skyla bounces around us and we all sway to the beat of the music, but before long I'm abruptly removed from my dance partners.

Lincoln has a tight grip on my wrist as he drags me towards the back of the restaurant. "What is wrong with you? Where are we going?"

He pushes a door open and shoves me inside. When I see where he's brought me I roll my eyes. "Seriously? What's your fetish with bathrooms?"

"What's your fetish with pissing me the fuck off?"

I roll my eyes, "I just wanted to dance, okay? Have some fun. Do you even know what that is?"

"Watching you trapped between two men who are grinding up on you isn't what I would call my version of fun," he growls.

"Then tell me, daddy," I tease, "what does your version look like?"

Lincoln pushes me against the door and turns the lock. "Taming brats."

His mouth is on me and it's releasing a moan I've been holding in for far too long. His lips travel to my chin and then my neck, where he nips my skin.

"They had no right to touch you. You're mine."

"Then prove it," I challenge.

His lips meet my neck again, this time sucking hard enough to mark the skin. He's claiming me and I fucking love it. His hand grabs at my thigh, pulling it around his hip and he begins to grind against me, but it's not enough.

"More, please," I beg and he runs his hand up under my dress.

"What the fuck are these?" Lincoln growls, clearly annoyed at the fabric barrier.

"Umm, shorts."

"And why the fuck are you wearing shorts when you have a dress on?"

Exasperated, I let out a sigh. "I don't expect your fine ass, zero percent body fat, chiseled self to understand, but when you have thighs as thick as mine, they tend to rub together. These shorts prevent that."

He pulls away from me, not too far, but enough to look down at where he has my dress hiked up and he's gripping the waistband of the fabric currently annoying the ever-loving fuck out of him. "But you had a dress on the first night we met and you weren't wearing any."

I roll my eyes, "I was hoping the date would go well and I don't typically wear them when I think I may get fucked."

A hard crack sounds as a delicious sting runs over my ass. "That's for rolling your eyes at me. And as far as I'm concerned, when I'm around, you should always be prepared to be fucked."

A loud rip sounds and I look down to see him holding the torn fabric of my anti-chafing shorts in his hands.

It's unhinged.

It's barbaric.

It's hot as hell.

He hikes my dress back up and I'm so ready for him to plunge his hard, thick length into me, but instead another sound of displeasure releases from him.

"And what the fuck are these?" He snaps the thong I'm wearing.

"You've never seen a pair of panties?"

He raises an eyebrow at me, "You know I have. In fact, I have a very special pair that I keep in my bedside drawer for special occasions."

I scrunch my nose up at that. He just keeps dirty panties in a drawer like that? Gross.

"You have a problem with me pleasuring myself to something that once covered your sweet cunt?"

"Don't turn this around on me," I say, "you have a panty problem."

"You're right," Lincoln growls, "I do." Another rip sounds and I stare at him as he holds up my destroyed black lace.

"Would you stop ripping all of my clothes?"

"Stop wearing them and I won't have to."

Before I can say another word, Lincoln reaches for the top of my chest and begins to pull, but I scream like a mad woman. His hands quickly move from his task to cover my mouth. "What the fuck is wrong with you? Are you trying to get someone to walk in here and catch us?"

"I told you to stop ripping my clothes. Take it off like a civilized person. I happen to like this dress. Even more than I like you most days."

He smirks at me and I'm ashamed of the liquid that leaks from my core from how hot he is when he makes that damn face.

Okay, fine. No I'm not.

"The moment we get back to the house, you're losing that dress."

He buries his face where he had just attempted to rip and sucks at each breast before sliding down my body. "Spread those legs for me. Let me see what's mine."

I do what he says and his tongue dives between them, lapping up all the arousal he's managed to build in a short amount of time.

"Mmm," he groans, "how can a brat like you taste so fucking sweet?"

His tongue continues to dip into me and I reach behind me, grabbing the doorknob for purchase. I'm so close that my legs begin to shake and that's when he runs his tongue over my clit one last time and then pulls away.

"What? What are you doing?" I whine.

"You've teased me all night in this fucking dress, so this is a little payback. Be a good girl until we get home, and then you'll get what you want."

"You're a dick," I huff.

He places gentle kisses on my inner thighs before pulling my dress back down over me and picking up the ripped material to throw it away. "Yeah, and you fucking love it."

I don't say anything, because, yeah I fucking do.

Chapter Thirty-Three
Lincoln

When Sierra and I walk back to the table, my brothers give me shit-eating grins and Anna and Skyla are sporting knowing looks. I shake my head to downplay what happened between us, and when I do, I see the light that was in Sierra's midnight eyes begin to fade.

Charlie yawns loudly, pulling everyone's attention from Sierra and myself and I have never loved my daughter more than in this moment. "I'm tired," she says before loudly yawning again.

I pick up my daughter, "Yup, it's bedtime for everybody."

When we get back to the beach house I pass a sleeping Charlie off to Camden. Anna and Keaton head to their room and Skyla heads outside for a walk on the beach.

Now that it's only the two of us, I press my lips to Sierra's forehead, then take her hand and lead her to my room. Leaving her in the middle of the room, I sit on the edge of the bed.

"Umm, what's this?" she asks, looking adorable with her crinkled, confused nose.

"You said you wanted to dance. So dance."

"How am I supposed to put on a show for you when there's no music?"

I pick up my phone that's sitting beside me and find the perfect song. When I place it back down on the bed beside me, the deep base of Ginuwine's greatest hit begins to thump and Sierra crosses her arms, accentuating her breasts in that damn halter dress she's wearing.

"This is a stripper song."

"Then strip for me. Fucking tease me. Get me so ready that I won't be able to stop until I have filled every single one of your holes."

"Lincoln, this is ridiculous," she complains, but I raise an eyebrow at her to show her that I'm serious.

She huffs her annoyance at me, then her hips begin to sway, trying to find the rhythm and failing miserably. She does a bobbing motion that I think is supposed to mimic her on a pole, but she isn't pulling it off. In fact, she's a pretty fucking terrible dancer.

And it's sexy as hell.

"Now strip, Sierra. Show me what you've got."

Sierra reaches up and unclasps the clip at the nape of her neck, allowing the two pieces to come undone and expose her throat. She twirls them like tassels and I bite my lip to keep a laugh from escaping.

When she slides the dress down over her breasts, they pop out and I see her rose-colored nipples are already pebbled with desire. "Squeeze those tits for me. Pinch those perfect nipples."

I grow hard watching Sierra follow my instructions. She's being such a good girl for me and I'm going to have to reward her for it. "That's right, now slide that dress off the rest of the way. I want to see all of you."

Once again she obeys my command and I begin to undo my pants to give myself some relief. When I pull my length out, I hear a whimper from Sierra.

"Is this what you want? You want daddy's cock?"

She bites her bottom lip and nods.

"Then come and get it."

I shuck off my shoes and slide my pants off my legs just in time for Sierra to make her way over and straddle my thighs. Her heat is hovering over my tip and it's taking everything in me not to shove her down.

She rocks her hips so that my tip brushes her lips and I can feel the precum begin to leak out. Sierra steps back, "Oh no, you're making a mess. I better clean that up."

Bending over, she licks my shaft from bottom to tip, making sure to get every drop that leaked out of me. I palm her ass and give it a squeeze. "All better," she says, straddling me again and not giving me a moment to think before she sits down on my cock, burying it completely inside of her.

"Fuck, Sierra, you feel so good." I thrust my hips in an upward motion, plunging myself into her over and over again, enjoying watching her bounce on top of me. The position she's in is going to have me coming way too soon, so I push her off of me. "Turn around."

She's such a good girl and does as she's told, and I pull her back into my lap, allowing my dick to fill her cunt, but bending her at the waist so I can cup her full ass. I lean down and spit on that forbidden hole of hers, needing to stake my claim there, too. I rub the natural lubricant around my thumb, gently dipping it inside and hearing her gasp. "Can you take me here?"

She nods, causing herself to bounce that much faster. "I need words, Sierra. Do you want me to fill up this tight ass of yours?"

"Yes," she moans, "please, daddy. I want it."

I pull at her skin to expose her even more and spit a couple more times, then I slowly work my thumb inside. "One day I'm going to fill this hole with my cock, Sierra, and you're gonna take it like a fucking champ."

"Yes, Lincoln, yes. Oh god, that feels so good. I'm so full."

I continue thrusting my cock and thumb in and out of her simultaneously until she's sobbing for relief. "Touch yourself. Rub that clit and make yourself come."

My good girl comes undone seconds after my command and I pull her off of me so the thick, white jets releasing from me cover the area where my thumb just fucked her. I use the same digit to swirl the sticky substance and dip it into her there, marking my territory. "You're mine, Sierra."

"Yours," she gasps.

And that word on her lips is the best fucking sound I've heard all night.

The next morning everyone headed out to the pool while I had some numbers to crunch.

Vacation, my ass.

When I finally finish up, I close my laptop and pull on my swim trunks to head outside. I expect to see my daughter splashing in the pool and maybe my brothers in there acting like idiots. I expect the girls to be sunbathing on the loungers. I don't expect to walk out and see Sierra bent over with her full ass on display, looking like a fucking snack.

Furious, I go straight over to her and pull her back into the beach house.

"What the hell is wrong with you?" she demands.

"Do you really think that is an appropriate swimsuit to be wearing in front of a six-year-old? In front of my brothers?" I ask her between gritted teeth. The smirk she gives me lets me know she knew exactly what she was doing when she put the damn thing on.

"Oh, this old thing? I believe it covers everything up, but maybe you can help be the judge of that." She trails a finger down her cleavage. "Now, these aren't the easiest things to contain, but I do believe they are covered. Tell me Lincoln, are my breasts on display?"

While the woman is displaying a decent amount of skin, I do have to admit that her tits are covered. Though the only thing I want them covered with right now is my mouth.

"Hmm, since it's a one piece, we don't have to worry about my belly on display, so everyone is in luck there."

"Don't do that," I snap at her.

Sierra looks at me, confused. "What?"

"Don't act like people wouldn't want to see every goddamn inch of your body." The two of us stare at each other for several seconds in silence, but then her lips begin to tilt up, ever so slightly.

"Noted. Then let's be sure to go over every inch and move down to my legs. They're going to show no matter what swimsuit I have on, right?"

I nod.

"Right. So then I guess we need to check that this ass is covered. I do understand the importance of covering one's own ass."

"Don't be a brat," I warn her.

"I wouldn't dream of it, Mr. Fisher." There's a gleam in her eye as she teases me and begins to bend over, causing my dick to harden at the sight of her luscious ass being stretched against the fabric.

"What the hell are you doing?"

She looks back at me and smiles, "I just wanted to make sure I was still covered when I bent over. Can you see anything, Mr. Fisher? Take a good look. I wouldn't want to be inappropriate." She bites her bottom lip and wiggles her ass in the air.

My hand twitches. This fucking brat is begging for a punishment, and lucky for her, I'm happy to oblige.

Walking over to her, I run my hand down her spine, feeling her shudder beneath me. "You do seem to be covered pretty well," I admit, "but you are wrong about something."

"What's that?" Sierra pants out, her breath shaky with desire.

"You seem to want to be very inappropriate." I run my hands over her ass, wanting to stop at the puckered hole my thumb got a taste of last night and my cock is dying for its turn.

But not today. Instead I trace her lips through the fabric, causing a ripple to run through her whole body. "And little brats who are inappropriate get punished." In a quick move I pull the fabric away from her pussy, exposing her so that I can thrust two fingers inside. Her heat is enough to have me coming in my pants if I don't slow things down. "So fucking wet, Sierra. Does being a brat turn you on?"

She grinds on my fingers and in between her moans manages to grind out the words, "Fuck you."

I'm thankful her back is to me so she can't see the smile spreading across my face. "I don't believe we have time for you to have the pleasure," I whisper in her ear, "now come for me, Sierra." She whimpers and writhes against me, but refuses to give in to her impending orgasm. "I said come for me."

"Don't tell me," she pants, "what to do."

I add a third finger and begin pulsing my fingers into her. My other hand lowers the top half of her swimsuit so I can cup her breast. "When I tell you to come, brat, you fucking come." I pinch her nipple, causing her to cry out.

And when her body gives into my demand, I pull my fingers from her core. "Stand up," I demand, and can't help but smile when she gives in to my command. "Open your mouth."

Sierra's confused expression is adorable. "Why?"

"Do what I say."

She rolls her eyes at me. "You can't tell me what to do, Lincoln, I..." as her mouth opens to say whatever nonsense she was thinking, I thrust my fingers inside.

"Suck. Taste how sweet you are when you listen to me and do as you're told."

Her eyes shoot daggers at me, but her body can't help but react to my words. Slowly, she sucks her flavor off my fingers and I'm seconds away from embarrassing myself. She must realize I'm in need of some relief, because Sierra begins tugging down my swim trunks, all the while focused on her task.

She reaches in and grabs my dick, pushing her thumb on the tip and causing me to moan. But before she can give me the release I so desperately need, a little voice calls out to me.

"Dad! Where did you go? I...ahhh!"

I shove Sierra away from me and manage to tuck myself in before Camden, Skyla, and Charlie make it to my bedroom, my daughter screaming.

"Why is your butt out? Eww. Why is it so white? What's wrong with your butt?"

"Stop saying butt," I tell my daughter.

"But what's wrong with it?"

"Nothing is wrong with it," I try to explain, at the same time shooting daggers at Camden as he's bent over in laughter.

I look over at Sierra who's covering herself while on the bed, a defeated look on her face. First I have to make things right with my daughter. And then I have to make things right with the woman who looks heartbroken.

Chapter Thirty-Four
Sierra

I'm sitting on the bed in nothing but my towel when Skyla comes into the room. I had to take a shower after this morning's events. It's not only that the family walked in on me and Lincoln, it's that he shoved me to the side like he was disgraced. I'm tired of being a dirty little secret. I want to be loved out loud. I want him to show the world that I'm his. I want no doubts when it comes to the way he feels about me.

"You okay?" Sky asks, sitting beside me.

I give her a weak smile, "Not really, but I'm not supposed to talk about it."

Skyla scrunches up her nose, "I think the cat's out of the bag, Sierra."

I groan, leaning back on the bed. "But he keeps trying to shove the damn cat back in the bag."

She joins me, sighing, and together we lay there until there's a knock on the door.

"Who is it?" Skyla hollers.

The doorknob turns and Lincoln pokes his head in, "Hey Sky, do you think Sierra and I could have a minute?"

Skyla looks at me and I give her a weak nod so she heads out the door, allowing Lincoln to enter the room. He sits down beside me, and that's how we remain for several minutes. Eventually I can't take it any longer and I go to stand so I can put some clothes on, but Lincoln grips my wrist, halting me.

"I hurt you."

It's not a question. He's stating a fact.

"You did."

He pulls me in his direction, wrapping his arms around my waist. "I'm sorry."

I let the two words linger in the air between us. It's not an uncomfortable silence, but still one that says a lot is still being left unsaid.

"Can you tell me how I can be better?"

The vulnerable question tugs at my heart and tears begin to form in my eyes. Still in his arms, I trail the vines of the Morning Glory that snakes up his arms and then disappears into the short sleeves of his shirt.

With a deep sigh I give him my honest answer, "I don't know."

He presses a kiss to my forehead and it eases some of the hurt. His lips cascade down my face, covering the tip of my nose, a chaste touch to my lips, and then traveling down my throat. He peppers my shoulder blades and when he reaches the top of my towel, I've all but forgotten why I was upset in the first place.

Fuck his lips are magic.

"Let me make you feel better, Sierra."

His demand is soft as he gently tugs where my towel comes together to barely cover my body. When it opens for him, a slight groan spills from his lips. "Fuck, your tits are great. Even better than Anna's, no matter what Keaton says."

He takes one nipple into his mouth and begins teasing it with his tongue while grabbing hold and massaging the other. "Can you not talk about another woman's body when you're with me?"

Lincoln quickly plucks himself off of me and when he casts his eyes to mine, the look on his face is one of horror. "I'm so sorry. I wasn't thinking about her body. It's just that Keaton goes on and on about hers and, well, I like yours even better. They're perfect. Perfect for me. Better than Anna's. No, I don't mean that. Don't tell her I said that. Don't tell Keaton either. He will kill me. I know he acts like he's nice and everything, but I've watched him beat somebody to a pulp over his girl and I have no doubt he would do the same to me."

I smile at his rambling, finding it off kilter and utterly adorable. "Your secret is safe with me."

He presses another tender kiss to my lips before returning to my breasts that are apparently perfect for him. The way he's handling my body right now is so different than how he normally does and I could definitely get used to it.

Once he's given the pair equal attention, he returns to my lips. "Feeling better?"

"Getting there," I answer.

"What do you need?"

"I need to know," I answer, shocking myself with my confession.

"You need to know what?" Lincoln asks, looking confused.

I gulp down the nerves that have built and am determined to be the confident and bold woman my mom raised me to be. "I need to know how you feel. About me. I don't want to have any doubts about what's going on between us."

I stand there in his arms watching the crease deepen between his eyes, until he finally speaks. "Get dressed."

I worry I've made him mad, or pushed him too far. The night we met he warned me he didn't want a relationship. He made it clear that it was supposed to be a one night thing. Then when things escalated between us, he was adamant that our involvement stay behind the scenes. If he wanted more, he'd be kissing me, touching me, demanding the opposite of putting more clothes on my body. Right?

Slowly and silently I begin to pull on one of my sundresses I brought with me. When I pull open the drawer and retrieve a pair of panties to put on, Lincoln speaks up again. "No. Just the dress is fine."

"I guess no shorts either?"

"Absolutely the fuck not. The dress is fine. You look perfect."

His words confuse me, but I place the underwear back into the drawer and then cross the room to stand beside him again. "Any other demands, daddy?"

An amused smirk tugs at his lips, but is quickly replaced with an undeterminable gaze. "Follow me."

Lincoln opens the door and together we walk down the short hallway into the living space. Skyla, Anna and Keaton are seated on the couch laughing as they watch Camden and Charlie. Cam is on the ground, flat on his back, with his knees bent to his chest and his feet up. Charlie lies across them, gripping his hands as he flies her through the air.

"Superman," I say smiling.

"What was that?" Lincoln asks, but I shake my head at my personal superhero who is much more likely to Hulk out than fly through the skies.

Lincoln clears his throat. "I'm glad you're all here. I have something to say. It's pretty important."

The room quiets down, eager to find out Lincoln's news, and I'm right there with them.

"Someone has come into my life in a pretty significant manner. I certainly didn't expect it and now that she's a part of my life, I can't imagine a world in which she isn't."

"It's about damn time," Skyla mutters.

"What do you mean?" I ask.

Keaton rolls his eyes, "Go ahead and get over yourselves and admit what we all already know."

My eyes go wide. No matter what I may want, I know Lincoln prefers what's going on between us to stay underwraps. "Umm," I manage, attempting to keep things the way Lincoln wants them. "I don't know what you're thinking, but there's nothing going on here."

"Stop," Lincoln interrupts me, causing my head to snap in his direction, looking into his eyes with so many questions behind my own.

"Fuck it," he says, crossing over to me and gripping my neck to tilt my chin up to him so he can claim my lips. He releases them and turns back to his family. "I'm in love with Sierra."

I'm deceased. This is how I die. Stunned into silence, completely forgetting how to breathe and completely blissed out. Beautiful, blue eyes belonging to the man who just confessed to his family that he loves me—fucking loves me—stare into mine. Nobody says a word as they wait for my reaction, but I can't muster one.

"Duh," Charlie says, cutting the silence.

Lincoln's eyes leave mine and travel to his daughter, where my own follow. Her braided brown pigtails hang crooked as she looks up at us like we're the dumbest people on this planet.

"What do you mean, duh?"

Keaton guffaws, "Umm, the two of you aren't exactly subtle."

"You're a much better spy behind the screen than in the real world," Camden adds.

"And you kiss like all the time," Charlie states loudly.

Lincoln stares at his daughter, "Now when have you seen us kiss?"

"You kiss everywhere. Yesterday the two of you tried to sneak behind the waterfall so you could kiss. Guess what, Dad, you can see through water."

"You all saw that?" Everyone in the room nods.

He runs his hand through his short hair and looks over at me, "What do you think of all this?"

I feel the smile bloom across my face and shrug, "I think I love you, too."

This man looks damn good in a suit. He looks phenomenal in a pair of swim trunks. When he's in dad mode, he's fucking stunning. But there's no better look on him than happy and in love. He pulls me to him and kisses me, claiming me, right here in front of everyone we know, leaving nobody with any doubts as to how we feel about one another.

"Eww, Dad. We can see through air, too."

Chapter Thirty-Five
Lincoln

"Yes, Lincoln, you feel so good."

Sierra moans as I kiss the column of her neck, satisfying a need in me I wasn't aware I had, but they're also loud enough for everyone else on the plane to hear. I made sure when I purchased the plane that we chose one with a bedroom in case Charlie needed to lay down for a nap, or in this case, her father needed to do something a bit more nefarious. "Keep quiet. All those delicious sounds of yours are for my ears only and if you keep it up, I'll have to kill my brothers. You wouldn't want Keaton's child to grow up without a father, would you?"

Shortly after I made my feelings about Sierra known to my family, Keaton and Anna shared the news that their family will be growing, not with just one baby, but with twins. It was a great fucking day. Now we're headed back home with everything out in the open and I can honestly say I'm the happiest I've ever been.

"Make me." Sierra's eyes are devilish with desire.

"My fucking pleasure."

Peeling off the lace panties covering her pretty pussy, I wad them up into a ball. "Open," I demand and my slutty little nanny does exactly as she's told. I love her bratty side, but I fucking come undone when she follows my commands.

"Such a good girl for me, Sierra. And do you know what good girls get?"

Her eyebrows shoot up in question.

"They get to come." The makeshift gag barely muffles her cries as I plunge two fingers into that perfect space between her legs. "Always so fucking wet for me." I continue teasing her until my cock is standing at full attention, begging to be buried inside. I make quick work of pulling my pants down far enough that I can line up with her and help us both officially become members of the mile high club.

Spread out on the bed, Sierra traces the ink on my chest. "Have I ever told you how hot your tattoos are?"

I snort. "Can't say that you have."

She hums, "I mean, everything about you is sexy as hell, but these," she moans, "well they're getting me wet all over again."

And it's that proclamation that helps the two of us kill some more time as we fly over the Atlantic, heading back home.

When we do finally manage to emerge from the back room, my family greets us with hoots and hollers, making catcalls and shouting comments like "get a room" followed by "they already did." It doesn't matter, though, I have Sierra in my arms and I can publicly claim that she's mine now. When we break our confirming kiss, I look around for my other girl. Charlie is beaming at us with tears in her eyes and I kneel in front of her.

"Is this okay with you, Little Bit. This thing between me and Sierra, I mean."

She nods, but her lip quivers and tears begin to fall down her face.

"Then why are you crying?"

"Because first I asked for a mom for Christmas. Then I asked for a family. Now all my dreams came true."

I pull my daughter into my arms and stand as I press a kiss to the back of her head. When I lift up, I find Sierra and wrap an arm around her, pressing a kiss to her head as well. "Mine too, Little Bit. Mine too."

As we approach the house I get the nervous feeling I always do after leaving my mom after any period of time. Typically we take a couple of weeks for our trip, but an uneasy feeling had me shortening this trip to only one. Which is unfortunate, because fucking Sierra in the ocean, on the beach, in the pool, and on every single surface of the beach was something I would have loved more time of.

As the white farmhouse with black accents comes into view, I put the Bronco in park and am immediately out the door and rushing inside. I know Sierra will get Charlie and I'll come back for the bags later, but I've spent a week with two of the most important women in my life, and now it's time to check on the third.

"Mama? We're home."

Keaton and Camden burst through my front door and with the three of us standing here, the spacious entryway turns crowded quick.

"Is something wrong? You ran like a bat out of hell," Keaton huffs.

My eyes scan over the living room and the adjoining kitchen, not seeing our mother anywhere in sight. "Just an eerie feeling," I admit.

"Mama!" Cam calls, heading for her bedroom. "You taking a nap?"

Pushing open the door, Cam peeks inside and then turns to look at us, shaking his head.

Where the hell could she be?

The three of us spread out around the house, ignoring the girls as they walk in on the search and ask what's going on. When Mama has one of her spells, she confines herself to her bedroom. Otherwise she's in the living room reading a book or watching her soaps. Sometimes she's in the garden, but the brisk, winter air will keep her from being out there today.

"What the fuck are you doing?" Keaton wails, and I pop my head out of the laundry room to see him standing just outside my office.

Camden hauls ass in that direction and I'm right behind him, but stumble when I see him throw his hands up as though he's under arrest.

I arrive at the scene unsure of what to expect, but never in my life could I have imagined what was unfolding in front of me. Speaking slowly, I talk to the woman who has only ever shown us love and understanding.

"Mama, put the gun down."

"And so I told her that if she ever showed back up on my property again, I wouldn't wait for the cops and would just take care of her myself."

Camden groans, "Mama, you can't say shit like that."

"I didn't even know there was a gun in this house. When did you get that, Lincoln?" Keaton asks in an accusatory tone.

"It's not mine," I say, and we all look at our mother.

She huffs, "It belonged to your dad. I stashed it in here years ago."

I pinch the bridge of my nose, trying to swallow down the anger building inside of me. "You mean to tell me that there has been a weapon concealed in my home all these years. With my daughter here. And I didn't know a fucking thing about it?"

"Well it's not like it was loaded, Lincoln." Mama huffs and crosses her arms like a petulant child.

"That's not the point and you know it. It was reckless and I should have been informed that a firearm was under my roof."

"It was my roof first," she mutters under her breath, but I hear it anyway.

Sierra takes a seat beside Mama in the additional leather wingback chair I have in my home office. "Sharon, I know it must have been scary having Nicole show back up here at the house like that and with you all by yourself. Did she threaten you?"

Mama's demeanor softens as she looks at my girl. "She threatened Charlie."

I'm immediately on edge and stand up. "What the fuck do you mean she threatened Charlie."

Tears begin to well up in Mama's eyes and I curse myself for my harsh tone, but she speaks anyway.

"She said that if you didn't agree to meet with her, she would try to reinstate her parental rights. I told her she was dimwitted if she thought any of us would allow that to happen, but she had a man with her and he mentioned that with the right judge, it could be done."

"Reinstating your terminated parental rights is extremely rare. And I do mean extremely. Even if it were to happen, it would be a long, drawn-out process and we all know Nicole isn't one for sticking around," Camden explains.

Mama shakes her head, "Oh I know she doesn't have a chance of winning any sort of rights to Charlie, but the idea of that cruel woman even setting her sights on my sweet grandbaby made me so damn mad."

"And that's when you threatened her?" Sierra asks.

"That's when I protected my family," Mama corrected. "And I would do it again and again."

We all look around at one another, knowing that we would all stand up for this family if anyone ever threatened one of us. I look at Anna, knowing we already have.

"Can you two get things squared away here?" I ask my two brothers.

"Where are you going?" Sierra asks, a look of panic in her eyes.

"To protect my family."

Chapter Thirty-Six
Sierra

I look at the clock for about the millionth time since Lincoln left this afternoon, wringing my hands to see that another hour has past and we haven't heard from him. My knowledge of Nicole is limited, but if she was able to leave the little girl who has her art supplies strewn all over the table, well then, she can't be mentally stable. I try to distract myself and sit next to Charlie, twirling one of her brown braids around my finger.

"Whatcha doing there, Little Bit?" I ask, watching her concentrate so hard her little tongue is poking out between her lips.

She doesn't answer me right away, instead taking her time to finish the final touch on whatever she's been working so hard on, then she holds it up proudly for me to look at. The illustration she shows me brings me to tears as I take in the crayon drawings of each member of our little makeshift family. Sharon stands proudly on the end with a blue, bespectacled Camden and his long brown hair towering over her and a cherry dress wearing Skyla on the other side of him. A very large chested Anna is standing next to her and on her belly is written the word baby. Charlie took a few liberties with Keaton, giving him a few more gray hairs than he actually has and I know Lincoln is going to love it. He's next in the lineup, looking just as handsome in red crayon as he does in real life. A tiny Charlie holds his hand, and her other hand grips mine. Seeing how Charlie views me is enough to have me on the verge of tears, but it's the word written above me that has me choking back sobs. I brush my finger over the word mommy.

"Is that okay?" Charlie whispers, concern in her voice.

Sharon comes up behind me and takes a peek at the picture. "Looks right to me."

"Sierra?" Charlie asks, still waiting for an answer, but the tears have begun to stream down my face and I can't manage to get any words out. I nod my head and my little girl leaps into my arms, embracing me like she's been mine all along.

I hope wherever Lincoln is at right now, he's giving Nicole hell, because nobody messes with my family.

It's half past midnight when I see the headlights shine in through the window, alerting me that Lincoln is finally home. Sharon and Charlie went to bed hours ago, but I knew I'd be tossing and turning all night waiting for the man I love to return. I set my newest obsession on the coffee table and toss the blanket off of me so I can greet Lincoln at the door. How this Kentucky girl who has never watched a single game in her life can become crazy over a hockey romance doesn't make sense to me, but here we are. Those men with big sticks aren't pucking around.

The door opens and in walks my strong, handsome man, though he looks slightly beaten down.

"Hey, you okay?" I ask, though I fear I already know the answer.

Lincoln's response is to wrap me in his arms and embrace me in a hug. It isn't sensual. It isn't flirtatious. It's perfect. And it's exactly what we both need at this moment.

He releases the hug, but still keeps his hands on my hip, "I don't know. She claims a bunch of shit and I never know what to believe when it comes to her."

"Do you want to tell me about it?"

Lincoln shakes his head. "No, I just want to go to bed and forget this day ever fucking existed."

Completely understanding, I give him a small smile and a peck on the cheek. "I get it. Let's go to bed and then tomorrow we can all start fresh."

I begin to head down the hallway toward our rooms, but Lincoln's deep voice stops me. "What's this?"

When I look back he's holding the picture Charlie drew earlier. The picture where she named me something I'm not sure her dad will take kindly. "Umm, Charlie drew that earlier tonight."

"Is this you?"

Gulping, I nod my head.

"She wrote the word mommy above it."

I nod again and he remains silent. While the tense silence probably only lasts seconds, my nerves get the best of me and I begin to ramble. "You know how kids are, they say the darndest things." I laugh, but Lincoln remains stoic. "Listen, I'm sure she didn't mean anything by it. I can set her straight tomorrow."

He puts the picture back down on the table and passes me, heading to his room. I blink back tears and silently follow behind him. Even if I only got to pretend to be the little girl's mommy for a few hours, they were the best moments of my life.

I twist the knob to my room, but before I can enter, Lincoln's gruff tone has me stopping.

"Where the fuck are you going?"

I look at him, then to my room, and repeat that enough times to test his patience.

"I asked you where the fuck you were going," he says again.

"To bed?" My statement somehow turns into a question.

He cocks his head, looking at me inquisitively, "Don't mommy and daddy sleep in the same room?"

I blink at him, trying to make sense of the roller coaster of emotions swarming inside me. Does he seriously want me to sleep with him in his room?

Once again, my processing time takes too long because before I know it he's barking an order at me. "Sierra, get the fuck in my room."

I do as he says, proving I'm not always a brat, and when I enter, I climb into the massive bed. The black silk sheets are smooth against my skin and I can't help but moan when my head hits the pillow, causing Lincoln to swat my ass.

"When you make those noises, it's because I'm inside of you. Do you understand?"

"Yes, daddy."

He shakes his head and walks over to the master bathroom to prepare for bed. By the time he crawls in, I'm halfway out of it, but sink into him as he wraps his arms around me.

"Hey, Sierra?"

"Yes?"

"I'm okay with it, you know?"

"Okay with what?"

"Her calling you Mommy."

I manage to rouse myself slightly more awake and twist to look at him. "You are?"

"Yeah, I am. Now go to sleep."

I give him a kiss before spinning back around to get situated.

"Hey Sierra?"

"Mmmhmm."

"Did you see how fucking gray she made Keaton's hair?"

I let out a laugh and Lincoln wraps his arms around me tighter. Then, for the first time, but hopefully not the last, I fall asleep in the arms of the man I love.

And when the clock strikes 3:47, I sleep straight through it.

Chapter Thirty-Seven
Lincoln

I wake up with the most beautiful woman I've ever seen in my arms and it makes it incredibly difficult to get up and going. Alas, there's work to be done at the office and to try and stop my insane ex who for whatever reason has shown back up in my life.

Gently, I roll out of bed so as not to wake Sierra, and head to my home gym to begin my morning routine. Before I start my mile run, I pop a text off to my brothers.

Lincoln

Meeting in my office this morning.

Keaton

This client related?

Lincoln

Family business.

Camden

I'll be there.

Keaton

Same.

I take out my aggression on the treadmill as I replay the conversation I had with Nicole last night. She's blackmailing me. Fucking blackmailing me. Demanding money or else she's going to release evidence that shows I'm unstable so that a judge will reinstate her parental rights so she can have sole custody of Charlie.

Over my dead fucking body.

First of all, any evidence she produces is absolutely, without a doubt, one hundred percent bullshit. I haven't even spoken to Nicole since the last time she showed up asking for money and I sent her on her way without so much as a dime.

I may have enough money to not worry about missing what she's asking for, but I'd much rather donate that money to people who actually need it instead of a money hungry, bloodsucking bitch like Nicole. The dude she was with was just as bad. In fact, I wouldn't be surprised if he's the one who was encouraging her to go about this whole thing.

The treadmill clicks over to show my mile is complete and I step down to make my way over to the pull-up bar. I'm on the ninth rep of my second set when a tall, curvy nanny catches my eye.

"If you were looking for a workout, you could have woken me up for one."

I smile because she's right. Last night I got to sleep with the woman I love, the woman my daughter loves, right beside me. It's what I've been searching after for years. And I could have easily stayed there all fucking day, but unfortunately life has thrown another wrench my way.

"I was tempted, trust me. But I need to work some stuff out."

She cocks an eyebrow at me. "Wanna talk about it?"

"I'd rather see your body in action. Come here."

Sierra walks my way with a cautious look on her face, unsure of the journey I plan to take her on. When she's within arms reach, I pull her in and kiss her like it's my last chance. When we pull away, she's breathless, and my heart is pounding in my chest harder than any workout has ever pushed it.

"Let's see what you can do, Sierra. I wanna see what you can lift." I nod my chin at the bench press and she follows my motion, staring at it, then back at me.

"Lincoln, I'm not built for that. Do you not see this flab?" She lifts her arm and gives it a little jiggle.

I resist the urge to make her signature move and roll my eyes. "What I see is the strongest woman I've ever met. Now get on the fucking bench, Sierra."

Sighing, she relents and takes her position.

"I'm going to start you out with just the bar so you can get used to the feel and find your grip. Are you ready?"

"No," she huffs, "but hand it here." She gets her arms into position and I place the bar in them. Slowly, she brings it down to her chest and back up, then repeats the motion several more times.

"Good girl," I say, taking pride in the pinkening of her cheeks that I'm pretty sure are caused by my words and not the physical exertion. I'm going to add five pounds onto each end now."

I rack the bar and add the weight like I promised.

"You ready?" I check in and she nods, giving me the go ahead.

She fumbles a little, but quickly regains her composure. "This isn't too bad."

"Go ahead and touch it to your chest, then bring it back up. I want to check your form." Sierra does as she's told and is a little shaky as she thrusts the bar into the air. "Slow down, lifting's not a sprint, it's a marathon."

She snorts, "I figure the faster I do these damn reps for you, the faster I can leave this gym and forget it exists."

As she lowers the bar once more, I strike her a deal. "How about for every rep you do, that's a minute I go down on you?"

Sierra finishes her workout , and then after seventeen blissful minutes between her thighs, I figure it's time to head into work and face my brothers.

I'm on my second cup of coffee by the time my brothers make it into my office and head over to pour themselves a cup from my fancy machine that keeps me going most days. They each take a seat across from my desk and when I finish going over the details Nicole laid out for me last night, they look as pissed as I was. My mood was so fucking sour, I had to go to Kalli's and have a beer before I could head back home so I wouldn't snap at anyone when I got there.

"Blackmail. She's resorting to blackmail?" Camden says, running a hand through his long locks. Where mine and Keaton's hair typically grows straight up out of our heads, our younger brother has long, thick waves like something out of a shampoo commercial.

"And what's all this evidence she claims to have?" Keaton asks, eyeing me skeptically.

"Well it's obviously bullshit," I tell him. "I don't know what she thinks she has on me, but I haven't done any of the shit she claims."

Camden adjust himself and winces, "Fuck that shit hurts."

"You okay baby bro?" Keaton asks, as we both eye him like he's contagious.

He ignores the question and instead directs us back to the woman currently causing me a plethora of issues. "She probably has generated something with AI. It's all over the fucking courts these days. And it's been a bitch to try and determine the authenticity of some of the evidence because of it."

"Text messages. Emails. Voice recordings. She says she has all that shit." I run a hand through my hair, wishing it wasn't such a close cut and I could actually pull on it. "Out to ruin my life and my daughter's for five million."

Keaton sighs, "I mean we have the money. We can give it to her and hope she walks away."

"She won't. She'll be back for more. She's always back. And this guy she's with," I think back to the man who was with her last night, "something is off with him. This isn't his first time scamming someone."

"Do you have his name?" Cam asks, taking his seat again.

I shake my head. "Just called himself Nicole's close, personal friend. Like I give two shits what poor sucker she has between her legs these days."

Camden sighs, "We can ask around and see if anybody knows who he is and see if he's connected to anything. Is Nicole staying with one of her friends"

"I don't fucking know or care where she's staying."

"I get that," he explains, "but we are going to have to keep an eye on her and make sure that you're on your best behavior whenever she's around."

"On my best behavior? What am I, a fucking toddler?"

Keaton snorts, "Sometimes."

Cam stands up and I catch him wincing again as he does. Either the guy has one hell of a case of blue balls or he needs to see a doctor about things down south. "You sure you're okay? Do you have something going on down there?"

"I'm fine, but you aren't right now. We don't know what fabricated evidence she has against you, but if it looks real and is hard to prove otherwise, there's no telling what a judge might decide. Throw in the fact that you have a pretty nasty temper, and she could make it look like you aren't fit to raise your daughter, at least not for some time."

Keaton stands now, "And just like that Nicole gets Charlie?"

Thankfully Camden shakes his head, "No. She has no rights so if Linc does something crazy, custody would be granted to one of us more than likely. But visitation would be limited. So don't go pulling a Keaton and thinking that beating the shit out of somebody is gonna solve anything."

I throw my hands up, "Fine. Best behavior it is. But I'm supposed to meet with her again on Friday and tell her whether or not I'm giving her the money, so maybe we can figure something out by then."

Keaton nods, "That gives us four days. If we can dig something up, we will. Between the two of us maybe we can hack into her hard drive. There's nobody better at decrypting hidden material than you."

Camden heads for the door, "I didn't hear any of that."

Chapter Thirty-Eight
Sierra

S haron wanted sandwiches for lunch and I wasn't about to turn down such deliciousness, so I head into town. Unfortunately after our last visit here, Sharon has refused to try leaving the house again, so I'm on my own. As I walk into Crumb and Get It to pick up our lunch, the woman I now know as Nicole and the bane of Lincoln's existence, is seated amongst three people, two of whom I've had the misfortune of meeting before.

Caroline and Wanda are a couple of moms I've met at the school who had nothing but snide remarks to make towards me regarding my size, and suggestive comments about what Lincoln and I do behind closed doors.

If they only knew...

I look around, but there's really no way of bypassing the crew. The counter to pick up our food is directly behind where they're seated. So I hold my head high and march past them, hoping Nicole won't acknowledge me.

"Oh, Sara!" She waves, because I have absolutely no luck on my side. I bite my tongue at the temper that wants to fly off of it because this woman knows my damn name.

I wave at Nicole and her group of friends before gritting out, "It's Sierra."

"Oh of course. I'm so sorry about that," Nicole says and her posse giggles. "We were just talking about you, weren't we ladies?"

A few of them nod. One even has the decency to look uncomfortable with this conversation. But one of the women must really want to be on Nicole's good side. She's the only one to speak up, "Yes, we were talking about how desperate Lincoln must be if he's going for little girls who, well, aren't exactly little." Wanda snickers while Caroline and the mystery woman eye me carefully to gauge my reaction.

"Yes, well, I'm here to pick up some sandwiches. Best be off." I don't say what I want to say. I don't let them know that I would much rather be a curvy and carefree woman than a Stepford Wife. I want to tell Nicole that I'm more of a mother to her little girl than she ever will be. I want to tell them that their husbands are probably miserable having to be married to such uppity bitches. But I don't say anything. Instead, I tap the tray underneath Nicole's picked-at sandwich. "If you want Lincoln back, Nicole, I'd suggest eating up. Apparently he likes his women with curves nowadays."

She gasps dramatically, carrying on to her friends about how she can't believe how people have the audacity and whatever else she cares to spew, but I'm walking away, her voice blissfully fading into the background.

When I reach the counter, I smile politely at the lanky boy standing behind it. "Pick up for Fisher, please," I say, giving

Lincoln's last name like Sharon insisted because apparently they have some sort of account here set up for rewards and she's after a free cupcake. I look in the clear case at the desserts on display and have to admit they do look delicious.

The boy gives me a pained look, "I'm sorry but it's not ready just yet. It should be finished soon though if you can wait about five more minutes?"

"No problem at all," I smile at him. "Would you mind adding one chocolate and one strawberry cupcake to the order, please?"

After paying for my updated order, I head to the bathroom and someone immediately follows me inside. The much-thinner-than-me, brunette-turned-bottle-blonde crosses her arms, pushing up her barely there chest. My heart lurches at the action when it draws attention to the charm necklace she's wearing. It looks nearly identical to one my mother had, and the sudden memory has me blinking back tears I wouldn't dare show in front of my present company. "Hi, Nicole. How can I help you?"

She gives me a cruel grin and I realize she isn't near as beautiful as I gave her credit for when we first met. Now I wonder what Lincoln ever saw in this woman. How could this evil being be the mother of such an incredible girl like Charlie? "You can act like Lincoln doesn't want me anymore, but we all know that's a lie."

"Nicole, I'm not looking to start anything, but if you truly think Lincoln wants anything to do with you, then you're clearly deranged."

The evil smirk on her face only grows wider. "Well if that's the case, then why was he with me last night?"

I think back to last night and recall the late hour Lincoln walked in the door. He was slightly disheveled, and smelled a bit like alcohol, and the look on his face was pained. Was it from regret? I shake my head, trying to convince myself but also letting her know that I don't believe her for one second. "The only reason Lincoln was with you was to tell you to leave him the hell alone."

"Then explain these." Nicole thrusts her phone in my face and I manage to grab ahold of it before it drops on the bathroom floor, though I should have let it go ahead and hit the dingy tile so she'd have to hold whatever germs accumulated on it right up to her face. When I bring the device up to look at, right there on Nicole's phone was a text thread between her and Lincoln. And the exchange between them had me ready to be sick.

Nicole

> It's always so good to see you. When are you going to ditch the girl and come back to me?

Lincoln

> soon, angel

Lincoln

> i promise

Nicole

> It's not fair that she gets to lay in bed with you every night. I don't even know how you fit in it with her by your side.

Lincoln

> uncomfortably

Lincoln

> i would much rather be curled up next to u

Lincoln

> or under u while u ride my dick

Nicole

> Come over tonight and I can make that happen.

I swallow down the sickness that's built up while reading the words she shoved in my face. Nicole's smug smile tells me that she accomplished what she came in here for. "Mind if I take a picture of this?" I ask her, giving her a politeness she doesn't deserve.

Nicole sticks her bottom lip out and nods, "Whatever you need to do to help you get through this, sweetie."

I pull my phone out and snap a picture of her screen, then hand Nicole her phone and get the hell out of that bathroom. Thankfully my food is ready, so I grab it and head back out to my car. But when I get there, a man is leaning up against it, and I stagger back in surprise.

"Got my money yet?"

I lift my chin, showing him that he no longer intimidates me. "Go away, Jason."

I shove at my stepdad so I can get into my vehicle, but he grips my wrist, pulling me into him so he can spit his words into my face.

"Don't worry, Sierra. I'll get your money, and all of your boyfriend's too."

I jerk my wrist from his grasp and he steps aside so I can get into my car. Why the hell is he here in Cheatham? How does he know about me and Lincoln? Why did I have to run into both him and Nicole today?

I turn on my car and reverse out of my spot. There's one more stop I need to make before I can get back home to Sharon with her sandwich.

Lincoln Fisher and I need to have a talk.

I step off the elevator at Phisherman's Cybersecurity, making a beeline for the woman I know is Lincoln's assistant.

"Hi, Amanda," I say before charging right into the office and slamming the door behind me.

"I'll have to call you back," Lincoln slams the phone down and stands, startled to see me, but seemingly determined to figure out what the hell I'm doing here. "What's wrong? Is it Charlie? Mama?"

"Jason."

Lincoln's face screws up in confusion and even like that he's sinfully delicious. But then the vein in the middle of his forehead begins to bulge and he turns an especially deep shade of crimson. "Is he fucking messaging you again?"

"He's here," I say quietly, hoping my gentle tone will calm him down.

"In the building?" he starts to the door, but I step in front of him, placing my hands on his chest and visibly watching him relax with my touch

"In Cheatham. I ran into him right after Nicole accused you of cheating on me with her."

The red rages through him again, and I fear if I don't get the man I love to calm down, a stroke is going to be imminent. "She fucking what?"

"Lincoln, I need you to sit down. I need you to drink some water and just listen to me right now."

"What the fuck is wrong with you? You can't fucking say fuck like that for everyone to hear," Keaton says unironically as he walks into Lincoln's office and shuts the door. "Oh shit, what's wrong?"

I ask Keaton to get Lincoln a bottle of water, hoping it will give me some time alone with the hulking man in front of me, but of course he walks over to the bar located here in Lincoln's office.

"Sit down, Linc. Let's talk this out." Lincoln's older brother speaks softly, more of how he speaks with his wife than the typical tone I hear in the banter between the brothers.

Lincoln does as Keaton says, placing his head in his hands and bending it down to his knees. I kneel down in front of him. "Talk to me, Lincoln. Please."

His voice is muffled, but cracks as he speaks, not looking up from where his face is buried. "Sierra, I swear I didn't."

"Lincoln, look at me." He doesn't budge, so I begin to push his hands down, hoping he will give into my demand. When he finally does, those beautiful blue eyes of his are filled with sorrow.

"I would never hurt you."

"I know."

The look on his face is one that doesn't believe my words, but I continue staring at him until his features begin to morph. "You know?"

I nod.

"How?"

"She showed me the texts you supposedly sent." I fish out my phone from my pocket and show him the picture I took of Nicole's screen. "Jason never capitalizes words or uses punctuation. You always do."

"You knew from that?" Keaton asks, and I have to admit that I forgot he was standing there.

"These are also texts from different operating systems than what we use. We don't use those rotten apples," I clarify with a smirk.

"They're working together," Lincoln huffs out. Then a smile tugs at his lips and he runs a hand over my brown locks. "My clever brat."

I smile back at him, happy to know I've helped him calm down. "But even if I didn't, I would have known. You came home last night looking defeated, not deceitful. You held me like I'm yours and like there's nobody else in the world you would want to be with." I swallow down the lump in my throat that has formed with the thick emotion coming over me. "All my life I have felt discarded. I've watched families and couples and knew that one day I wanted the same. I wanted to be loved. Wholly. Without question. And with you, Lincoln Fisher, I have no doubts. I love you and I know you love me, too."

"I do, Sierra. I love you so fucking much." He crushes his lips to mine, and our feelings for each other seep through the touch. I run my hands up his arms, needing to touch him, demanding him to be closer.

"Fuck, Sierra, I love you. I want to take you right now on this fucking desk."

A throat clears from the back of the office. "It would be hypocritical of me to advise you to not do that, but I would ask that you please wait for me to leave the room."

Lincoln turns and looks back at his brother with a smirk. "Then you better fucking run."

Chapter Thirty-Nine
Lincoln

J ason. Fucking. Raleigh.

A deep dive has led me to discovering that this motherfucker of a man has been scamming dying women for years. When he was twenty-one years old, his fiancée at the time passed away with some rare form of brain cancer. Upon her death, he inherited a large sum of money and it was either the grief from her passing, the greed from his earnings, or a mixture of both that created some sick, fucking twisted monster.

The money fell away from his account almost as quickly as it was added, thanks to what looked like trips to a casino across the river. As I watched his funds trickle away, I was also able to pull up a marriage license to a woman fifty years his senior. Twenty-five year old Jason married Edith, a childless woman who wanted to find love before she passed with the terminal diagnosis she had just received. The one she received from the doctor's office where Jason worked as an admissions clerk. When Edith passed a couple of years later, she left everything to her beloved husband, Jason.

Once again his money went to the casinos and wild transactions for outrageous sums. He kept his job as an admitting clerk and met Alice Davis. Alice was a bit younger than Edith, at only fifty, but her diagnosis was graver. Stage four hit her hard and fast, and while her last days were painful, the love of her new beau kept her strong. Alice took her last breath two weeks after she and Jason signed the papers that legally made them husband and wife.

Jason's cycle continued for decades. He would find these dying women, marry them, take their money, and then waste away at the casino. I waded through dates and transactions for hours until my head felt like it was going to explode, until I finally reached a name that had me hesitant to investigate.

Eleanor Thomas. Sierra's mom. The same dark blue eyes I get lost in are staring back at me, along with a shorter pixie-style version of the dark waves Sierra wears. The other files I've looked through have been enough to churn my stomach, and now this one hits closer to home, so I let out a breath of relief when I go to open her medical file and Keaton walks in.

"Dario's on the phone. He'd like to speak with us about adding another layer of protection on the jackpot server. Claims someone has been trying to manipulate it." Keaton explains, pulling me from the only work I've been focused on since Sierra gave me the name of Nicole's accomplice.

The three of us discuss strategy and ultimately decide on what's going to be best to strengthen things at the Las Vegas casino Dario and his brothers run. There's been some speculation as to what all the Caruso Family is involved in, and it makes me wonder what other business ventures they take part in.

Before we end the call, I work up the nerve to ask the question that's been brewing in my head. "So, now that we have business squared away Dario, do you think I could speak to you regarding a personal matter?"

"Holy fuck. Don't move."

Dario and I had an enlightening conversation that helped ease the pain of having to rifle through the facts and figures between Jason and Sierra's mom. The scam he pulled on that sweet woman and the way he tried to fuck the woman I love over is going to mean a lot of pain and suffering will be headed his way. My plan was to come home and share all the information I gathered with Sierra and let her in on the next steps, but the scene in front of me is going to put a pause on that.

When I walked into my house from work this afternoon, I expected to see the usual scene – Charlie and Sierra in the kitchen and Mama either reading a romance novel or watching one of the classic shows from her childhood she likes to watch in the evening. What I didn't expect was my porn fantasy come to life. Seeing Sierra bent over into the drum of the dryer had my cock standing at attention so fast I'm surprised I didn't strain something.

"Where are Mama and Charlie?" She begins to back out of the appliance to answer my question, causing my hand to slap against her perfect, round ass. "I said don't move."

Her grumble is muffled, but I smile as I have no doubt she's cursing me at this moment. "They're in the greenhouse. Your mom said something about seed pods and Charlie got super excited about it."

I walk over to the small window that looks over my backyard and see their two shadows hard at work in the greenhouse we bought Mama for Mother's Day several years ago. This time of year, she and Charlie like to begin plotting out the vegetable garden and filling pods with seeds of more vegetables than we know what to do with. I think I gave away at least a couple hundred tomatoes last year, and that's after we kept a few hundred for ourselves.

I glance back to the dryer and see Sierra trying to shift her way out of it again. The slap of my palm against her ass halts her actions and releases a cry that makes me begin to leak inside my pants. "Are you going to be a good girl or a brat for me today?"

"Probably both," Sierra admits, causing me to smile.

"My fucking favorite."

Tugging her black joggers down, I find that she's bare underneath and swat her ass, "Were you hoping I'd come home and find you like this? Is that why your cunt is so hot and ready for me?" I slap her bare pussy and hear a thud from inside the dryer, followed by a string of curse words.

"Are you okay?"

"Oh sure, I'm fucking great. I'm just stuck inside an appliance while you're teasing me with your cock. This isn't exactly the most comfortable of angles and I'm dying for you to be inside of me, so could you just go ahead and fuck me now?"

"Well since you asked so nicely," I tease.

I make quick work of unbuckling my belt and shoving my pants and boxer briefs down far enough that my erection can spring free. At this angle, Sierra's hole that has teased me for so long is in perfect position, but I won't take the plunge there just yet. Instead, I slide my dick through her slit, collecting the moisture that's gathered there so quickly.

"Ugh, Lincoln. Fuck me already."

I thrust into her tight cunt as her cries echo within the drum of the dryer, nearly causing me to lose control. "Fuck, Sierra. You feel so good. You're like my wet dream come to life and I can't believe this is reality."

She begins to rock back and forth, pulling my dick in and out of her and I'm not sure how much longer I can last. "Fuck, Sierra, your pussy is amazing. You have no idea what you do to me."

Grunts and groans are all I can make out of her as I continue pumping inside, matching her thrusts with my own. I reach my hand down and find that tight bud of hers, ready to make her detonate so I can quickly follow behind her. "Need to come now. Be a good girl for me Sierra and come first." My fingers make quick work of rubbing circles and then when I gently tug, the orgasm crashes through her, sending shockwaves into me that cause my own orgasm to spill.

I pull out of her, grabbing a towel nearby to clean up my mess and noting the convenience of fucking in the laundry room. Sierra slowly backs herself out of the appliance and I help her clean up and pull her pants back into place. She turns and gives me a gentle kiss, completely opposite to the rough manner in which we were taking things just moments before.

"So that was one of your fantasies?" she asks, pulling a sheepish smile from me.

"Yeah. Thanks for making it come true."

"Oh, anytime. I can't wait for you to return the favor."

She sashays out of the laundry room and I look after her in wonder, before I wise up and fear begins to sink in. "Wait, what kind of fantasies do you have?"

I chase down my girl as her evil laughs bounce off the hallway walls.

Chapter Forty
Sierra

"Lincoln, I don't know that I can do this."

We've gone over the plan on how we are going to confront Jason at least a dozen times, but the idea of speaking to, or so much as looking at, my stepfather has me ready to bolt. I knew something was off about him, but he did seem to make my mom genuinely happy. He may not be a good man, but he's one hell of a con artist.

"Sierra, you're the strongest person I know. You are going to go in there, we are going to lay everything out to him, and then I have a special surprise for him at the end. I'll be with you every step of the way."

I look at the man who was once nothing but a one night fling and has somehow become my everything. Giving him a nod we walk into Kalli's Corral and find Jason sitting at the bar, nursing a beer. When Lincoln steps up to him, Jason gives him a smarmy smirk and it makes me want to go all Road House on him and take his beer bottle to his head. Since I'm neither talented when it comes to fighting, or bold enough to make the first hit, I let Lincoln take the reins.

"Jason, I've heard a lot about you. I'm Lincoln Fisher."

Jason goes to stand and there's an odd satisfaction when he comes up short and has to look up to my handsome, tattooed, fella. "You have the money?"

Lincoln nods at Kalli who gives him one in return. "Oh Jason, you should know a proper businessman isn't going to address such things in public like this. We have a private booth set up, let's head back there."

I follow the two men silently through the bar, and see a familiar face I wish I had never had the pleasure of seeing before. A small groan releases from me and Lincoln catches my eye to check in. I tilt my chin at the young man getting incredibly handsy with a woman on the dance floor. Lincoln looks over at him and then returns to me with a confused expression. "Elton," I mouth, and an understanding seems to click.

Before long, Lincoln parts the black curtain of a part of the bar I've never seen before. The large, bulky amps and a drumset tell me that this must be the backstage area for the bands who frequently perform on the weekends. A booth sits to the left and a man I've never met is sitting there. A man whose face screams "I've killed before and I'll do it again," and the nerves I had about this evening double.

"Luca, so nice to finally meet you," Lincoln says and the man greets him with a grunt and goes to stand.

Holy shitballs. When this man lifts up from the booth, it's like when a transformer goes from a tiny sports car to, well, the robot-looking things they transform into. My neck strains as I look up and find that he's every inch the same height as Cam. But where Camden has more of a slender build, this man's muscles have muscles. I'm pretty sure he can do that trick where he crushes a watermelon between his thighs, only with three of them at the same damn time. His olive complexion and dark waves have me assuming he is of Italian descent, and the suit he wears has me thinking he's involved in organized crime. I'm not sure how the hell Lincoln would know someone like this, but I figure it's better to ask questions later.

Lincoln's hand on the small of my back has me letting out a tiny yelp and I realize I've been staring. "Luca, this is Sierra Thomas. She's mine."

The man tips his head in my direction, but the scowl on his face remains. I'm pretty sure the man was born into the world wearing one and a smile has never graced his face.

"And this is Jason."

Luca cracks his knuckles and it's enough to intimidate my stepfather so that a small shudder runs through him. Maybe he's smarter than I thought.

"Shall we?" Lincoln says, gesturing to the booth, grabbing me so that I'm sitting flush against him. Luca and Jason sit across from us and I have to bite my lip to hold back the laugh that wants to bubble up at the sight of the two men scrunched closely together.

"So now that you've hidden us from the prying eyes of your tiny town, do you have my money?" Jason's smug smile is on his face again and a visual of Luca wiping it off with a swift punch in the face pops into my brain. God, I'd love to see it.

"Sierra?" Lincoln probes, and I shake the lovely image from my brain to confront the man in front of me.

"There is no money, Jason. Not anymore. Not for you." I surprise myself with the steadiness in my voice, but the evil grin that spreads across his face has my confidence faltering.

A low laugh sounds out of him, "I don't think you understand. You will give me the money that Nicole and I asked for, or the two of you will lose absolutely everything."

"I think it's going to be the other way around, actually," Lincoln states. "You see, we will not be giving you any more money to blow on casinos and whatever else you're into. And Luca here is going to make sure you don't scam any other women for as long as you live, which might not be that long depending on how quickly you piss off the big guy there."

Jason looks over at Luca and his face pales, "What? No. No, this wasn't my idea. It was Nicole who wanted to come after your money and your little girl. That wasn't my plan."

"Your plan was to just scam my mother and once she passed, scam me, right? You didn't realize she had a daughter when you sought her as your next target, and so I put a wrench in your plans when she passed and left everything to me. We know you falsified those hospital bills to get me to send you more money, but the gig is up, Jason."

Panic begins to set in as Jason realizes he's been caught and Luca's role in all of this. He tries to dart out of the booth, but the big man grabs a hold of him and by the cringe on Jason's face, it wasn't lightly. "Seriously, she has your kid. She plans to kidnap her until you give her the money. I may be a scammer, but she's dangerous."

Lincoln snorts, "Those documents she's created aren't going to fool the courts. Neither of you will be getting a dime from us. Nicole is a lot of things, but I don't think dangerous is the word I would use to describe her."

He motions for me to slide out of the booth, and the two of us stand looking down at a fearful Jason. "Luca, you good here?"

"I'll take care of it."

Jason goes to scream, but before he can, Luca does some weird grip with his fingers and Jason's body goes slack. I stare at him with wide eyes and the man shrugs. "It's quieter this way."

"Time to go," Lincoln says, pulling my hand and separating us from whatever Luca plans to do to my stepfather. He pulls us through the curtain and abruptly halts when he runs into somebody.

I glance around him to see Elton, having the nerve to look offended. "Hey, watch where you're going, bruh."

Lincoln's grin grows and he looks at me. "This is the man that told you all that bullshit on your date?"

I nod nervously, expecting Lincoln to punch the poor boy's lights out. Instead, I watch Lincoln extend his hand and give a smile. "Nice to meet you, big fan of your work."

Umm, excuse me. What the fuck?

Elton takes Lincoln's hand and the second he does, Lincoln tightens his grip and I watch Elton try to squirm away, but there's not a chance in hell he can overpower my man. "If it wasn't for all that shit you said, I may not have met the woman I love, so thanks. Oh, and, too bad you didn't get that blowy," Lincoln leans into him, "she's really fucking great at them."

Chapter Forty-One
Lincoln

I don't typically step out into the sunshine when I leave Kalli's Corral, but it feels like a sign that my life is ready to take on some warmth and brightness. Sierra and I buckle into the Bronco and smile as I watch the woman I love visibly relax against the leather seat.

"Thank you. Thank you for helping me get him out of my life. And not only for that, but for helping him stop doing that to other women too. What a fucking creep."

Her whole body shudders and I lean over the console to kiss her, "I'd do anything for you, Sierra."

"Ugh, when did you get so damn cheesy?" she groans, laughing.

"Shut up, brat." I grab her again, kissing her in a far more punishing way to give her a preview of what's to come. When we break apart she sighs and grows quiet.

I run my hand over her thigh and she grips it with her own, but I can tell something is still troubling her. "What is it?"

"Do you think Luca is going to kill Jason?"

The image of the incredibly intimidating Italian man conjures in my brain. I have no doubt that he has killed people before and wouldn't think twice about doing the same to a piece of scum like Jason.

"I'm not sure what he'll do with him," I answer honestly.

Sierra bites her bottom lip, clearly concerned. I pull it from her teeth and run my thumb over soft skin.

"Am I a horrible person if I hope he does?" she whispers, and the question breaks my heart.

The console restricts me from pulling Sierra into my arms and I curse myself for not having purchased a pickup with a bench seat so she can be directly beside me. I manage to do the best I can, wrapping my arms around her in an awkward, but sincere, hug. "I don't think you're horrible for wanting a man who abused you and your mother to get the justice he deserves. You're the best person I know, Sierra."

She reaches up and wipes a small tear that has leaked from the corner of her left eye, then sniffs a couple of times before she motions to the dash.

"We should probably go ahead and pick up Charlie. Then maybe we can all go out for ice cream to celebrate the end of an era." A small smile tugs at the corner of Sierra's mouth and a feeling of peace settles into my bones.

I give her a kiss to the forehead before releasing my hold and agreeing with her. "Let's go get our girl."

The convenient thing about living in a small town like Cheatham is that it doesn't take you long to get to whatever destination you desire. The elementary school Charlie attends was only five minutes from Kalli's, and was just the right amount of time to have Sierra come to terms with whatever fate Luca decides for Jason.

I parked the car in the large lot in front of the building and Sierra and I step up to the buzzer hand-in-hand.

"How can I help you?"

"Hey, Colleen," I say to the school secretary who has been here since Camden attended. "I'm here to pick up Charlie."

We're about an hour ahead of dismissal, so I have to go through the process of being buzzed in and signing Charlie out. I don't do it often, but I can't recall a time where the doors weren't opened immediately. Instead, I wait in silence and wonder what the hell is going on.

I glance over at Sierra, who is worrying that bottom lip of hers again. She juts her chin in the direction of the buzzer on the wall of the school. I push it again.

"Mr. Fisher, I'm sorry, but Charlie isn't here. She was picked up earlier."

Colleen's words shock me. The only ones approved to pick up Charlie are my mom, who hasn't left the house since the gazebo incident, my brothers, and the two of us currently standing outside the locked doors. Neither Camden or Keaton would pick Charlie up without asking me first, and generally it's me asking them to pick her up if I'm running behind at work.

I press the little intercom button and my voice comes out haunted, "Who picked her up, Colleen?"

The school secretary's stuttered words hit me so fucking hard I can't find air. "Umm, her mom."

Her mom?

What mom?

The only mother figure that Charlie has is standing beside me and as soon as I can make it official, she's the only mom Charlie will know.

My body begins to shake and all the oxygen in my lungs leaves my body.

My daughter isn't here.

My daughter has been taken.

My daughter is missing.

The steel door opens and the cherub face I've seen hundreds of times steps out into the sunshine that no longer feels right. Where Colleen's face is always warm and cheerful, today it's etched in despair. I try to speak, but words evade me.

Sierra speaks on my behalf, "Do you mean to say Mr. Fisher's mother picked her up? Sharon Fisher?"

The secretary shakes her head, and though everything sounds muffled, I hear the name she gives Sierra.

Nicole Pierce.

Nicole fucking took Charlie. She kidnapped my daughter and I can't even fathom how this happened. Concern quickly morphs into anger.

"And why the fuck did you just let anybody pick up my kid?

The secretary looks flummoxed as she answers my question. "Well there was never any paperwork on file before, but she brought it in with her. It states that her parental rights were reinstated and that she has custodial rights for Charlie. I looked it over and even had the principal and our school resource officer check. We take the safety of our students very seriously and would never have allowed someone without clearance walk away with her."

"But you fucking did!" I'm seething, taking my anger out on the wrong person, maybe, but my baby girl is missing and right now it's everyone's fucking fault.

"We didn't," Colleen insisted. "She had the paperwork, Lincoln."

"They're fucking fake!" I roar, slamming my fist into the brick of the building. It should hurt. I know it should hurt. But right now the pain of not knowing where my daughter is at hurts more than anything this brick building could do to me.

The officer that was hired to be on the duty for additional security rushes out of the building. I've seen him around town, but we didn't grow up together. Still, he must know who I am because he calls me by my name when he speaks.

"Lincoln, you're going to need to calm down."

What a stupid fucking thing to say. "Calm down? You gave my kid to a total stranger. Did she act like she knew who she was when she came to pick her up? Did you ask Charlie?"

Colleen wrings her hands. "Well she was visibly upset, but we couldn't tell her she wasn't allowed to take Charlie."

"And you didn't think to fucking call me?"

"That's not protocol," the officer says and my hand grows into a fist.

Sierra pries my fingers apart and holds my hand. Somehow the touch instantly soothes me. I'm still fucking pissed and scared beyond belief, but I'm not alone. "Lincoln, I know this is the absolute worst thing that could be happening right now, but standing outside the elementary school and cursing at people is not going to help us find Charlie."

"Well it makes me feel better," I say between gritted teeth.

"I know it does, but the best thing we can do is work together to find out where Charlie could be." She turns and looks at the man with a puffed out chest who is seriously a fucking moron if he thinks he could take me. "Can you file a missing person's report for us?"

He shakes his head, "She had the paperwork. I can't file it when she has the rights to have her daughter."

"Those papers are fucking forged!" I rage again, and Sierra puts a hand on my chest in an attempt to calm me.

"Do you have a copy of those papers?" Sierra asks calmly. I look at the gorgeous woman beside me and I know she's hurting as much as I am right now. Charlie may be my biological daughter, but she's ours. And Sierra is doing everything she can to help us get her back.

Colleen nods frantically, "Yes, I had to make a copy to keep with our records. Let me go grab you a copy."

She scans her badge and darts back inside, leaving Officer My-Ego-Is-Bigger-Than-My-Dick to stand here and watch over us. I glare at him, my fingers twitch to start a fight, but Sierra notices and gives me a task.

"Lincoln, call your brothers. Explain to them what's going on and have them meet you at the house. Why don't you call them from the car?"

I furrow my brows, but she pushes me in the direction of the Bronco. "You go on and call them. I'll be there as soon as I get the paperwork."

My stomps are loud and aggressive as I march back to the vehicle and wedge myself inside. I bought this vehicle because of the way it could accommodate my larger body, but without Charlie, nothing feels right.

Pulling up my phone, I call my brothers and tell them to meet me at the house.

We're going to get her back.

We have to get her back.

Camden pushes up his glasses as he looks over the papers Sierra handed to him. Our entire family is in the living room as we go over all possibilities of where my daughter could be.

Anna's silent tears fall as Keaton holds her in his arms.

Skyla sits next to Sierra, holding her hand tightly.

Mama sits in the recliner, a vacant expression on her face.

When Camden throws the papers down on the table, everyone's heads snap up and we all focus our eyes on him. "They're definitely fake."

"I fucking knew it."

Cam shakes his head, "But there's no way they would have. This isn't the school's fault. She did a really good job of creating these documents and if you don't know exactly what you're looking for, it would be easy to believe they were real."

"It doesn't matter if it's the school's fault. They aren't the ones who know where she would be. Have you tried calling Nicole's parents?"

One of the reasons Nicole wanted to get out of Cheatham so damn bad was because of the horrible people who abused and neglected her and yet the state still allowed them to call themselves her parents. I think of the scars on Nicole's back left by the cigarette burns and shake my head, "She wouldn't have gone to them. There's no way."

"What about her friends?" Anna suggests, "She has to have some still in town, right?"

Sierra speaks up. "She was with a group of women the other day at Crumb and Get It. I knew two of them. Wanda and Caroline, but I don't know their last names."

I knew them. Wanda Bleumel and Caroline Gray, Nicole's best friends from high school. In retrospect, they were pretty shitty friends and I'm not sure why Nicole would have come back to hang out with them. "I don't think they're in on it, but we could definitely show up on their doorsteps and ask questions. Actually, Amanda lives next door to Wanda. Anna, could you text her?"

My sister-in-law wipes the tears from her eyes and gives me a determined look. "On it." She stands and as she walks out of the living room, her phone is pressed to her ear.

"Jason," Sierra whispers.

"Who?" Skyla asks.

Sierra looks at her friend and clarifies, "Jason. My stepfather." She turns her head towards me. "Jason knows where that bitch took her."

Fuck. The idea that the man we just met with would have any idea where my daughter might be at this moment completely eluded me.

I charge out of the living room in the opposite direction of Anna and dial the number I have for Luca Caruso, praying it's not too late. When he answers after two rings, I all but yell my words, "Please tell me you're still with that prick."

His deep voice is low, "You'll have to be specific."

"Jason. Jason Raleigh. Are you still with him?"

"I'm with most of him," the scary Italian man says and a shudder runs down my spine thinking about the type of torture I'm sure this man could inflict.

"Can he speak?"

Silence greets me on the other line for a painful amount of time. Every second without Charlie is like another dagger sinking into my skin.

"For now."

Relief begins to pour into me knowing that someone may have knowledge about where my daughter could be.

"I need to speak with him."

A long silence greets me again and my brief moment of comfort begins to evaporate.

"Luca?" I finally ask.

"I'll text you a location."

The line goes dead and for the first time since walking out of the town bar, hope begins to fill my body. My phone vibrates in my hand and I see a single message from Luca Caruso. An address. Nothing more.

I walk into my office and find the item my mom stashed in the safe, a 9mm semiautomatic pistol I was unaware of for so many years. My hands shake as I hold the item so foreign to me. I'm one of three brothers, so I've had my fair share of physical altercations, but never have I considered violence with a deadly weapon. But when it comes to my daughter, I'll do whatever it takes, so I shove the gun into my waistband just as Sierra comes into the room.

"What are you doing?"

I don't answer her, instead breezing past her and heading to the front door.

Sierra's words come out frantic, "Lincoln I'm in full agreement of getting Charlie back and doing what it takes, but do you think Nicole is armed? Do you really think taking a loaded weapon into the place where your daughter is being held captive is the answer?"

I stop at the exit to my home, and turn and stare into Sierra's pained midnight eyes, momentarily getting lost as I look at the real mother of my child. Planting a kiss on her forehead I make Sierra a promise. "I'm bringing our baby home."

1 1 1 1 0 0 0 0 1 0 1 0 0 0 0 0 0 0 1 1 1 0 0 0
1 1 0 0 1 1 0 0 0 1 0 1 0 1 1 1 1 0 0 1 0 0
0 0 0 0 0 0 0 1 1 0 0 1 1 0 0 0 0 0 1 0 1 1
1 0 1 0 1 0 1 0 0 0 1 1 0 0 0 1 1 0 0 1 0 0
0 0 0 0 1 1 1 1 0 0 1 0 0 1 0 0 0 1 0
0 1 0 1 1 1 0 0 1 0 0 1 1 1 0 1 0 1

Chapter Forty-Two

Sierra

"**B**ring our baby home," I whisper as the door slams behind Lincoln and his brothers. That's what Charlie is, our baby. I fell in love with that little girl from the first moment I saw her gum-coated hair. Knowing Lincoln sees her as mine means everything to me.

The idea of Lincoln walking out of this house armed does little to settle my nerves, but I can't blame him. There's nothing I wouldn't do to make sure Charlie is back home and in our arms again.

Anna walks back into the room, putting her phone back into her jeans pocket. "Where did the guys go?"

I explain to the girls about my stepfather and all he's done to me, my mom, and several other women throughout the years.

"What a fucking creep," Skyla says, and I nod my head in agreement.

Anna runs her hand over mine. "I'm so sorry that happened to you Sierra, but I'm so glad you were able to face him and take him down."

I give her a small smile. I don't know all of Anna's story, but Lincoln has told me enough to know that Anna had to face an abuser of her own not too long ago.

"Oh!" she gasps, "Amanda said that Wanda had just pulled into the driveway. Seems like as good a time as any to go and question her. What do you think?"

Skyla, Anna and I stare at each other

Skyla jumps up and shouts, "We ride at dawn!"

Anna and I give her confused looks.

"Dawn? Why dawn?" I ask.

Sky groans, "Because we ride in five minutes doesn't have the same effect."

It doesn't take us long to get ready and prepare to confront Nicole's friend. She may not know where Charlie and Nicole are, but I'll be damned if I'm going to sit around here and do nothing when it comes to finding my kid.

My chest blooms at the thought of Charlie being mine. Lincoln calls her ours and those words are even more beautiful to me than when he said he loved me. I mean, those words were incredible too, but knowing he trusts me enough to allow me to love his daughter the way a mother should, that means everything.

As I make my way to the door, I pass by Sharon, who is still sitting in the recliner like she has all afternoon. Seeing all her boys under the same roof had her smiling, but when she found out Charlie was missing, all emotion drained from her face. She's been a statue ever since. I head her way, crouching down so that we're eye-to-eye.

"Sharon, we're going to go and find Charlie. Would you like to go with us?" She blinks, but doesn't react, and I can't help the annoyance that builds inside me.

"Do you care that she's gone? That we can't find her? That she's out there with some psycho woman who was willing to give her away in the first place?" My voice comes out louder than I expect and I can see Skyla and Anna in my peripheral vision, taking it all in.

Sharon blinks again and whispers, "I care. I care very much."

"Then where's the fiery woman I saw when Nicole showed up at this house? That woman wouldn't be sitting here in a daze."

She runs a finger over the wedding band she continues to wear every day. "I can't go out there." Her voice is so soft I barely hear her. "I've lost so much."

I shake my head. I love this woman, but she has been testing my patience since I moved in and at this point, I'm fed up. "Sharon, all my classes taught me that when dealing with grief you must be patient. Everyone heals in their own way, and you can't rush progress, but you can be there to listen to people when they need it the most. It's not my job as a therapist to tell people what to do, but to instead offer suggestions that help them figure it out themselves. And in most cases, that's true. But when it comes to you," I take a deep breath, "well Sharon, it's the biggest pile of horseshit Keeneland has ever seen."

From behind me Skyla hoots and Anna gasps.

"Excuse me?" Sharon says, her voice louder now and her mouth agape.

"Your granddaughter is missing. Your family is hurting. Your son is breaking. He needs you. He needs his mom to get out of this damn house and help him find his daughter. Yes, you were a wife and I am so incredibly sorry you lost the love of your life. You're right. You have lost so much. But you're also a mother. You have three other loves of your life who need you right now. Scratch that, you have four. Charlie needs you, too. Actually, scratch that, because dammit Sharon I need you."

"Six," Anna says. "I need you too, Sharon."

"Seven, because so do I," Skyla adds.

I glance back and give the best friends I've ever had, friends who have somehow become more like the sisters I've always wanted, a small smile. I turn back to Sharon who still sits expressionless, as though all emotions have just blipped right out of her body.

"I know the last time you left this house was painful. We thought you were ready and maybe it was all too soon. But you're ready now, Sharon. You're strong. You're a survivor. And is there really any better time to get out of this fortress you've created than to go and kick this bitch's ass?"

Sharon blinks and then stares at me. I return her stare, looking for any sign that my words sank in. And I see it. It's small. A miniscule smirk that tilts her lip up so fast that had I blinked I would have missed it.

"Well," Sharon says, and I close my eyes waiting to hear the powerful blow I know this small but mighty woman is capable of handing out. I anticipate her telling me that I'm out of line. That I had no right to raise my voice at her. I expect her to tell me exactly where me and my opinions can go. What I don't expect are the words that come out of her mouth and put a smile on mine.

"Let's go kick the bitch's ass."

Amanda is standing in her driveway waving at us as Skyla, Anna, Sharon, and myself pull up in Keaton's truck. When Anna kills the engine, she hops out and hugs her friend.

"I'm so sorry," Amanda says as she hugs Anna, but she's looking at me. I give her a nod of gratitude, unable to say anything from the grief that has built up in my throat on the ride over.

I texted Lincoln, but he hasn't replied. Luca seemed like the type to kill first and ask questions later, so there's a solid chance that there won't be much left of Jason when Lincoln and his brothers arrive. A shudder runs down my spine at the thought and I look over at the house next door to Amanda's to focus on the task at hand.

Through the window I can see her. Walking through her house without a care in the world. Wanda has never been particularly kind to me, but I wouldn't have gone out to say we were adversaries. But now I know she's friends with the woman trying to rip my family apart. So today, she pays.

Our group of women gather around and head up the short sidewalk to Wanda's home. I smile as I see that Amanda has joined us. There really is solidarity in numbers and I'm grateful for all the women who are here with me today.

I ring the doorbell, but clearly my patience has snapped, because the next thing I know, I'm beating on the door. The door that never opens. I glance back through the front window and see Wanda standing there, staring at her phone.

Banging on the door again, I shout, "I know you're in there Wanda. Open up!"

Noise sounds from the little black box attached to the house, "Can I help you?"

I grit my teeth, pissed at her cowardice. "Where's Nicole?"

"I'm sorry, who?" She plays dumb. Honestly, I'm not sure she's playing much.

I take in the ranch style home and look around for another point of entry. There's a garage, but the doors are closed, and I don't see another door to access it.

I pinch the bridge of my nose and try again, "Wanda, I just want to talk. Charlie is missing."

Silence greets us, but as we watch her through the window, I can see the confusion on her face. Finally we hear her voice again, "What do you mean missing?"

A voice I'm all too familiar with sounds, but not from behind me where I think I would hear it. Instead, Sharon's voice is coming through the little box where we've been hearing Wanda's.

"Missing, you twat. Because you're friends with a damn psychopath. Now tell us where she's at."

Wanda screams and we all rush over to the window. Sharon has a hold of Wanda's perfectly smooth auburn hair in her hands. "How the hell did you get in my house?"

We watch Sharon roll her eyes, "It's called a backdoor. Maybe don't leave it unlocked all the time you dumbass. Now where's your friend?"

Wanda screams again as Sharon yanks her head back one more time. I step into the little rock bed that's lined up with boxwoods and knock my fist against the window. "Let her go, Sharon, and unlock the door."

"I can manage to unlock it without letting her go," Sharon hollers back and I bite my lip to keep from laughing. The situation should not be amusing, but I'm genuinely enjoying the scene in front of me.

"Let her go," I say again. This time Sharon listens and Wanda backs the hell away. We all rush over to the door as Sharon unlocks it and opens it for us. As we step into the house, I shake my head at Sharon, but a smile is on my face. Skyla steps in and gives the woman a huge hug, calling her a badass.

I've never seen Sharon look as proud of herself as she does right now. And I don't think I've ever been more proud of her, either.

1 1 1 1 0 0 0 0 1 0 1 0 0 0 0 0 0 0 1 1 1 0 0
1 1 0 0 1 1 0 0 0 1 0 1 0 1 0 1 1 1 1 0 0 1 0 0
0 0 0 0 0 0 0 1 1 0 0 1 1 0 0 0 0 0 0 1 0 1 1
1 0 1 0 1 0 1 0 1 0 0 0 1 1 0 0 0 1 1 0 0 1 0 0
0 0 0   0 1 1 1   1 0 0 1   0 0 0 1 0 0 1 0
0 1 0   1 1 1 0   0 1 0 0   1 1 1 0 1   0 1

Chapter Forty-Three
Lincoln

Jason's spit lands at my feet and I stare down at the glob of bloodied saliva. "Well that wasn't very nice. I just asked a simple question."

The man looks like shit. Luca has roughed him up well. Where his brown hair was slicked back, it's now sticking up every which way. Blood trickles down from a swollen lip. Even a few of Jason's fingers are missing and I have to keep myself from glancing down so that the stuff currently churning in my stomach doesn't try to rise to the surface. When I bring my eyes up from his missing digits, I notice the reddened skin where he's thrashed against the rope currently holding him to a very uncomfortable looking wooden chair.

It's official. Luca Caruso is one scary motherfucker.

When I reached out to the Caruso brothers, I was simply looking for some assistance with intimidation. I wanted to make sure Jason was scared enough to never scam another woman in his life. Maybe pee his pants in front of Sierra so her last memory of him can be him cowering in fear. According to Luca, however, it's been several of their casinos where Jason has not only been blowing his inheritances, but building debts and never paying for them.

You don't want to fuck with a family like the Caruso's and Jason has been fucking them over for years.

"Just tell us where Nicole took her," Camden says, looking up at the ceiling. He refused to stay outside the abandoned warehouse, determined to help us find Charlie. Still, he says he can't watch the scene in front of us and keep a good conscious, so he's been staring at the ceiling since he walked in.

Jason's voice comes out strained, "I ain't telling you nothing."

Luca grabs the back of Jason's head, causing the jerk to wail in what's probably both terror and pain. He bends down and speaks in his deep, low voice, "Well, if we aren't going to get any information from you, I can go ahead and cut out your tongue. I need you quiet for the plans I have anyway."

I look at the big man with wide eyes, knowing he isn't kidding, and thankful that the business I have with my brothers isn't the same line of work. The click of a blade opening sounds and I look over to Keaton whose face is a bit green.

Jason squirms as Luca grips his face, trying to force his tongue out. "Alright! Alright!" Jason squeals like a pig. "She was taking her to my place."

"I think you mean Sierra's home," I state. "The one where she and her mother were living when you came into their lives and tried to fuck them both over."

He huffs, "Whatever. It's where Nicole and I have been living. She was taking that bitch of a kid of yours there until you came through with the money."

I see red and my hands ball up into fists at how this piece of shit sitting in front of me describes my kid, but when I step forward to land a punch, I'm too late. Keaton's arms are wrapped around Jason's neck as Camden is landing blows to his stomach.

"That kid is fucking perfect," Keaton growls as Jason struggles for air.

When they step back, I look at my brothers and realize I've never been more proud of them than at this moment. Keaton is gonna make one hell of a dad.

Since we're done here and know where Nicole has taken off with Charlie, I'm in a hurry to get the hell out of this makeshift torture chamber. I nod at Luca, thanking him for allowing us to bust in on his session.

Jason's screams sound as my brothers and I exit the warehouse, but as soon as the doors close behind us, all noise is silenced. There's an eerie stillness and it sends a shudder down my spine.

"Remind me never to piss off Caruso Enterprises," Keaton says, and I nod in agreement.

Camden speaks up, "I'm so glad the two of you are mild hackers and not whatever the fuck that was."

I smirk as Keaton pats Cam on the back. I'd much rather decrypt information from a screen than literally pry it out of a person any day.

The mission hasn't changed, so I pull out my phone to call Sierra and find out what her old address was so we can get my daughter back. She picks up after the first ring, but it's not her voice I hear first.

"Keep that crazy old woman away from me!"

"Sierra? Are you okay? Where are you?"

She sighs on the other line. "I'm fine. That's just Wanda being dramatic. Your mom is here."

I blink a few times as I take in Sierra's words. "What do you mean my mom is there? Mom is where?"

Camden and Keaton's heads snap up at that. We assumed that her little meltdown in the park a few weeks ago would have set her back and it would be years before we could ever talk her out of leaving the house again.

Sierra sighs again, this time heavier, "We're at Wanda's. Your mom may be slightly terrorizing her."

"I told you what I know, now get this woman out of my house!" Wanda screams so loudly I have to pull the phone away from my ear.

Shaking my head, I hang up and climb in the vehicle so I can get my baby girl.

"What a fucking bitch."

"Charlene Elizabeth Fisher," I scold, but when I look at my beautiful girl's face, I can't help the smile that begins to spread across my face. "You're absolutely right."

When we got to the house, Nicole was sitting in the kitchen with her head in her hands, literally pulling at her hair as Charlie was talking her head off. I expected her to be startled at the arrival of all of us, but instead she looked crazed.

"Does this kid ever shut up?" She wanted to know, and I couldn't help but smile at the sight of my girl and give Nicole the God's honest truth.

Nope.

Nicole demanded her money, but we were all very adamant that she wasn't getting a single cent from our family and there was no way we would be leaving without my child.

Skyla had made the call to the police on their way to Sierra's former home, and they arrived shortly after we made our appearance. Nicole was arrested for forging legal documents and kidnapping for ransom. Camden made sure to let her know she will also not be able to reach out or be near anyone in our family for the foreseeable future.

With Nicole locked away and with Jason, well, wherever Luca puts him, my little family will finally be able to have some peace. It will be great knowing that Charlie, Sierra and I can spend the rest of our lives no longer having to worry about my ex or Sierra's stepfather.

I give Charlie a squeeze, savoring this moment of having her in my arms, but when I glance around the kitchen, there's someone missing. I pass my daughter over to her favorite uncle and let Camden know I'm going to look for Sierra.

The house Sierra was raised in is cozy and full of character. Since it's on the smaller side, it doesn't take me long to go from room to room and note Sierra's absence.

"We're gonna head on out," Keaton says from behind me as I stand in front of a fireplace. The mantle is adorned with photographs of Sierra and her mother from over the years.

"Would you mind taking Charlie back with you? I think Sierra needs a moment." My big brother nods his understanding, and they load up, discussing who will be riding with whom since they have Keaton's truck and Amanda's minivan to escort everyone back.

I ascend the wooden stairs that lead up to a small upstairs area with a bathroom directly at the top and two bedrooms, one to the left and the other to the right. I take three short strides to my left to where Sierra is sitting in the middle of the bed, a picture frame in her hands and tears streaming down her cheeks.

1 1 1 1 0 0 0 0 1 0 1 0 0 0 0 0 0 0 1 1 1 0 0
1 1 0 0 1 1 0 0 0 1 0 1 0 1 1 1 1 0 0 1 0 0
0 0 0 0 0 0 0 1 1 0 0 1 1 0 0 0 0 0 1 0 1 1
1 0 1 0 1 0 1 0 1 0 0 0 1 1 0 0 0 1 1 0 0 1 0 0
0 0 0 0 1 1 1 1 0 0 1 0 0 0 1 0 0 1 0
0 1 0 1 1 1 0 0 1 0 0 1 1 1 0 1 0 1
0 0 1 1 0 0 0 0
0 0 0 1 1 0 0 0 0 0 0
1 0 0 0 0 1 1
1 0 0
0 1 0 1

Chapter Forty-Four

Sierra

F inding Charlie safe and knowing she had been driving Nicole insane the whole time made me happier than I could ever imagine. But as the hours stretched on and the police spoke to us about the events that occurred and took each of our statements, memories from this house came flooding in.

Lincoln refused to let go of Charlie as soon as she jumped into his arms and seeing the love the two shared reminded me so much of the bond my own mother and I had. I slipped out of the kitchen where everyone was gathered and began taking in all the things I once took for granted.

My hands ran down the worn, gray recliner where Mom would sit most days. When she was exhausted from treatments, there was no way she could climb the stairs, so instead of retreating to her room, the recliner became her bed. Near the end, Hospice brought in a hospital-style bed that has since been wheeled out. We had it located beside the electric fireplace so she could look at the pictures of the two of us throughout the years. It also helped warm her because I can't recall a time she wasn't shivering from the cold in those last days.

Tears began to form as I climbed the stairs. Her bedroom was to the right and mine was to the left. Though there was a bathroom downstairs, we shared the one that was nestled between our rooms. I stepped to the right and walked in, expecting to find pieces of my mom strewn about. Instead, Nicole's clothes were tossed around, mixing in with Jason's. The pictures my mom had hung of her and Jason's wedding were missing. I walked to the closet where her clothes had hung, but just as I suspected, they were all gone.

The pain of knowing Jason had tossed her aside like she meant nothing to him at all was too much for me to bear. I walked into my bedroom, clutched the framed picture I had of the two of us on my nightstand, and began to sob. The creak of the floors has me looking up to see the most handsome man standing in the doorway with heartache and concern on his face.

"Hey," Lincoln whispers.

Instead of replying, the sobs come harder and the floodgates open behind my eyes. I'm an absolute disgusting mess, but this man of mine comes into my childhood bedroom, sits on the bed, and gently takes me into his arms.

"It isn't fair," I cry into his chest. "She was so good. She deserved to be loved. He didn't love her."

Lincoln doesn't speak. He strokes my hair, kissing the top of my head.

"I had doubts, you know? From the very beginning I thought something was off with him, but I couldn't figure it out."

"That's not your fault, Sierra. Jason was a skilled con artist. He knew exactly what to say and do to make these women fall for him."

I shake my head and the tears begin to fall again. "I don't want to remember her like that. I don't want to remember her with him, being played a fool."

Lincoln extracts the framed photo from my grip. "Then don't. Tell me about this picture."

I blink back the tears trying to push their way through and stare at the image of my mother kissing me on the cheek the night of my senior prom. My date took the picture, and while things didn't work out between the two of us, I will forever be grateful to him for capturing this moment.

I tell Lincoln the story and his arms wrap around me, providing me the comfort and encouragement I need. When I finish, his lips begin to graze my neck.

"Do I need to be worried about this prom date of yours?" His voice is low and rumbly and does things to my insides.

"You don't need to worry about any man, Lincoln."

"Because you're mine, Sierra."

"I'm yours."

Lincoln places the photo back on the nightstand before he lowers me to the bed. "Did that prom date of yours bring you back to your bedroom at the end of the night?"

I shake my head. "No. Nobody has ever had me in this bedroom."

"Mine," he growls again, tugging at the leggings and panties I'm wearing and tossing them to the hardwood floor.

Lincoln places his hands on my knees and shoves them apart, exposing my core to him. "So fucking wet."

"For you," I reiterate, "only for you."

He leans forward, flattening his tongue and licking all the way up my seam. A whimper breaks from my throat as he repeats the motion.

"And this is mine."

"Yes, yours."

His mouth attacks. He's sucking on my clit, tonguing inside my pussy, and driving me completely insane.

"Lincoln, I'm going to come." I warn him, but he doesn't let up. Instead, he plunges two fingers into me, rocking them back and forth as his lips suction around my bundle of nerves that are about to explode.

And when he crooks his fingers, hitting that spot within me, I do.

When I come down from the orgasm Lincoln gave me, I notice his phenomenal body is on full display. He grabs at my shirt, pulling it over my head, then unclasps my bra. When the material uncovers my nipples, he dips his mouth down to take them in. His tongue swirls around the hardened tips just before he nips at them and I'm already about to come again.

"I need you inside of me," I beg him.

Lincoln grunts. "Not finished with these, yet."

A smirk plays on my lips. "Well if you don't want to be inside of me, I think I still have my prom date's number stored in my phone."

"You fucking brat," he smiles at me. "You're going to pay for that."

God I hope so.

Lincoln straddles my body and places his cock on my chest. "Squeeze those perfect tits of yours while I fuck them." I do as he says while he moves his hand to my head, gripping my hair and pushing it forward. "And suck. Hard."

He glides his dick between my breasts, giving me just enough of him to wrap my mouth around the tip. I flick my tongue across the tip as I do what he says. "Fuck Sierra, your mouth feels so fucking good."

I pull off of him with a pop. "Bet my pussy feels better."

A roar from within him comes out and it's so fucking hot.

"Flip over," he demands and I eagerly do as I'm told.

Lincoln slaps my ass and I cry out as he thrusts into me without warning. "So fucking tight, Sierra. You feel so fucking amazing."

"Told ya," I sass as I rock against him, feeling him deeper with each movement.

He continues pumping into me, grabbing a handful of my cheeks and squeezing so hard it's a mix of pleasure and pain. Liquid lands on me and I gasp as Lincoln rubs his finger in it, dipping down into the hole I know he's been eager to fuck.

"Still want to take you here," he grunts, enunciating each word with a thrust.

My mind rushes with everything this man makes me feel. In the months we've been together, he has given me the safety and love I've desired my entire life. He's given me a home and a family. He's given me a daughter.

"Then do it," I blurt out, wanting to give him one thing I know he's been wanting.

His movements halt and I can't help but whine. "Are you sure?"

"If it means you'll keep fucking me then yes, please. I love you, Lincoln. I want to be yours completely."

He pulls himself from me and I cry out at the loss of him, but then he's hauling me into his arms and turning my face to his. "I love you, Sierra. I love you so fucking much."

Lincoln's lips crash down on mine and fireworks explode in my brain. When he pulls away, I'm left dizzy and wanting more. "You're sure about this? I want you to want it too, Sierra."

The sweetness of my grumpy man has my heart pounding in my chest. I take his face in my hands and place a soft kiss on his lips. "I want this, Lincoln. I want you."

"Do you have any lube?" he asks and I can't help but giggle.

"Umm, not here."

His hand dips down and he swipes his fingers through the moisture between my thighs. "Good thing you're always so fucking wet."

Laying me down, he moves one hand down to the hole nobody has ever explored before while using his other hands to bend my knees up to my chest. "It's a little easier to take you from behind," he explains, "but I want to see your face."

His fingers dip inside me, attempting to get me ready for him. He gathers more of my arousal and continues to do so until he's satisfied. "Are you ready?"

I nod. I am ready. I'm ready to be Lincoln's in every single way.

"It might hurt at first, but you tell me if you need me to stop. I promise I'm going to do everything I can to make you feel good."

His thick tip begins to push at my entrance and I gasp. "I don't want to hurt you, Sierra. Tell me if you need me to stop."

"I'll tell you," I say, and he pushes his tip further into me. There's a slight burning sensation as he continues to press, but the way his eyes are fixed on my face, making sure I'm alright with what's happening, eases the pain.

"Take a deep breath, Sierra."

I do as he says, and Lincoln plunges himself into me, causing me to cry out and him to freeze.

"Are you okay?"

I take quick inventory, and realize I am okay. I am so fucking okay.

"Yes," I stammer out. "Full. Feels good."

"You're sure?" The care in his voice has tears brimming in my eyes, but I know if I let them fall he'll think it's because he's hurting me.

"I'm sure. I'm good."

Lincoln nods and begins to slowly pull himself out and then back into me. I wasn't lying when I said it feels good. It's different, but in a very good way. I moan and Lincoln mimics the sound.

"Fuck, your ass is perfection. Fuck, Sierra, I'm not gonna last long."

"Me neither," I admit.

And we don't. He thrusts a few more times before our orgasms ripple through us.

When Lincoln collapses beside me, he pulls me onto his chest. He found me crying on this bed, and his sweet words cause the tears to return.

"I love you, Sierra. And I want you to be mine. Always."

Chapter Forty-Five
Lincoln

I t was a long day at work where we had another meeting with Caruso Enterprises. Dario and Giovanni were on the video call with us, and I was thankful to not see Luca after our encounter a couple of weeks ago. I'm sure the two of them are just as capable of the same things as their brother, but watching someone try to cut out a person's tongue definitely puts them in a different perspective.

As I reach the back door, I turn when I hear a loud thud. My mother is standing there, a large suitcase beside her, a taped up box at her feet, and a smile as vast as the Sahara Desert across her face.

"What the fuck is all this?"

Mama continues smiling, not the least bit bothered by my outburst. "Oh, Lincoln, I'm glad you're finally home. Do you think you could come help me with some things in my room?"

I follow her into her bedroom, a place I've been countless times, but everything is very different. For years I have checked on Mama in this room, and have seen it in all of its various stages. There has been the meticulously clean era where everything had to go in its precise spot and the room had to be vacuumed and dusted daily. I've seen clothes strewn everywhere, blankets and pillows thrown onto the floor, and broken glass that had been shattered in fits of rage. I've walked in to find her nearly lifeless, sheets soiled, the air pungent, and the feeling of despair so thick it could have smothered you.

But never have I walked in and found it covered in stacks of taped up boxes. "Mama, what is going on?"

She picks up one of the boxes and then motions for me to do the same. "I'm moving out!"

"You're moving out?"

"Lincoln, this home holds so many memories for me. Really incredible ones of you and your brothers growing up.

"I understand, Mama." I say, wrapping her up in my arms in a hug and placing a kiss to the top of her head.

"Besides, as much as I love you and am so happy things with you and Sierra worked out the way they did, there are certain things a mother shouldn't hear." I stare down at her and she pumps her eyebrows with a smirk, "Daddy."

Releasing her, I mock gagging and she cackles. It's a foreign, but beautiful, sound.

"So where exactly are you going?" I ask.

"Oh somewhere nearby. It's been recently renovated and the owner is giving me a steal of a deal."

"Either way, I should probably look over the contract." Dealing with Jason opened my eyes to how truly evil some men can be and how easily older women can be taken advantage of.

"Suit yourself. My new landlord is actually going to stop by today, so you can feel free to ask him any questions you want."

A smug grin pulls at her lips, but before I can question her any further, I hear my older brother's voice. "Hey, Pip. Where's your dad and Grammy?"

As Keaton steps into my mother's room, I do a sweeping motion with my hand at the scene in front of me. "Did you know about this?"

Anna comes in, taking the box out of my mom's arms. "Of course we knew," she says, "Where do you think she's moving?"

My jaw drops and my hand extends to the swollen stomach of my sister-in-law. "They fuck as much as Sierra and I do!"

"That may be true, but hopefully not in the guesthouse. Besides, they'll need Grammy nearby when the little ones are born. I'll be there to help them just like I was here to help you with Charlie."

"They definitely fuck in that guesthouse," I mutter.

Anna rolls her eyes and walks out of the room with the box she's holding. When I look at Keaton he shrugs, grabs a box, and follows his wife. Mama isn't wrong. She's going to be a heap of help to the two of them when their twin boys make an arrival. She played a crucial role in helping me raise Charlie into the incredible little girl she is, and I have no doubt that she'll have the same impact on my nephews.

My face drops as I think of how devastated my daughter will be when she finds out Grammy won't be living with us any longer. "Charlie," my voice cracks, "this will crush her."

Mama steps up to me and places a box in my arms. "Charlie has the family she needs now. She has a mother and a father who love her so much, they're willing to go to war for her. That child won't be devastated to see me move out. But I do expect to have her visit me from time to time. Her sass keeps me young."

"I think that's everything," Camden says, shutting the tailgate of Keaton's truck. "You ready, Mama?"

"I'm so ready. A new house and a ride in your new car. It's like a new life for Sharon Fisher."

Charlie stomps her foot and crosses her arms. "I wanna ride in Uncle Cam's new car."

I take a look at the shiny, red Corvette my younger brother just purchased. He's always been the practical one, but lately there's been an interesting shift in him.

"Yeah, that's not happening." I say, lifting her into the cab of Keaton's truck.

"Be good, Little Bit."

"I will!"

I watch my family drive off and my shoulders begin to deflate.

"You okay?"

"My mother's leaving."

Sierra rests her head on my shoulder and wraps her arm through mine.

"And how does that make you feel?"

I grab Sierra by her waist and pull her in for a kiss. "Horny. So fucking horny."

"Well we do have this whole house to ourselves for a while, what would you like to do?"

"Everything," I say, kissing her again while tugging the white shirt she's wearing out of her jeans.

"Mmm, that sounds amazing." She presses a hand to my crotch and I about come undone at her touch. Fuck, I love this woman. "And we can fuck anywhere in the house we want."

"Fuck, that sounds good. I want to fuck you in the kitchen. And the living room. And my office."

"Kitchen first. There's this thing with an ice cube I really want to try."

I smile at my kinky girl, "I do have one request, though."

Sierra speaks in between kisses as she makes her way up my neck, "And what's that?"

"I don't think you can call me daddy anymore."

1 1 1 1 0 0 0 0 1 0 1 0 0 0 0 0 0 0 1 1 1 0 0
1 1 0 0 1 1 0 0 0 1 0 1 0 1 0 1 1 1 1 0 0 1 0 0
0 0 0 0 0 0 0 1 1 0 0 1 1 0 0 0 0 0 1 0 1 1
1 0 1 0 1 0 1 0 0 0 1 1 0 0 0 1 1 0 0 1 0 0
0 0 0 1 1 1 1 0 0 1 0 0 0 1 0 0 0 1 0
0 1 0 1 1 1 0 0 1 0 0 1 1 1 0 1 0 1

Chapter Forty-Six
Epilogue

"Happy Mother's Day!"

Charlie's sweet voice wakes me up and I rapidly blink my eyes to clear the view of her and Lincoln bringing me in a tray. As I sit up in bed, they place it so it straddles my lap and I breathe in the comforting aroma of pancakes and bacon. Fresh berries with a dollop of cream are in a ramekin next to the plate. A glass of orange juice completes my breakfast in bed.

"This is incredible, you two. Thank you so much!" I pull Charlie in, kissing the top of her head while Lincoln smiles down at us.

"It's your very first Mother's Day, so we wanted this one to be extra special."

I blink back tears at Charlie's words, knowing my sweet girl truly means them. I may not be her biological mother, or technically have any rights to call her my own, but that's what she is. Mine.

"Well it's very special," I say, "you did a great job."

"I forgot your gift!" Charlie shouts, running out of the bedroom. Her absence gives time for Lincoln to lean down and give me a kiss with so many promises behind it. The two of us are officially living together in a couple capacity rather than the employer/employee situation one we started out in. We've also decided that while we very much love one another and Charlie, she's enough for the two of us and we aren't looking to add any future Fishers and Thomases to our little family.

The sound of little running feet alerts me of Charlie's return and Lincoln steps to the side for her incoming. I brace for impact, steadying the glass of juice, as she leaps onto the bed beside me.

"Here you go. I made you this."

Purple construction paper folded in half is thrusted into my face. I take the paper and smile at the misshaped heart where a tiny stick family is nestled inside. My tiny stick family. On the outside in pink crayon it reads Hapee Mom Day, and it couldn't be more perfect.

I open the homemade card to see another beautiful picture of the entire family I consider my own now. There may not be a ring on my finger or any legal documents that give me a rightful claim to them, but they're mine just the same. Someone must have helped Charlie with the inside of this card, because in perfect spelling and penmanship it says, Will you be my mom?

Since Charlie has been exclusively calling me by that title since around Christmas, I give her a confused look. She points her finger across the bed to where Lincoln is standing.

Well, he was standing. Now he's on one knee and my breath catches in my throat. I straighten up in the bed, moving the tray away from my lap and over to the side next to Charlie.

"Lincoln, what is this?" My question comes out strangled, causing him to smile. I glance down at his hands, but where I expect a ring box to be, there's a folded piece of paper.

"Sierra Thomas," he begins, but then is interrupted with the ringing of his phone.

A couple of curses fly from his mouth as he answers the call, putting it on speaker.

Instead of a standard hello, my grump gives a more true to him greeting. "What the fuck do you want?"

Keaton's voice sounds from the other end, "Are you on your way?"

"Not yet. I told you I'd text you when we were ready."

"Well Mama is up, and wants us to take her out to brunch."

"Y'all go ahead. I made Sierra breakfast in bed."

Charlie clarifies, "We made her breakfast in bed."

I give her a smile and wink, but Keaton continues to talk. "Did you ask her yet?"

"I'm trying, but some asshole decided to call me."

"Well hurry it up. We're waiting."

"Fine." Lincoln ends the call and there's something in his actions that makes me know he misses the days of where he would have been able to slam it down on the receiver.

Shaking his head, he puts his phone back in his pocket and I try to control my shoulders from the laughter I'm trying to contain.

"Umm, so what exactly are you supposed to ask her?"

"Yeah Dad, just go ahead and ask her."

Lincoln sighs heavily, but he's smiling at me. "Sierra Thomas, I love you so much. You complete me. You complete Charlie. You complete our family. I desperately await the day that you can become my wife and we can share our lives together, but I'm not going to ask you to do that today."

I can't help but feel my smile begin to wilt on my face. This Mother's Day really took a nosedive.

Lincoln continues, "I want us to share our lives together one day, Sierra, but today I'm asking you to share my daughter's. With me. As her mom. Legally."

Lincoln begins to unfold the documents in his hands, revealing a legal contract that once signed, and I'm sure notarized, approved by a judge, and whatever other steps we have to take, will officially make me Charlie's mother.

Charlie. My sweet girl with her brown braids.

Charlie. The blue-eyed beauty who looks exactly like her father.

Charlie. A sassy spitfire who has completely stolen my heart.

During Lincoln's speech, she managed to climb off the bed and join him on the floor, kneeling down beside him and looking at me with glassy eyes. "Will you be my mom?"

Tears begin to pour as I nod repeatedly because nothing would bring me greater joy than signing those papers and knowing that this precious child is officially mine. "Yes. Yes, Charlene Elizabeth Fisher. I'll be your mom."

She leaps up with a cry of joy and climbs into my arms. Lincoln stands up slightly slower than his daughter and leans over to kiss the tops of our heads. Then we get ready so I can have the best first Mother's Day a girl can have.

With my family.

Want to find out about the sticky situation Anna and
Keaton found themselves in on their trip to the Caribbean?
Click here to get the bonus scene or scan the QR code.
You can also find the bonus scene on my website
www.meribethrichards.com

Thank You

THANK YOU!

In a world with so many words, I truly appreciate you taking the time to read mine.

If you loved the story, I would love your review!

Please consider leaving one on Amazon, Goodreads, or your favorite platform.

Feel free to tag me!

Acknowledgements

"The most important things are the hardest to say." – **Stephen King**

To Mary Beth: I have no doubt that if you were still here you would be supporting me as hard as mama, but snickering as much as my sister. There were hard times in piecing this story together, but I never gave up on myself because I know you would never give up on me. I love you. I miss you. Until we meet again...

To my daughter: You are my biggest dream come true. Thank you for inspiring the character of Charlie. Hers are the only parts of this book you're allowed to read. I love you, Little Bit.

To my husband: The support and understanding you provide is limitless. From sitting through signings and shipping out books, to being my travel partner and helping me with the research - I appreciate every single thing you do for me. I love you infinity x infinity.

To my parents: Mom, thanks for telling me where I need to add in a motherfucker or two. Dad, your pride knows no bounds. You can tell everyone you know about this book now. I love you both a bushel and a peck.

To Alyssa: Thank you for putting up with me as you brought the image of Lincoln, Sierra, and Charlie to life. I'm so sorry I have zero artistic talents, but am so incredibly thankful for yours.

To Author Rebecca Gulley: Without all your help, I'm not sure this book would have happened. Thanks for being my tech support, my hype girl, and for never allowing me to give up. I can't wait to see all your dreams come true.

To Raven, Evie, Sharilyn, and Rebecca: You are the best beta team a girl could ask for. Lincoln and Sierra's story is so much stronger because of your support. Thank you for answering legal questions, reading and rereading, and finding time in your hectic schedules to see this book come to fruition. You helped me create a love story I can be proud of and I hope I have made each of you proud, as well.

To my ARC readers: There is not a thank you in this world large enough to show you my appreciation. It may be my words on the page, but it's your words that help readers find my story. I appreciate you taking the time to not only read it, but to hype it up so that the world can get to know the characters that live within me.

To local independent bookstores: Thank you for giving indie authors a chance and sharing our stories with others.

To my family and friends: I can't list every single one of your names, but you have no idea how much your presence means to me. Thank you for showing up. For reading. For telling others. For believing in my dream.

Also by

Want more from the Phishing for Love Series?
Decoded (*Keaton & Anna*) is available now!
Defended (*Camden & Skyla*) releases June 2026!

Want to know what's coming up next in the world of
Meribeth Richards? Visit www.meribethrichards.com and sign up
for the newsletter.

About the Author

A lover of love, Meribeth Richards writes contemporary romance
with relatable characters and plenty of banter. Her stories have
plenty of swoon, sass, and sexy, curvy ladies.

Meribeth resides in Kentucky with her husband, her daughter,
and their many pets. You can find her buddy reading with her
friend Jaime or talking books or general nonsense with her mom.
When her nose isn't stuck in a book, you may even find her seeking
inspiration for her next book in every scenario.

You can connect with Meribeth on her website
www.meribethrichards.com or follow her across most social media
platforms.

Hang out with other fans in Meribeth's Sweet & Spicy Society!

Instagram: @authormeribethrichards

Tiktok: @authormeribethrichards

Facebook: @authormeribethrichards

Threads: @wordymerdy13